The
WEDNESDAY
WARS

Other books by Gary D. Schmidt

Anson's Way
Straw into Gold
Lizzie Bright and the Buckminster Boy

The
WEDNESDAY
WARS

GARY D. SCHMIDT

sandpiper

HOUGHTON MIFFLIN HARCOURT
Boston New York

Library of Congress Cataloging-in-Publication Data

Schmidt, Gary D.
The Wednesday wars / by Gary D. Schmidt.
p. cm.
Summary: During the 1967 school year, on Wednesday afternoons when all his
classmates go to either Catechism or Hebrew school, seventh-grader Holling
Hoodhood stays in Mrs. Baker's classroom, where they read the plays of William
Shakespeare and Holling learns much of value about the world he lives in.
ISBN-13: 978-0-618-72483-3
ISBN-13: 978-0-547-23760-2 pb
[1. Coming of age—Fiction. 2. Shakespeare, William, 1564–1616. Plays—Fiction.
3. Junior high schools—Fiction. 4. Schools—Fiction. 5. Family life—Long Island
(N.Y.)—Fiction. 6. Long Island (N.Y.)—History—20th century—Fiction.] I. Title.

PZ7.S3527We 2007
[Fic]—dc22

2006023660

VB 10 9 8 7 6 5 4 3

For Sally Bulthuis and Camille De Boer,
and for all the gentle souls of
Pooh's Corner,
who, with grace and wisdom and love,
bring children and books together

The
WEDNESDAY
WARS

september

Of all the kids in the seventh grade at Camillo Junior High, there was one kid that Mrs. Baker hated with heat whiter than the sun.

Me.

And let me tell you, it wasn't for anything I'd done.

If it had been Doug Swieteck that Mrs. Baker hated, it would have made sense.

Doug Swieteck once made up a list of 410 ways to get a teacher to hate you. It began with "Spray deodorant in all her desk drawers" and got worse as it went along. A whole lot worse. I think that things became illegal around Number 167. You don't want to know what Number 400 was, and you *really* don't want to know what Number 410 was. But I'll tell you this much: They were the kinds of things that sent kids to juvenile detention homes in upstate New York, so far away that you never saw them again.

Doug Swieteck tried Number 6 on Mrs. Sidman last year. It was something about Wrigley gum and the teachers' water fountain (which was just outside the teachers' lounge) and the Polynesian Fruit Blend hair coloring that Mrs. Sidman used. It worked, and streams of juice the color of mangoes stained her face for the rest of the day, and the next day, and the next day—until, I suppose, those skin cells wore off.

Doug Swieteck was suspended for two whole weeks. Just before he left, he said that next year he was going to try Number 166 to see how much time that would get him.

The day before Doug Swieteck came back, our principal reported during Morning Announcements that Mrs. Sidman had accepted "voluntary reassignment to the Main Administrative Office." We were all supposed to congratulate her on the new post. But it was hard to congratulate her because she almost never peeked out of the Main Administrative Office. Even when she had to be the playground monitor during recess, she mostly kept away from us. If you did get close, she'd whip out a plastic rain hat and pull it on.

It's hard to congratulate someone who's holding a plastic rain hat over her Polynesian Fruit Blend–colored hair.

See? That's the kind of stuff that gets teachers to hate you.

But the thing was, I never did any of that stuff. Never. I even stayed as far away from Doug Swieteck as I could, so if he did decide to try Number 166 on anyone, I wouldn't get blamed for standing nearby.

But it didn't matter. Mrs. Baker hated me. She hated me a whole lot worse than Mrs. Sidman hated Doug Swieteck.

I knew it on Monday, the first day of seventh grade, when she called the class roll—which told you not only who was in the class but also where everyone lived. If your last name ended in "berg" or "zog" or "stein," you lived on the north side. If your last name ended in "elli" or "ini" or "o," you lived on the south side. Lee Avenue cut right between them, and if you walked out of Camillo Junior High and followed Lee Avenue across Main Street, past MacClean's Drug Store, Goldman's Best Bakery, and the Five & Ten-Cent Store, through another block and past the Free Public Library, and down one more block, you'd come to my house—

which my father had figured out was right smack in the middle of town. Not on the north side. Not on the south side. Just somewhere in between. "It's the Perfect House," he said.

But perfect or not, it was hard living in between. On Saturday morning, everyone north of us was at Temple Beth-El. Late on Saturday afternoon, everyone south of us was at mass at Saint Adelbert's—which had gone modern and figured that it didn't need to wake parishioners up early. But on Sunday morning—early—my family was at Saint Andrew Presbyterian Church listening to Pastor McClellan, who was old enough to have known Moses. This meant that out of the whole weekend there was only Sunday afternoon left over for full baseball teams.

This hadn't been too much of a disaster up until now. But last summer, Ben Cummings moved to Connecticut so his father could work in Groton, and Ian MacAlister moved to Biloxi so his father could be a chaplain at the base there instead of the pastor at Saint Andrew's—which is why we ended up with Pastor McClellan, who could have called Isaiah a personal friend, too.

So being a Presbyterian was now a disaster. Especially on Wednesday afternoons when, at 1:45 sharp, half of my class went to Hebrew School at Temple Beth-El, and, at 1:55, the other half went to Catechism at Saint Adelbert's. This left behind just the Presbyterians—of which there had been three, and now there was one.

Me.

I think Mrs. Baker suspected this when she came to my name on the class roll. Her voice got kind of crackly, like there was a secret code in the static underneath it.

"Holling Hoodhood," she said.

"Here." I raised my hand.

"Hoodhood."

"Yes."

Mrs. Baker sat on the edge of her desk. This should have sent me some kind of message, since teachers aren't supposed to sit on the edge of their desks on the first day of classes. There's a rule about that.

"Hoodhood," she said quietly. She thought for a moment. "Does your family attend Temple Beth-El?" she said.

I shook my head.

"Saint Adelbert's, then?" She asked this kind of hopefully.

I shook my head again.

"So on Wednesday afternoon you attend neither Hebrew School nor Catechism."

I nodded.

"You are here with me."

"I guess," I said.

Mrs. Baker looked hard at me. I think she rolled her eyes. "Since the mutilation of 'guess' into an intransitive verb is a crime against the language, perhaps you might wish a full sentence to avoid prosecution—something such as, 'I guess that Wednesday afternoons will be busy after all.'"

That's when I knew that she hated me. This look came over her face like the sun had winked out and was not going to shine again until next June.

And probably that's the same look that came over my face, since I felt the way you feel just before you throw up—cold and sweaty at the same time, and your stomach's doing things that stomachs aren't supposed to do, and you're wishing—you're really wishing—that the ham and cheese and broccoli omelet that your mother made for you for the first day of school had been Cheerios, like you really wanted, because they come up a whole lot easier, and not yellow.

If Mrs. Baker was feeling like she was going to throw up, too, she didn't show it. She looked down at the class roll. "Mai Thi Huong," she called. She looked up to find Mai Thi's raised hand, and nodded. But before she looked down, Mrs. Baker looked at me again, and this time her eyes really did roll. Then she looked down again at her list. "Daniel Hupfer," she called, and she looked up to find Danny's raised hand, and then she turned to look at me again. "Meryl Lee Kowalski," she called. She found Meryl Lee's hand, and looked at me again. She did this every time she looked up to find somebody's hand. She was watching me because she hated my guts.

I walked back to the Perfect House slowly that afternoon. I could always tell when I got there without looking up, because the sidewalk changed. Suddenly, all the cement squares were perfectly white, and none of them had a single crack. Not one. This was also true of the cement squares of the walkway leading up to the Perfect House, which were bordered by perfectly matching azalea bushes, all the same height, alternating between pink and white blossoms. The cement squares and azaleas stopped at the perfect stoop—three steps, like every other stoop on the block—and then you're up to the two-story colonial, with two windows on each side, and two dormers on the second floor. It was like every other house on the block, except neater, because my father had it painted perfectly white every other year, except for the fake aluminum shutters, which were black, and the aluminum screen door, which gleamed dully and never, ever squeaked when you opened it.

Inside, I dropped my books on the stairs. "Mom," I called.

I thought about getting something to eat. A Twinkie, maybe. Then chocolate milk that had more chocolate than milk. And then another Twinkie. After all that sugar, I figured I'd be able to come up with something on how to live with Mrs. Baker for nine months. Either that or I wouldn't care anymore.

"Mom," I called again.

I walked past the Perfect Living Room, where no one ever sat because all the seat cushions were covered in stiff, clear plastic. You could walk in there and think that everything was for sale, it was so perfect. The carpet looked like it had never been walked on—which it almost hadn't—and the baby grand by the window looked like it had never been played—which it hadn't, since none of us could. But if anyone had ever walked in and plinked a key or sniffed the artificial tropical flowers or straightened a tie in the gleaming mirror, they sure would have been impressed at the perfect life of an architect from Hoodhood and Associates.

My mother was in the kitchen, fanning air out the open window and putting out a cigarette, because I wasn't supposed to know that she smoked, and if I did know, I wasn't supposed to say anything, and I *really* wasn't supposed to tell my father.

And that's when it came to me, even before the Twinkie.

I needed to have an ally in the war against Mrs. Baker.

"How was your first day?" my mother said.

"Mom," I said, "Mrs. Baker hates my guts."

"Mrs. Baker doesn't hate your guts." She stopped fanning and closed the window.

"Yes, she does."

"Mrs. Baker hardly knows you."

"Mom, it's not like you have to know someone well to hate their guts. You don't sit around and have a long conversation and then decide whether or not to hate their guts. You just do. And she does."

"I'm sure that Mrs. Baker is a fine person, and she certainly does not hate your guts."

How do parents get to where they can say things like this? There must be some gene that switches on at the birth of the first-born child, and suddenly stuff like that starts to come out of their mouths. It's like they haven't figured out that the language you're using is English and they should be able to understand what you're saying. Instead, you pull a string on them, and a bad record plays.

I guess they can't help it.

Right after supper, I went to the den to look for a new ally.

"Dad, Mrs. Baker hates my guts."

"Can you see that the television is on and that I'm watching Walter Cronkite?" he said.

We listened to Walter Cronkite report on the new casualty figures from Vietnam, and how the air war was being widened, and how two new brigades of the 101st Airborne Division were being sent over, until CBS finally threw in a commercial.

"Dad, Mrs. Baker hates my guts."

"What did you do?"

"I didn't do anything. She just hates my guts."

"People don't just hate your guts unless you do something to them. So what did you do?"

"Nothing."

"This is Betty Baker, right?"

"I guess."

"The Betty Baker who belongs to the Baker family."

See what I mean about that gene thing? They miss the entire point of what you're saying.

"I guess she belongs to the Baker family," I said.

"The Baker family that owns the Baker Sporting Emporium."

"Dad, she hates my guts."

"The Baker Sporting Emporium, which is about to choose an

architect for its new building and which is considering Hoodhood and Associates among its top three choices."

"Dad . . ."

"So, Holling, what did you do that might make Mrs. Baker hate your guts, which will make other Baker family members hate the name of Hoodhood, which will lead the Baker Sporting Emporium to choose another architect, which will kill the deal for Hoodhood and Associates, which will drive us into bankruptcy, which will encourage several lending institutions around the state to send representatives to our front stoop holding papers that have lots of legal words on them—none of them good—and which will mean that there will be no Hoodhood and Associates for you to take over when I'm ready to retire?"

Even though there wasn't much left of the ham and cheese and broccoli omelet, it started to want to come up again.

"I guess things aren't so bad," I said.

"Keep them that way," he said.

This wasn't exactly what I had hoped for in an ally.

There was only my sister left. To ask your big sister to be your ally is like asking Nova Scotia to go into battle with you.

But I knocked on her door anyway. Loudly, since the Monkees were playing.

She pulled it open and stood there, her hands on her hips. Her lipstick was the color of a new fire engine.

"Mrs. Baker hates my guts," I told her.

"So do I," she said.

"I could use some help with this."

"Ask Mom."

"She says that Mrs. Baker doesn't hate my guts."

"Ask Dad."

Silence—if you call it silence when the Monkees are playing.

"Oh," she said. "It might hurt a business deal, right? So he won't help the Son Who Is Going to Inherit Hoodhood and Associates."

"What am I supposed to do?"

"If I were you, I'd head to California," she said.

"Try again."

She leaned against her door. "Mrs. Baker hates your guts, right?"

I nodded.

"Then, Holling, you might try getting some."

And she closed her door.

That night, I read *Treasure Island* again, and I don't want to brag, but I've read *Treasure Island* four times and *Kidnapped* twice and *The Black Arrow* twice. I even read *Ivanhoe* halfway through before I gave up, since I started *The Call of the Wild* and it was a whole lot better.

I skipped to the part where Jim Hawkins is stealing the *Hispaniola* and he's up on the mast and Israel Hands is climbing toward him, clutching a dagger. Even so, Jim's in pretty good shape, since he's got two pistols against a single dagger, and Israel Hands seems about to give in. "I'll have to strike, which comes hard," he says. I suppose he hates Jim's guts right at that moment. And Jim smiles, since he knows he's got him. That's guts.

But then Israel Hands throws the dagger, and it's just dumb luck that saves Jim.

And I didn't want to count on just dumb luck.

◦◦

Mrs. Baker eyed me all day on Tuesday, looking like she wanted something awful to happen—sort of like what Israel Hands wanted to happen to Jim Hawkins.

It started first thing in the morning, when I caught her watching me come out of the Coat Room and walk toward my desk.

By the way, if you're wondering why a seventh-grade classroom had a Coat Room, it isn't because we weren't old enough to have lockers. It's because Camillo Junior High used to be Camillo Elementary, until the town built a new Camillo Elementary and attached it to the old Camillo Elementary by the kitchen hallway and then made the old Camillo Elementary into the new Camillo Junior High. So all the rooms on the third floor where the seventh grade was had Coat Rooms. That's where we put our stuff—even though it was 1967 already, and we should have had hall lockers, like every other seventh grade in the civilized world.

So I caught Mrs. Baker watching me come out of the Coat Room and walk toward my desk. She leaned forward, as if she was looking for something in her desk. It was creepy.

But just before I sat down, I figured it out: She'd booby-trapped my desk—like Captain Flint would have. It all came to me in a sort of vision, the kind of thing that Pastor McClellan sometimes talked about, how God sends a message to you just before some disaster, and if you listen, you stay alive. But if you don't, you don't.

I looked at my desk. I didn't see any trip wires, so probably there weren't any explosives. I checked the screws. They were all still in, so it wouldn't fall flat when I sat down.

Maybe there was something inside. Something terrible inside. Something really awful inside. Something left over from the eighth-grade biology labs last spring.

I looked at Mrs. Baker again. She had looked away, a half-smile on her lips. Really. Talk about guilt.

So I asked Meryl Lee Kowalski, who has been in love with me since she first laid eyes on me in the third grade—I'm just saying what she told me—I asked her to open my desk first.

"How come?" she said. Sometimes even true love can be suspicious.

"Just because."

"'Just because' isn't much of a reason."

"Just because there might be a surprise."

"For who?"

"For you."

"For me?"

"For you."

She lifted the desk top. She looked under *English for You and Me, Mathematics for You and Me,* and *Geography for You and Me.* "I don't see anything," she said.

I looked inside. "Maybe I was wrong."

"Maybe *I* was wrong," said Meryl Lee, and dropped the desk top. Loudly. "Oh," she said. "Sorry. I was supposed to wait until you put your fingers there."

Love and hate in seventh grade are not far apart, let me tell you.

At lunchtime, I was afraid to go out for recess, since I figured that Mrs. Baker had probably recruited an eighth grader to do something awful to me. There was Doug Swieteck's brother, for one, who was already shaving and had been to three police stations in two states and who once spent a night in jail. No one knew what for, but I thought it might be for something in the Number 390s or maybe even Number 410 itself! Doug Swieteck said that if father hadn't bribed the judge, his brother would have been on Death Row.

We all believed him.

"Why don't you go out for lunch recess?" said Mrs. Baker to me. "Everyone else is gone."

I held up *English for You and Me.* "I thought I'd read in here," I said.

"Go out for recess," she said, criminal intent gleaming in her eyes.

"I'm comfortable here."

"Mr. Hoodhood," she said. She stood up and crossed her arms, and I realized I was alone in the room with no witnesses and no mast to climb to get away.

I went out for recess.

I kept a perimeter of about ten feet or so around me, and stayed in Mrs. Sidman's line of sight. I almost asked for her rain hat. You never know what might come in handy when something awful is about to happen to you.

Then, as if the Dread Day of Doom and Disaster had come to Camillo Junior High, I heard, "Hey, Hoodhood!"

It was Doug Swieteck's brother. He entered my perimeter.

I took three steps closer to Mrs. Sidman. She moved away and held her rain hat firmly.

"Hoodhood—you play soccer? We need another guy." Doug Swieteck's brother was moving toward me. The hair on his chest leaped over the neck of his T-shirt.

"Go ahead," called the helpful Mrs. Sidman from a distance. "If you don't play, someone will have to sit out."

If I don't play, I'll live another day, I thought.

"Hoodhood," said Doug Swieteck's brother, "you coming or not?"

What could I do? It was like walking into my own destiny.

"You're on that side." He pointed.

I already knew that.

"You're a back," he said.

I knew that, too. Destiny has a way of letting you know these things.

"I'm a forward."

I could have said it for him.

"That means you have to try to stop me."

I nodded.

"Think you can?"

I suppose I could stop you, I thought. I suppose I could stop you with a Bradley tank, armor two inches thick, three mounted machine guns, and a grenade launcher. Then I suppose I could stop you.

"I can try," I said.

"You can try." Doug Swieteck's brother laughed, and I bet that if I had looked over my shoulder, I would have seen Mrs. Baker peering out her third-floor classroom window, and she would have been laughing, too.

But the thing about soccer is that you can run around a whole lot and never, ever touch the ball. And if you do have to touch the ball, you can kick it away before anyone comes near you. That's what I figured on doing. Doug Swieteck's brother wouldn't even come near me, and I would foil Mrs. Baker's nefarious plan.

But Doug Swieteck's brother had clearly received instructions. The first time he got the ball, he looked around and then came right at me. He wasn't like a normal forward, who everyone knows is supposed to avoid the defense. He just came right at me, and there was a growl that rose out of him like he was some great clod of living earth that hadn't evolved out of the Mesozoic Era, howling and roaring and slobbering and coming to crush me.

I expect that the watching Mrs. Baker was almost giddy at the thought.

"Get in front of him!" screamed Danny Hupfer, who was our goalie. "In front of him!" His voice was cracking, probably because he was imagining the propulsion of a soccer ball as it left Doug Swieteck's brother's foot and hurtled toward the goal, and wondering what it might do to his chest.

I didn't move.

Danny screamed again. I think he screamed "In front!" But I'm not sure. I don't think he was using language at all. Imagine a sound with a whole lot of high vowels, and I think you'd have it.

But it didn't make any difference what he screamed, because of course I wasn't going to get in front. There was no way in the world I was going to get in front. If Doug Swieteck's brother scored, he scored. It was just a game, after all.

I stepped toward the sideline, away from the goal.

And Doug Swieteck's brother veered toward me.

I ran back a bit and stepped even closer to the sideline.

And he veered toward me again.

So as Danny Hupfer screamed vowels and Doug Swieteck's brother growled mesozoically, I felt my life come down to this one hard point, like it had been a funnel channeling everything I had ever done to this one moment, when it would all end.

And that was when I remembered Jim Hawkins, climbing up the side of the *Hispaniola* to steal her, tearing down the Jolly Roger flag, sitting in the crosstrees and holding Israel Hands back.

Guts.

So I glanced up at Mrs. Baker's window—she wasn't there, probably so she wouldn't be accused of being an accomplice—and then I ran toward the goal, turned, and stood. I waited for Doug Swieteck's brother to come.

It was probably kind of noble to see.

I stood my ground, and I stood my ground, and I stood my ground, until the howling and the roaring and the slobbering were about on top of me.

Then I closed my eyes—nothing says you have to look at your destiny—and stepped out of the way.

Almost.

I left my right foot behind.

And Doug Swieteck's hairy brother tripped over it.

Everything suddenly increased in volume—the howling and the roaring and the slobbering, the whistling of Doug Swieteck's brother's airborne body hurtling toward the goal, the screams of Danny Hupfer, my own hollering as I clutched my crushed foot. Then there came an iron thunk against the goal post, which bent at a sudden angle around Doug Swieteck's brother's head.

And everything was quiet.

I opened my eyes again.

Doug Swieteck's brother was standing and sort of wobbling. Mrs. Sidman was running over—though, properly speaking, what she did wasn't really running. It was more a panicky shuffle. She probably saw "Negligent Playground Monitor" headlines in her future. When she got to him, Doug Swieteck's brother was still wobbling, and he looked at her with his eyes kind of crossed. "Are you all right?" Mrs. Sidman asked, and held on to his arm.

He nodded once, then threw up on her.

He had eaten a liverwurst-and-egg sandwich for lunch. No one ever wants to see a liverwurst-and-egg sandwich twice.

And Mrs. Sidman's rain hat did not help at all.

That was the end of the soccer game, except that Danny Hupfer—a very relieved Danny Hupfer—ran up to thump me on the back. "You sure did take him out!"

"I didn't mean to take him out."

"Sure. Did you see him fly? Like a missile."

"I didn't mean to take him out," I hollered.

"I never saw anyone get taken out like that before."

Doug Swieteck ran over. "You took out my brother?"

"I didn't mean to take out your brother."

"Everyone says you took out my brother. I've been wanting to do that since I was out of the womb."

"It was like a missile," said Danny.

I limped back into school, trying not to look at an unhappy Mrs. Sidman, who was holding the wobbling Doug Swieteck's brother at the same time that she was using her rain hat to do not very much. Liverwurst is like that.

Meryl Lee was waiting for me at the door. "You took out Doug Swieteck's brother?" she asked.

"I didn't mean to take him out."

"Then how did he end up flying through the air?"

"I tripped him."

"You *tripped* him?"

"Yes, I tripped him."

"On purpose?"

"Sort of."

"Isn't that cheating?"

"He's three times bigger than I am."

"So that means you can cheat and make him look like an idiot."

"I didn't try to make him look like an idiot."

"Oh. And you didn't try to make me look like an idiot, opening your desk for some dumb surprise that wasn't even there."

"What's that got to do with it?"

"Everything," said Meryl Lee, and stomped away.

There are times when she makes me feel as stupid as asphalt. "Everything." What's that supposed to mean?

Mrs. Baker's face was pinched when we came back into the class—the disappointment of a failed assassination plot. Her face stayed pinched most of the afternoon, and got even pinchier when the P.A. announced that Doug Swieteck's brother was fine, that he would be back in school after ten days of observation, and that there was a need for a playground monitor for the rest of the week.

Mrs. Baker looked at me.

She hated my guts.

We spent the afternoon with *English for You and Me,* learning how to diagram sentences—as if there was some reason why anyone in the Western Hemisphere needed to know how to do this. One by one, Mrs. Baker called us to the blackboard to try our hand at it. Here's the sentence she gave to Meryl Lee:

The brook flows down the pretty mountain.

Here's the sentence she gave to Danny Hupfer:

He kicked the round ball into the goal.

Here's the sentence she gave to Mai Thi:

The girl walked home.

This was so short because it used about a third of Mai Thi's English vocabulary, since she'd only gotten here from Vietnam during the summer.

Here's the sentence she gave to Doug Swieteck:

I read a book.

There was a different reason why his sentence was so short—never mind that it was a flat-out lie on Doug Swieteck's part.

Here's the sentence she gave me:

For it so falls out, that what we have we prize not to the worth whiles we enjoy it; but being lacked and lost, why, then we rack the value, then we find the virtue that possession would not show us while it was ours.

No native speaker of the English language could diagram this sentence. The guy who wrote it couldn't diagram this sentence. I stood at the blackboard as hopeless as a seventh-grade kid could be.

"Mr. Hoodhood?" said Mrs. Baker.

I started to sweat. If Robert Louis Stevenson had written a sentence like that in *Treasure Island,* no one would have ever read the book, I thought.

"If you had been listening to my instructions, you should have been able to do this," said Mrs. Baker, which is sort of like saying that if you've ever flicked on a light switch, you should be able to build an atomic reactor.

"Start with 'what we have,'" she said, and smiled at me through her pinched face, and I saw in her eyes what would have been in Long John Silver's eyes if he had ever gotten hold of Captain Flint's treasure.

But the game wasn't over yet.

The P.A. crackled and screeched like a parrot.

It called my name.

It said I was to come to the principal's office.

Escape!

I put the chalk down and turned to Mrs. Baker with a song of victory on my lips.

But I saw that there was a song of victory on her lips already.

"Immediately," said the P.A.

I suddenly knew: It was the police. Mrs. Baker had reported me. It had to be the police. They had come to drag me to the station for taking out Doug Swieteck's brother. And I knew that my father would never bribe the judge. He'd just look at me and say, "What did you do?" as I headed off to Death Row.

"Immediately," Mrs. Baker said.

It was a long walk down to the principal's office. It is always a long walk down to the principal's office. And in those first days of school, your sneakers squeak on the waxed floors like you're torturing them, and everyone looks up as you walk by their classroom, and they all know you're going to see Mr. Guareschi in the principal's office, and they're all glad it's you and not them.

Which it was.

I had to wait outside his door. That was to make me nervous.

Mr. Guareschi's long ambition had been to become dictator of a small country. Danny Hupfer said that he had been waiting for the CIA to get rid of Fidel Castro and then send him down to Cuba, which Mr. Guareschi would then rename Guareschiland. Meryl Lee said that he was probably holding out for something in Eastern Europe. Maybe he was. But while he waited for his promotion, he kept the job of principal at Camillo Junior High and tested out his dictator-of-a-small-country techniques on us.

He stayed sitting behind his desk in a chair a lot higher than mine when I was finally called in.

"Holling Hood," he said. His voice was high-pitched and a little bit shrill, like he had spent a lot of time standing on balconies screaming speeches through bad P.A. systems at the multitudes down below who feared him.

"Hoodhood," I said.

"It says 'Holling Hood' on this form I'm holding."

"It says 'Holling Hoodhood' on my birth certificate."

Mr. Guareschi smiled his principal smile. "Let's not get off on the wrong foot here, Holling. Forms are how we organize this school, and forms are never wrong, are they?"

That's one of those dictator-of-a-small-country techniques at work, in case you missed it.

"Holling Hood," I said.

"Thank you," said Mr. Guareschi.

He looked down at his form again.

"But Holling," said Mr. Guareschi, "we do have a problem here. This form says that you passed sixth-grade mathematics—though with a decidedly below-average grade."

"Yes," I said. Of course I passed sixth-grade mathematics. Even Doug Swieteck had passed sixth-grade mathematics, and he had grades that were really decidedly below average.

Mr. Guareschi picked up a piece of paper from his desk.

"But I have received a memo from Mrs. Baker wondering whether you would profit by retaking that course."

"Retake sixth-grade math?"

"Perhaps she is not convinced that your skills are sufficiently developed to begin seventh-grade mathematics."

"But—"

"Do not interrupt, Holling Hood. Mrs. Baker suggests that on Wednesday afternoons, starting at one forty-five, you might sit in on Mrs. Harknett's class for their math lesson."

Somewhere, somewhere, there's got to be a place where a seventh-grade kid can go and leave the Mrs. Bakers and Mr. Guareschis and Camillo Junior Highs so far behind him that he can't even remember them. Maybe on board the *Hispaniola,* flying before the wind, mooring by a tropical island with green palms crowding the mountains and bright tropical flowers—real ones—poking out between them.

Or maybe California, which, if I ever get there, you can bet that I would find the virtue that possession would show us.

But Mr. Guareschi returned to his form and read it over again. He shook his head. "According to this record," he said, still reading, "you did pass sixth-grade mathematics."

I nodded. I held my breath. Maybe I could dare to believe that even a dictator of a small country might have a moment of unintended kindness.

"Mrs. Baker does have a legitimate concern, it would seem, but a passing grade is a passing grade."

I didn't say anything. I didn't want to jinx it.

"You'd better stay where you are for now," he said.

I nodded again.

"But"—Mr. Guareschi leaned toward me—"I'll double-check your permanent record, Holling Hood. Be prepared for a change, should one be necessary."

In case you missed it again, that's another one of the dictator-of-a-small-country techniques: Keep you always off balance.

Mr. Guareschi scribbled over Mrs. Baker's memo. He folded it, then took out an envelope from his desk. Looking at me the whole time, he placed the memo in the envelope, licked the flap, and sealed it. He wrote *Mrs. Baker* on the outside. Then he handed it to me.

"Return this to her," he said. "The envelope had better be sealed when she receives it. I will make a point of inquiring about it."

So I took the envelope—sealed—and carried it back to Mrs. Baker—sealed. She unsealed it as I sat back down in my seat. She read what Mr. Guareschi had written and slowly placed the letter in the top drawer of her desk. Then she looked up at me.

"Regrettable."

She said all four syllables very slowly.

She could probably diagram each one if she wanted to.

I watched her carefully for the rest of the day, but nothing ever gave away her murderous intentions. She kept her face as still as Mount Rushmore, even when Doug Swieteck's new pen broke and spread bright blue ink all over his desk, or when the Rand McNally Map of the World fell off its hangers as she pulled it down, or when Mr. Guareschi reported during Afternoon Announcements that Lieutenant Tybalt Baker would soon be deployed to Vietnam with the 101st Airborne Division and we should all wish him, together with Mrs. Baker, well. Her face never changed once.

That's how it is with people who are plotting something awful.

october

The Wednesdays of September passed in a cloudy haze of chalk dust.

At 1:45, the bus arrived from Temple Beth-El to spring half of my class.

At 1:55, the bus arrived from Saint Adelbert's to spring the other half—even Mai Thi, who had to go to Catechism since it was the Catholic Relief Agency that had brought her over from Vietnam, and I guess they figured that she owed them, even though she wasn't Catholic.

Then Mrs. Baker and I sat. Alone. Facing each other. The classroom clock clicked off the minutes. She was probably considering what she could legally do to remind me how regrettable it was that my family was Presbyterian.

"There's no point teaching you something new," she said. "You'd just hear it a second time tomorrow." So that first Wednesday I washed all the chalkboards. Then I straightened the *Thorndike* dictionaries. Then I washed all the chalkboards again since they were streaky. Then I went outside and pounded the erasers against the brick wall of Camillo Junior High until the white chalk dust spread up and around me, settling in my hair and in my eyes and up my nose and down my throat, so that I figured I was probably going to end up with some sort of lung disease that would kill me before the end of the school year. All because I happened to be Presbyterian.

The second Wednesday of September, and the third, and the fourth, and Wednesdays on into October were pretty much the same. I got good at the chalkboards, so Mrs. Baker added putting up her bulletin boards with microscopic pins and leveling tools, and sweeping down the cobwebs from the asbestos tiles on the ceiling, and wiping the grime of sweaty hands off the lower half of the windows, then pushing them all up so that, as Mrs. Baker said, fresh air could circulate into the classroom.

Which it really needed, since once air reached the Coat Room, it landed on all the stuff from all the lunches that had been chucked into the corners because they were too vile to eat even when they were fresh. Lunches like liverwurst sandwiches.

So after I got good at the windows, Mrs. Baker got me cleaning out the Coat Room.

But what I didn't clean out was the stash that Doug Swieteck was hiding to prepare for Number 166. So far, there was a box of tapioca pudding, a bag of marshmallows that had been smashed into a sticky pulp, a half-dozen ragged feathers, a bottle of red ink, and a plastic bag with something awful in it. Probably something dead. He had it all in a small box from the A&P, stuffed on the shelf above the coats.

I didn't touch any of it.

And do you think I complained about this? Do you think I complained about picking up old lunches that had fungus growing on them and sweeping asbestos tiles and straightening *Thorndike* dictionaries? No, I didn't. Not once. Not even when I looked out the clean lower windows as the afternoon light of autumn changed to mellow and full yellows, and the air turned so sweet and cool that you wanted to drink it, and as people began to burn leaves on the sides of the streets and the lovely smoke came into the back of your nose and told you it was autumn, and what were you doing smelling chalk dust and old liverwurst sandwiches instead?

And why didn't I complain?

Because after the first week in October, the Baker Sporting Emporium narrowed its architect choices down to two—Hood-hood and Associates, and Kowalski and Associates—and so every single night after supper but before Walter Cronkite began reporting, my father said to me, "So Holling, everything all right with Mrs. Baker?" and I answered, "Just swell."

"Keep it that way," he'd say.

So I didn't complain.

Still, you would have thought that since all this was happening because I was a Presbyterian, God would have seen to it that the Yankees would have played in the World Series to pay me back for my persecution. But were they? Of course not. The world isn't fair that way. The Boston Red Sox were playing instead. And let me tell you, everyone knows that the Boston Red Sox are never going to win another World Series. Never. Not even if they have three Carl Yastrzemskis. Which they don't.

Doug Swieteck's brother was still not back in school, and Doug Swieteck told us why: The ten days of observation had been pure delight for him, but when no one had found any behavior beyond his usual weirdness, he realized that he would be coming back to school again pretty soon. So the evening before he was to return, when he came to his classroom with Mrs. Swie-teck to meet with his teacher, Doug Swieteck's brother walked up to the chalkboard and pounded the erasers against his head. Since

Mr. Ludema didn't have someone like me around to pound them against the brick walls every Wednesday afternoon, Doug Swieteck's brother's hair turned white after about four poundings. Then he took two long pieces of chalk, stuck them into his mouth like fangs, and went howling and roaring and slobbering out into the hallway.

The school was mostly deserted, so it really was just dumb luck that Mrs. Sidman, who had decided to leave her new post in the Main Administrative Office, had come into school that particular evening to clean out the last of her personal effects.

I think her screams echoed up and down the halls of Camillo Junior High until dawn.

That bought Doug Swieteck's brother another four weeks of medical observation. And it was pretty clear from Mrs. Baker's glares the next morning that, somehow, she thought this was all my fault. Which it wasn't. I didn't have a thing to do with it. But when someone hates your guts, truth, justice, and the American way don't mean all that much.

On Wednesday, when we all stood up to go to Mr. Petrelli's geography class, Mrs. Baker stopped glaring. In fact, as we walked out with *Geography for You and Me* in our hands, she started to smile at me. Then I got worried. She looked like those evil geniuses who suddenly figure out a plan to conquer the world and can already imagine earth's population quivering in their grasp.

It was all I could do not to sprint out of Mrs. Baker's classroom—even though we weren't supposed to run in the halls—to the safe world of junior high geography.

Mr. Petrelli believed that no class was worth anything without a Study Question Data Sheet. He dittoed these off like a major publisher. His hands were always blue from the ink, mostly because he hauled the dittos out from the machine while they were still wet from the alcohol—the smell of which gave the room a tang.

"Fill these out in pairs," he said. "You have forty-three minutes."

Forty-three minutes. Teachers don't reckon time the way normal people do.

When Meryl Lee came over to be my study partner, I was still wondering why Mrs. Baker had smiled.

"Are you all right?" Meryl Lee asked.

"Just swell."

"You're holding your pen upside down."

"Thanks for pointing that out, Detective Kowalski."

"You're very welcome. Do you think you can figure out the answers while I write them down on the sheet?"

"Why don't you figure out the answers while I write them down on the sheet?"

"Because I know how to write. What's the first state?"

"Delaware. Do you think Mrs. Baker looks like an evil genius?"

"Not unless you're paranoid. What's the second state?"

"I'm not paranoid. Pennsylvania. Mrs. Baker hates my guts."

"Mrs. Baker doesn't hate your guts, and you are, too, paranoid. What's the third state?"

"Well, thank you for your vote of confidence. New York."

Meryl Lee looked over at *Geography for You and Me*. "New York wasn't the third state. It was New Jersey, not New York."

"How do you know that?"

"Everybody knows that," she said.

Oh, out beyond Mr. Petrelli's not-so-clean lower windows it was one of those perfect blue autumn days, when the sun is warm and the grass is still green and the leaves are red and tipped with yellow.

A few white clouds drifted high, teased along by a breeze as gentle as a breath.

"What's the fourth state?" said Meryl Lee.

That's pretty much how it went for Meryl Lee and me until recess, which had become a whole lot safer since Mrs. Baker's failed assassination plot. I figured that most of her would-be assassins had seen what had happened to Doug Swieteck's brother and were worried I might take them out, too. So when we left Mr. Petrelli and went back to Mrs. Baker's classroom, I believed I could actually run out into the perfect October day and hope to come back alive.

I could feel the warm sun on my back already.

But then I found out why Mrs. Baker had been smiling.

"Mr. Hoodhood," she called from her desk as the school clock clicked to noon, "I have a quick job for you. Everyone else, enjoy your recess."

I looked at Meryl Lee. "See?" I whispered.

"You are paranoid," she said, and abandoned me.

"Mr. Hoodhood," said Mrs. Baker, "there are some pastries that Mrs. Bigio has spent the morning baking for me that need to be brought up to this room. Would you go down to the kitchen and bring them here? And do not start any rumors. These are not for the class. They are for the Wives of Vietnam Soldiers' gathering at Saint Adelbert's this afternoon. Not for anyone else."

"Is that all?" I said.

"Don't look so suspicious," she said. "Suspicion is an unbecoming passion."

I took my unbecoming passion and left to find Mrs. Bigio. This didn't seem like it would take too long, even though the seventh-grade classrooms were on the third floor and the kitchen was on the first floor, at the very end of the hallway—probably so that the wind could blow the fumes away. Sometimes that worked. And sometimes it didn't. When it didn't, the halls filled up with the scent of Hamburger-and-Pepper Surprise, a scent that lingered like the smell of a dead animal caught underneath the floorboards.

I think that Mrs. Bigio couldn't smell the scents, either because she wore a cotton mask over her face all the time or because she had worked in the kitchen of Camillo Junior High for so long that she could no longer smell.

But I didn't have a mask and I could smell, so when I reached the kitchen, I got ready to take a deep breath before I walked in. But then I realized I didn't need to. There were no fumes. There was only the delicious, extravagant, warm, tasty scent of buttery baking crust, and of vanilla cream, and of powdered sugar, still drifting in the heated air. And stretched out on the long tables, far from Whatever Surprise was being fed to Camillo Junior High for lunch that day, were a dozen trays of cream puffs—brown, light, perfect cream puffs.

"Mrs. Baker send you?" said Mrs. Bigio.

I nodded.

"You can start with that one," she said, pointing.

I thought, Shouldn't Mrs. Bigio be grateful for my willingness to help? Wouldn't any human being with a beating heart hand me one of the brown, light, perfect cream puffs? Was that so unlikely?

Yes. It was unlikely.

"Now would be a good time to start," said Mrs. Bigio. "And don't drop any."

I won't drop any, I thought, and you're very welcome.

I picked up a tray in each hand.

"One tray at a time," said Mrs. Bigio.

I looked at her. "That will take me twelve trips to the third floor," I said.

"So, Mr. Samowitz is teaching you some arithmetic after all. Don't drop any."

It took me the rest of lunch recess to carry the trays—one at a time—up to the classroom. Mrs. Baker smiled sweetly as I brought each one in. "Place them on the shelf by the windows. The cool air will keep them from getting soggy."

I thought of my father and the future of Hoodhood and Associates. I did not complain. Even when Mrs. Baker asked me to open the windows a little wider and I had to move all the trays—one at a time—so that I could reach over the shelf and jerk all the windows open a little wider, I did not complain.

"Thank you," said Mrs. Baker, as the school clock clicked to 12:30 and the classroom began to fill and Danny Hupfer came to punch me on the shoulder because he thought the cream puffs might be for us, which they weren't. He figured that out when Mrs. Baker told us to take our *Mathematics for You and Me* books, line up by the door, and then head to Mr. Samowitz's class.

Let me tell you, it is hard to care much about set theory when there are twelve trays of brown, light, perfect cream puffs cooling deliciously on a shelf back in your own classroom. Twelve sets of cream puffs divided by twenty-three kids plus Mrs. Baker meant half a set of cream puffs for every person in that room. And don't think we weren't all figuring out that same equation. And don't think we weren't all worrying that Mr. Samowitz's homeroom class, who had walked past us with *English for You and Me* in their hands, was trying to get those same hands on our cream puffs.

But they didn't, and when we came back in after set theory, the cream puffs were still there, cooling in the circulating air coming in beneath the clean lower windows. But Mrs. Baker acted like the cream puffs weren't there at all. And I suppose that in the end it didn't really matter that they were there. They may as well have been over with the Wives of Vietnam Soldiers at Saint Adelbert's already, for all the chance we had of getting one.

When 1:45 came, half the class left, and Danny Hupfer whispered, "If she gives you a cream puff after we leave, I'm going to kill you"—which was not something that someone headed off to prepare for his bar mitzvah should be thinking.

When 1:55 came and the other half of the class left, Meryl Lee whispered, "If she gives you one after we leave, I'm going to do Number 408 to you." I didn't remember what Number 408 was, but it was probably pretty close to what Danny Hupfer had promised.

Even Mai Thi looked at me with narrowed eyes and said, "I know your home." Which sounded pretty ominous.

But I knew I was safe. It was just as likely that President Lyndon B. Johnson himself would walk into the classroom as Mrs. Baker would give me a cream puff.

Actually, though, someone did come to the door after everyone had left. It wasn't President Johnson. It was a fifth grader from Camillo Elementary. He was carrying a box.

"There you are, Charles," said Mrs. Baker. "Did you get them all?"

"I think so."

"From Mr. Petrelli's class? And Mr. Samowitz?"

Charles nodded.

"And did you remember Mrs. Harknett downstairs?"

"Yes."

"And Mr. Ludema?"

"I got them all," Charles said.

"Thank you. You may put them here on the desk."

Charles put the box on Mrs. Baker's desk. He looked once at me—kind of sadly, I thought—then left, brushing his hands off.

Chalk dust fell from them.

"Mr. Hoodhood," said Mrs. Baker, "recent events have led the junior high school teachers to conclude that we need to be keeping our chalkboard erasers much cleaner. So I asked Charles to gather them from the classrooms and bring them here each Wednesday." She gestured toward the box on her desk. "Would you take care of them, please?"

If there ever was a time to complain, this was it. I walked over and looked into the box. There must have been thirty erasers in there. White with six weeks' worth of chalk.

This was really the time to complain.

But I thought of the future of Hoodhood and Associates.

I picked up the box of erasers.

"I'll be in the ditto room," said Mrs. Baker.

Just swell, I thought.

But then Mrs. Baker said something that made the world spin backward. "If we both finish in time, you may have one of the cream puffs."

I think I must have gone white.

"You needn't look so shocked," she said.

But I was shocked. She had offered the hope of a cream puff. A brown, light, perfect cream puff. It was as if Mrs. Baker had suddenly become not Mrs. Baker. It was like I had had another vision, only this one was real.

So before the vision could fade, I carried the box of erasers down the hall, down two flights of steps, and outside.

The day was still a perfect blue October day, as if it had been waiting for me since I'd missed it at lunch recess. It smelled of baseball, and the last cut of grass, and leaves drying out but still holding on. And for a while I could smell all of it.

But the cloud of white chalk that comes out of thirty erasers is pretty impressive, let me tell you. I pounded and pounded them against the wall. And the chalk dust that didn't get into my lungs flew and twisted with the breeze that curled against the first-floor classrooms, coating all the windows—the teachers had learned to close them on Wednesday afternoons now.

A cream puff. At the end of a long school day. Brown, light, and perfect. And no one—not Danny Hupfer, not Meryl Lee, not Mai Thi—no one needed to know.

The cloud of chalk dust wafted higher. It flew up to the second-floor windows—all closed.

Maybe Mrs. Baker would give me two. After all, there were twelve trays of the things. Maybe two.

The chalk dust wafted with the swirling breeze—past the second-floor windows and then up to the third-floor windows.

Maybe she would give me a third cream puff to take home.

The chalk dust gathered by the seventh-grade windows.

Windows someone had left open so the air could circulate.

Mrs. Baker's windows.

Open next to the brown, light, perfect cream puffs so that they wouldn't get soggy!

I ran up desperately, lugging the box of thirty erasers, twenty-three of which had sent their chalk dust toward Mrs. Baker's windows.

But I was too late.

The cloud of chalk dust had drifted in, and then gravity had taken over. The chalk had fallen gently upon each one of the cream puffs. They looked like Mrs. Bigio had spread an extra-thick layer of powdered sugar on top.

"Are you picking out the one you would like?" Mrs. Baker came back into the room with a pile of blue dittos.

"Not really," I said.

"Choose quickly, then," she said, "and we'll carry the trays down to my car."

I picked one up off the tray. It felt a little gritty.

Then I helped Mrs. Baker carry all the trays down to her car—one at a time—hoping that the Wives of Vietnam Soldiers would not notice the chalk dust all that much.

Between trips, I threw my own cream puff into the Coat Room, beside the moldering lunches.

You know how a story gets told in a small town, and how every time someone tells it, it gets bigger and bigger, until it's a flat-out lie? That's what happened to the story of the cream puffs at Saint Adelbert's that afternoon. By the time the story got back to my father—which took only sixteen hours, since he heard it the moment he arrived at Hoodhood and Associates Thursday morning—it said that every single one of the Wives of Vietnam Soldiers had nearly choked to death while eating cream puffs—which had to have been an exaggeration. At first, according to the story, they had turned on Mrs. Baker, but when they realized that Mrs. Baker could not even imagine pulling a practical joke, they had turned on Mrs. Bigio, who was also one of the Wives of Vietnam Soldiers. When Mrs. Bigio assured them that there must have been something wrong with the powdered sugar and she would be sure to write the company to complain, they decided that they would not expel her from the Wives of Vietnam Soldiers. However, she would never again be their Official Cook. Never.

At this, Mrs. Bigio had tearfully insisted that the cream puffs were really not that bad after all, and she had put a whole one into her mouth, chewed, and swallowed.

The doctor at Saint Ignatius Hospital said that the spell had come on when she refused to let herself cough even once.

That night at supper, my father looked at me with an unbecoming passion.

"Holling," he said, "everything all right with Mrs. Baker?"

"Just swell," I said.

"You didn't help to make her cream puffs yesterday, did you?"

"No, sir."

"You didn't sneak down to the school kitchen and do anything to Mrs. Bigio's powdered sugar?"

"No, sir. No sneaking."

"So everything is all right?"

"Just swell."

"You don't know anything about—"

Okay, this is where God broke in to pay me back for all that had happened because I was a Presbyterian, because if my father had finished this question, I might have had to give him something pretty far from the truth. But he never finished it, because my sister came in and sat down across from me, and on her cheek she had painted a bright yellow flower.

My father stared at it, then turned to my mother.

"Tell your daughter that she has a bright yellow flower painted on her cheek."

"I know I have a flower painted on my cheek," said my sister.

"Why?" said my father.

"Isn't it obvious?"

"Not unless you want us to believe that you're a flower child."

My sister didn't say anything.

There was a little pause while the whole world sucked in its breath.

"No," said my father, "you're not a flower child."

"A flower child is beautiful and doesn't do anything to harm anyone," said my sister.

My father closed his eyes.

"We believe in peace and understanding and freedom. We believe in sharing and helping each other. We're going to change the world."

"A flower child," said my father, opening his eyes, "is a hippie who lives in Greenwich Village in dirty jeans and beads and who can't change a pair of socks."

"Fifty thousand flower children protested the war at the Pentagon today. They all say you're wrong."

"Fortunately, right and wrong don't depend on math."

"They don't depend on President Johnson, either."

"Thank you, Miss Political Analyst," said my father. "Now analyze this: The person to whom you are now speaking is a candidate for the Chamber of Commerce Businessman of 1967. This is an honor that he has wanted for a long time. It is also an honor that will lead to larger, more profitable ventures than he has yet seen. It is not an honor that is awarded to a man who has a daughter who calls herself a flower child. So go wash your face."

There was another one of those long pauses because the world still hadn't let out its breath. It was a really long pause. The world must have been about ready to have a spell.

Then my sister shoved back her chair and went upstairs. She came down with only a yellow smudge.

"Pass the lima beans," said my father.

౧౦

That night, my sister opened my door.

"Thanks for all your help, Holling."

"A flower child? You want support for being a flower child?"

"I want support for believing in something bigger than just me."

"Then don't paint a bright yellow flower on your face. You looked stupid."

"Imagine that," she said. "And *you* don't have to paint anything on your face to look stupid."

"You're not going to get my support that way," I pointed out.

"Fifty thousand people at the Pentagon, Holling. Fifty thousand. Something big is happening, and it's starting right now. Maybe it's time to think about growing up."

"So I can become a flower child?"

"So you can become who you're supposed to be: Holling Hoodhood."

"In case you haven't noticed, I *am* Holling Hoodhood."

"Isn't it comforting to think so? But when I look at you, you're just the Son Who Is Going to Inherit Hoodhood and Associates."

"It's the same thing," I said.

"Only if you let it be the same thing. Why do you let him bully you? Why don't you ever stand up to him?"

"And it works so well when you stand up to him."

My sister put her hand up to her cheek.

"So why do it?" I said.

"To let him know that I don't like being told who I am, and who I'm going to be."

"You don't have a flower on your cheek now. It doesn't look like it made a whole lot of difference."

"It makes a difference to me," she said, and went to her bedroom to play the Monkees. Loudly.

The next morning, Mrs. Baker was waiting for me by the Coat Room. "Mr. Hoodhood, I have been thinking about our Wednesday afternoon routines, and we need to make some changes."

Remember the ham and cheese and broccoli omelet?

"We do?" I said.

"We do. We'll talk about it on Wednesday. But no more chores—or perhaps, just one more."

"One more?"

"For another cream puff, perhaps."

I felt my unbecoming passion rising.

"Okay," I said. "One more chore. But I don't need the cream puff."

"Imagine that," said Mrs. Baker, and walked away. This was a new strategy, I was sure. But I didn't have time to figure it out.

"You got one of the cream puffs?" said Meryl Lee.

"Not exactly," I said.

"Mrs. Baker just said, 'For another cream puff.' *Another.* And you said, 'Okay.' So how is that 'not exactly'?"

Danny Hupfer came over. "You got one of the cream puffs?"

"I didn't eat it."

"Sure, you didn't eat it. You put it up high on a shelf so you could just look at it."

"No. I really didn't eat it."

"You owe us all cream puffs," said Meryl Lee.

"What do you mean, I owe you all cream puffs?"

"I'll speak slowly and clearly: You . . . owe . . . us . . . all . . . cream . . . puffs."

"Where am I supposed to get cream puffs for the whole class?"

"That's your problem," said Danny Hupfer. "Find the cream puffs or die."

Mai Thi looked at me, and narrowed her eyes.

Let me tell you, it's a pretty hard thing to be a seventh grader with new death threats hanging over you just about every day.

On the way home that day, I stopped at Goldman's Best Bakery. They had cream puffs, too—without chalk dust. But you wouldn't believe how much they wanted for them! It would take three weeks' worth of allowance to be able to pay for twenty-two cream puffs. Three weeks!

The world is not a fair place.

On Monday, I told Danny and Meryl Lee and Mai Thi that I needed three weeks. They agreed. Sort of. But the death threats were repeated every day, along with new and colorful descriptions of what would happen if the cream puffs didn't appear. Let me tell you, Danny Hupfer has one bloody imagination, but he is nothing compared to Meryl Lee. I was almost glad when Wednesday came and Mrs. Baker and I were alone again.

Can you believe it? I felt safer with Mrs. Baker!

Even if I still hadn't figured out the new strategy.

"Mr. Hoodhood," said Mrs. Baker, "we have been wasting our opportunities."

"We have?"

"We have. On Wednesday afternoons from now on, we will be reading Shakespeare together."

"Shakespeare."

"You don't need to repeat everything I say. I presume you know the English language well enough or I wouldn't ask you to read Shakespeare."

I nodded.

"First we'll read *The Merchant of Venice* aloud together, so that I can be sure that you are following the dialogue. Afterward, you'll be reading on your own."

Reading Shakespeare. Of all the strategies Mrs. Baker could come up with, this must be the worst. Teachers bring up Shakespeare only to bore students to death. And I was going to be bored to death for eight months. No human being could stand it.

"Are you sure you don't want me to pound erasers instead?"

Mrs. Baker shook her head. "There's only one last chore," she said. "Sycorax and Caliban need their cage cleaned out."

I looked across the classroom at Sycorax and Caliban.

I haven't told you about Sycorax and Caliban yet, and you might want to skip over this next part, since it's pretty awful.

Because Sycorax and Caliban were rats.

Every other classroom in Camillo Junior High had fish or hamsters or gerbils or mice.

We had rats.

The reason we had rats, Mrs. Baker told us, is that Lieutenant Tybalt Baker had picked them out for her when they were only cute balls of fuzz and pink snouts playing in clean and aromatic cedar shavings. He had seen them in a pet-shop window, and when he went inside and put his finger to their cage, one of them had come and licked it. Right then, he decided that they needed a home.

So here they were in our classroom, and Mrs. Baker wasn't going to get rid of anything that Lieutenant Baker had given her—even if she wouldn't go near them herself.

Actually, no one in the class had ever gone near Sycorax and Caliban—not even Doug Swieteck, and he would do anything—because they weren't cute balls of fuzz anymore. They looked like they weighed about fifteen pounds each. They had hair the color of cardboard in splotches over parts of their bodies, but mostly they were just yellow and scabby skinned. If anyone even looked at them, they threw themselves against the sides of their cage and stuck their scabby snouts out as far as they could and clacked their long yellow teeth together. The sounds that came out of their throats were never heard anywhere else in Nature.

They probably carried plague.

"I can't clean the cage with them in it," I said.

"In the cupboard beneath the counter is a smaller cage. Pour some food into it, put the door to that cage next to the door in the bigger cage, and open them both. Sycorax and Caliban will run into the smaller cage. Then you can clean their cage."

It sounded too easy, and I looked at Mrs. Baker to see if something in her eyes said "Plot." But I couldn't see her eyes, because she was opening an ancient green book and turning thin pages. "Hurry, Mr. Hoodhood, so we can enjoy the play," she said.

I found the small cage in the cupboard, and even though I didn't think it would work out just like Mrs. Baker had said, it actually did. The rats were so hungry, I guess, that they would have done anything to get at the food. They probably would have eaten chalk-covered cream puffs. So when I opened the doors, Sycorax and Caliban laid off sticking out their scabby snouts and clacking their yellow teeth and rioted into the smaller cage. Then I carried the big cage outside to the garbage cans, holding it as far away from me as I could reach. I dumped everything, then carried the cage to the faucet near Mr. Vendleri's office. I hosed it down from about twenty feet away. I wasn't going to touch anything I didn't have to.

I got paper towels from the boys' restroom and dried the whole thing off. Then I carried it back upstairs into the classroom, spread new sawdust—there was a whole bucket of it in the back of the cup-board—and filled the food and water dishes in the big cage.

In the small cage, Caliban and Sycorax were back to their scabby-snout-and-yellow-teeth routine, but they were a little less frantic about it, probably because they had just stuffed themselves. The blacks of their eyes seemed almost natural, not like they were possessed.

I slid the two cages together, held them tightly against each other, and opened the two doors. Sycorax and Caliban started to clamber in.

"By the way," said Mrs. Baker from her desk, "teachers do not bring up Shakespeare to bore their students to death."

She knew! She could tell what I had been thinking!

And so you see, what happened next wasn't my fault at all.

I turned around, sort of stunned, to look at Mrs. Baker, and I felt the two cages move apart.

"Mr. Hoodhood!" cried Mrs. Baker, suddenly standing up.

Sycorax and Caliban each had half their bodies pushed into the space between the two cages. Their scabby snouts were twitching triumphantly, and their teeth were clacking as close to my thumbs as they could get. I smashed the two cages together, hard, and they let out a high, awful rat screech. They both turned their little black eyes toward me—bulging with demonic light—and clawed hysteri-cally at the bars that were hardly holding them from escape. And they kept on screeching.

"Don't hurt them!" cried Mrs. Baker, who was now halfway across the room. So I pulled apart the two cages just a little bit, and Sycorax whirled, hissed, threw herself on top of Caliban, and pushed through. Then she leaped at my thumb, her yellow jaws open.

"Oh!" I said, and jumped back from the cages.

"*Hiss,*" said Caliban, and jumped out from the cages.

"*Screech,*" said Sycorax, and jumped down from the counter.

"*Hiss,*" said Caliban again, and jumped down from the counter over the cupboard after her.

"Oh!" said Mrs. Baker, and jumped onto Danny Hupfer's desk.

"Oh!" I said again, as Sycorax and Caliban ran over my foot— over my foot!—and headed into the Coat Room, where they threw themselves into the pile of fungused lunch remnants.

Mrs. Baker and I were both breathing pretty hard by this time, so what she said next came out in a sort of strangled whisper. "Go get Mr. Vendleri. Quickly."

I did, jumping from desk to desk, since I wasn't going to take any chances—Over My Foot!

I didn't tell Mr. Vendleri what we needed him for until we got to the classroom, because I wasn't certain he would come if I did. He looked at us with wide eyes while we told him. (I was back up on a desk.) Then he nodded, went down the hall to the supply closet, and came back with a shovel and two brooms. "You two flush them out from that side," he said. "I'll be waiting with the shovel."

"Flush them out?" I said.

"Don't hurt them," said Mrs. Baker.

"Flush them out?" I said again. I guess they hadn't heard me.

"I won't hurt them unless they're going to hurt me," said Mr. Vendleri—which is exactly what they tried to do.

Mrs. Baker and I climbed down from the desks.

"Flush them out?" I said a third time.

"Mr. Hoodhood, be bold," said Mrs. Baker.

Let me tell you, we probably did not look bold as we crept toward the Coat Room with our brooms. Or when we poked at the moldering lunch remnants. Or when we peered behind the coats still hanging there. And I know we didn't look bold when the rats erupted from Doug Swieteck's coat with a full scale of screeches. They howled and roared and slobbered toward Mr. Vendleri, Sycorax with a decaying cream puff still in her yellow jaws. We heard Mr. Vendleri holler "Oh!" and by the time we got to the other side of the Coat Room, Mr. Vendleri was up on Danny Hupfer's desk.

"Climbed into the radiators," he said, pointing.

But they weren't there long.

We heard hissing. We heard scrambling up the walls. We heard heavy pattering across the asbestos ceiling tiles. Then all was silence. The only thing that remained of their passing was the cream puff, abandoned before Sycorax had climbed into the radiator.

"I'd better tell Mr. Guareschi," said Mr. Vendleri.

Mrs. Baker, who had somehow gotten up onto her desk, looked at me, then at the cream puff, and then back at me. "Perhaps you had better hurry," she said.

And that was all. Nothing about the cream puff.

Whatever this new strategy was, it was good.

So Mr. Vendleri went to report, and soon Mr. Guareschi arrived at the scene of the escape. He was breathing heavily, since principals and dictators of small countries aren't used to running. He looked over the two cages, peered into the Coat Room, and then put his ear to the walls. "I don't hear a thing," he said. None of us did, either.

"They might be gone," said Mr. Vendleri hopefully.

"How did they get out in the first place?" Mr. Guareschi asked, as if that made a whole lot of difference now.

"I was cleaning their cage," I said.

"It was my fault," said Mrs. Baker. "I shouldn't have had him do it."

"Indeed not," said Mr. Guareschi. He rubbed his chin, considering. "But they're out now, and we can't let anyone know. Do you all understand? Until the . . . escapees . . . are caught, not a soul outside of this room hears about the incident." Mr. Guareschi's voice got low and menacing. "Not. One. Soul."

And so began Mr. Guareschi's Campaign Against the Escapees.

And by the way, for the record, I didn't exactly say "Oh" when Sycorax and Caliban jumped out from the cages.

Neither did Mr. Vendleri.

And neither did Mrs. Baker.

I wasn't sure that I wanted to be left in the classroom alone with Mrs. Baker after Mr. Guareschi and Mr. Vendleri left to begin planning campaign strategy. She still hadn't said anything about the cream puff, and I figured it had to come sooner or later. It turned out to be sooner.

As soon as the door closed, Mrs. Baker put her hands on her hips and looked at me thoughtfully.

"You never did eat the cream puff, did you?" she said.

I shook my head slowly. I tried to look guiltless.

"But you pretended that you did."

I said nothing. The future of Hoodhood and Associates was suddenly shaky.

"You made a wise culinary choice. Go sit down."

And that was it. Really. That was all she said.

I was about to climb down off my desk, but first I looked around to be sure that nothing was lurking on the floor.

"Mr. Hoodhood," said Mrs. Baker impatiently.

I wanted to point out that she was still standing on her own desk, but since Hoodhood and Associates was suddenly okay again, I didn't. But when Mrs. Baker saw me hesitate, she looked around, then climbed down from the desk to the chair to the floor. She hesitated a bit herself before she put her feet on the floor. "Now go sit down," she said. She opened the lowest drawer of her desk. She pulled out an ancient black book to match the ancient green book, and blew away cobwebs from it. Then she brought the black book to my desk and thumped it down. It smelled of must and dust.

"The plays of William Shakespeare," said Mrs. Baker, "which can never be boring to the true soul. Open it to *The Merchant of Venice*."

I did.

The rest of that afternoon, we both held our feet up off the floor and took turns reading parts from *The Merchant of Venice* — even though the print was made for tiny insects with multiple eyes and all the pictures in the book were ridiculous. I mean, no one really stands as if they're posing to be a flower, and no one would wear the stuff they were wearing and dare to go outside.

But it turned out that Mrs. Baker's strategy didn't work after all! She had wanted to bore me to death, even though she said that she didn't — which was all part of the strategy. But *The Merchant of Venice* was okay.

There's no Jim Hawkins. And the stuff about Shylock was slow at first. But it picks up with him in the courtroom, ready to cut out a pound of Antonio's flesh because Antonio hasn't been able to pay — which is exactly what Long John Silver would have done. And then Portia comes in and gives this speech that turns everything upside down.

> But mercy is above this sceptred sway;
> It is enthroned in the hearts of kings.

When Mrs. Baker read that, I had shivers running up and down me.

But Shylock didn't. He was ready to get to work with his knife, when Portia turns everything upside down again and the judge ends up freeing Antonio.

> *The quality of mercy is not strained,*
> *It droppeth as the gentle rain from heaven*
> *Upon the place beneath.*

Those are words to make you shiver.

So, another nefarious Mrs. Baker plot foiled.

That night, I dreamed about Doug Swieteck's brother as Shylock, and him bending over me with a soccer ball in his hand, about to smash it into my face because I had taken him out. And then Meryl Lee comes up, and Doug Swieteck's brother looks at her, and I look at her, and I'm waiting for the quality-of-mercy-dropping-like-a-gentle-rain-upon-the-place-beneath speech, and Meryl Lee opens her mouth and says to Doug Swieteck's brother,

> *Go thou ahead.*
> *Droppeth thine soccer ball as thunder from the clouds*
> *Upon his head beneath thee.*

Those are words to make you shiver, too.

And then I look over at Mrs. Baker, who is the judge standing by, and she is smiling because she's wearing a yellow flower on her cheek. And then I look around the courtroom, and there's my father, and I'm thinking, Maybe he can bribe the judge, and he says, "Is everything all right with Mrs. Baker?" and I say, "Just swell" and he says, "Then what did you do?" And Mrs. Baker keeps smiling.

Let me tell you, if Shakespeare had known about me and Meryl

Lee and Doug Swieteck's brother and Mrs. Baker, he really would have had something to write about.

We read *The Merchant of Venice* the next Wednesday, too, and finished it on the last Wednesday of October. After we closed our books, Mrs. Baker asked me to discuss the character of Shylock.

"He isn't really a villain," I said, "is he?"

"No," said Mrs. Baker, "he isn't."

"He's more like someone who wants . . ."

"Who wants what, Mr. Hoodhood?"

"Someone who wants to become who he's supposed to be," I said.

Mrs. Baker considered that. "And why couldn't he?" she asked.

"Because they wouldn't let him. They decided he had to be a certain way, and he was trapped. He couldn't be anything except for what he was," I said.

"And that is why the play is called a tragedy," said Mrs. Baker.

november

November dripped onto Long Island, as it did every year. The days turned gray and damp, and a hovering mist licked everything. The perfect white cement sidewalk in front of the Perfect House was always wet. The azaleas lost the remnants of their white and pink blossoms, and then many of their leaves, and since they were half-naked and embarrassed, my father wrapped them in tight burlap— which also got wet. On the first Saturday, I cut the lawn for the last time, and then my father cut the lawn again to get it right, since it was going to look this way until spring, he said, and it had better look good. The next Saturday we climbed up to the roof and cleaned out the gutters, since they were overflowing now every time it rained and the dirty water was staining the corners of the Perfect House. Which made my father really mad.

But not as mad as the stain on the ceiling of the Perfect Living Room made him. No one knew how long water had been dripping down onto it, because no one ever went in there. So by the time my mother discovered it while vacuuming, the stain was as wide as a garbage can lid, and dark with mold. That night, when my father reached up to feel it, a handful of plaster came down on his face. Some of the moldy stuff got into his mouth.

It was a very quiet supper.

But that's November. It's the kind of month where you're grateful for every single glimpse of the sun, or any sign of blue sky above the clouds, because you're not sure that they're there anymore. And if you can't have sun or blue sky, then you wish it would snow and cover all the gray world with a sparkling white so bright that your eye can't take it in.

But it doesn't snow on Long Island in November. It rains. And rains and rains.

Which is how, I think, Mrs. Baker got the idea of assigning me *The Tempest*.

But her nefarious plot to bore me to death failed again, because *The Tempest* was even better than *The Merchant of Venice*. In fact, it almost beat out *Treasure Island*—which is saying something.

It was surprising how much good stuff there was. A storm, attempted murders, witches, wizards, invisible spirits, revolutions, characters drinking until they're dead drunk, an angry monster named Caliban—can you believe it? I was amazed that Mrs. Baker was letting me read this. It's got to be censored all over the place. I figured that she hadn't read it herself, otherwise she would never have let me at it.

Caliban—the monster in the play, not the escaped rat—he knew cuss words. I mean, he really knew cuss words. What Mr. Vendleri said while standing on Danny Hupfer's desk didn't come close. Even Doug Swieteck's brother couldn't cuss like that—and he could cuss the yellow off a school bus.

I decided to learn them all by heart—even if I didn't know exactly what they meant. I didn't know what most of Doug Swieteck's brother's cusses meant, either, and it didn't make all that much difference. It's all in the delivery anyway. So I practiced in my bedroom, thinking of my sister.

A southwest blow on ye and blister you all o'er!

I know, it doesn't sound like much. But if you say it slow and menacing, especially when you get to "blister," it'll do. Keep your eyes half-closed, and it will really do. But for the rest of the Caliban curses, it's a lot better to say them loud and fast, like:

The red plague rid you!

and:

Toads, beetles, bats, light on you!

and:

As wicked dew as e'er my mother brushed with raven's feather from unwholesome fen drop on you.

I'm not exactly sure what that last one means, but if you really hit the last three words hard, it will do its stuff.

I told you that Mrs. Baker wouldn't have let me read this if she'd read it herself.

Every night after supper, I practiced in front of the dresser mirror—without my shirt, because I could look more menacing that way. I decided to perfect the "Toads, beetles, bats" one first, since that was the one I understood the best and because when I said it, a little bit of spit came out with the "beetles."

By the second Tuesday night, I had gotten it about down and could say "toads" with a bloodcurdling croak when my mother knocked on my bedroom door.

"Holling?" she said. "Are you all right?"

"I'm fine," I called.

"It sounds like you're talking to someone."

"I'm practicing for a speech," I said, which was sort of true.

"Oh," she said. "Oh. Then I'll leave you to finish."

I worked on the "red plague" for a bit, because that one is all in the timing.

Then my father knocked on the door. There must have been a commercial on.

"I can hear you all the way down in the den. What are you doing?"

"Practicing Shakespeare," I said.

"What do you need Shakespeare for?"

"For Mrs. Baker."

"For Mrs. Baker?"

"Yes."

"Then get it right," he said, and walked away.

I went back to the "toads, beetles, bats" until my sister knocked on the door.

"Holling?"

"Yeah."

"Shut up."

"A southwest blow on ye and blister you all o'er," I said.

She threw open my door. "*What* did you say to me?"

In the face of a sixteen-year-old sister who's about to drop something on you from heaven, even Shakespeare fails. "Nothing," I said.

"Keep it that way," she said, "and put your shirt on, you weirdo." She slammed the door shut.

I decided I was done with practicing for the night.

I went to school early the next day, since I needed some private place to practice the curses. When I reached the third floor, I found

Mr. Vendleri holding a ladder steady in the middle of the hall. He had half a dozen spring traps in his hand, which he was holding up toward Mr. Guareschi. I could see only Mr. Guareschi's legs, since the rest of him was poked up through an opening where he'd removed some asbestos tiles.

"Hand me the rest," Mr. Guareschi called down, and Mr. Vendleri did.

"Now the cheese."

Mr. Vendleri reached into his bib overalls and pulled out a plastic bag with cubes of yellow cheese.

"Now, I'll just pull this spring back," Mr. Guareschi said, "and set the bait right beneath—"

There was a sudden loud snap, and then it wasn't mercy dropping down as the gentle rain on the place beneath. It was Mr. Guareschi.

"Oh," he said.

(Not really "Oh," but it wasn't as good as Shakespeare. Not even as good as Mrs. Baker.)

Mr. Guareschi looked up from the floor. His face was red, and his fingers redder. He shook them wildly, as if he wanted them to separate from the rest of him. "Oh," he said again.

(Not really.)

"You could try 'The red plague rid you!'" I said.

Mr. Guareschi, still on the ground, looked up at me. "What are you doing in school so early?" he said.

"Or 'Scurvy patch!'" I said.

Mr. Guareschi shook his fingers again. "You're not supposed to be here this early," he said.

"He saw us putting up the cages," said Mr. Vendleri.

Mr. Guareschi stared at him. "This is the student who let the rats go," he said. "He already knows."

Mr. Vendleri looked hard at me. Then he put his finger up to his lips. "Not a word," he said.

"Toads, beetles, bats light on me if I let it out," I said, and I got the timing just right—even the little bit of spit on the "beetles."

Mr. Guareschi looked at me strangely, and then he slowly stood, picked up the spring traps that had fallen around him, and turned to climb back up the ladder. Considering the condition of his red fingers, I thought it was pretty brave of him.

"Go to class, Holling Hood," he said.

Mrs. Baker was already in her classroom. She was looking up at the ceiling when I came in, listening to the scrambling and pattering of feet scurrying across the asbestos tiles overhead. We listened together for a moment until the scurrying stopped.

"Not a word, Mr. Hoodhood," she said.

"Not a word," I said, and went to my desk.

"Did you finish *The Tempest*?" asked Mrs. Baker.

"Yes," I said.

"We'll see this afternoon," she said, and she turned back to a pile of essays on her desk, spreading a red plague over them with her pen.

Even though I didn't have the private place to practice that I wanted, I figured I could work on the Caliban curses to see if I could get them down just right in a pressure situation. So I whispered into my desk, "Strange stuff, the dropsy drown you"—which was cheating a little, because I put two together. But I thought it sounded right. I tried it again, thinking about Caliban and Sycorax—the rats, not the monsters in the play—because I wanted to make the "strange stuff" come out more like a hiss.

"Strange stuff, the dropsy drown you," I whispered.

"Is there something you have to say?" asked Mrs. Baker.

I sat up. "No," I said.

"Are you speaking to someone hiding in your desk?"

I shook my head.

She put her red pen down. "Since there are only two of us in the room—a situation which has become very familiar to us these past months—and since you were speaking, I assumed that you must be addressing me. What did you say?"

"Nothing."

"Mr. Hoodhood, what did you say?"

"'Strange stuff, the dropsy drown you.'"

Mrs. Baker considered me for a moment. "Was that what you said?"

"Yes."

"A curious line to recite, especially since the combination never occurs in the play. Are you trying to improve on Shakespeare?"

"I like the rhythm of it," I said.

"The rhythm of it."

"Yes."

Mrs. Baker considered this for a moment. Then she nodded. "So do I," she said, and turned back to spreading the red plague.

That had been close.

But I watched her with something like amazement.

She had known the curses! Both of them!

She had read the play!

And she had still let me read it!

Whatever she was plotting, it was a whole lot more devious than I had given her credit for.

I decided to ease into things more naturally, to let Caliban curses come where they might fit in without any fuss.

At lunch, I found that my mother had given me a bologna

sandwich with no mayonnaise, a stalk of celery that had been wilting since the weekend, and a cookie with something growing on it that wasn't supposed to be there.

"Strange stuff," I whispered.

At lunch recess, Doug Swieteck's brother lurched across the field, sixth graders scurrying out of his way as if he was a southwest wind about to blister them all over.

"Thou jesting monkey thou," I said.

Not so that he could hear it.

Right after recess, I found that the eighth graders had filled the boys' restroom with smoke so thick you couldn't even smell the disinfectant.

"Apes with foreheads villainous low," I said.

Not so that they could hear it.

In Geography, Mr. Petrelli announced a unit project: "The Mississippi River and You." I raised my hand and told Mr. Petrelli that I had never been to the Mississippi River and had no plans to go soon. I didn't feel any kind of personal stake in it at all, so I didn't understand the "You" part.

"Must all history center around your own personal experience, Hoodhood?" Mr. Petrelli asked.

It did seem that since we were talking about the Mississippi River and You—or in this case, Me—one possible answer to his question would be yes. But in Camillo Junior High, and especially in Mr. Petrelli's class, the right answer is usually just shutting up.

"Your report," Mr. Petrelli continued to the class, "can be on . . ."

I whispered the "Toads, beetles, bats" one here and got it just right.

In Chorus, Miss Violet of the Very Spiky Heels—the "Very Spiky Heels" line isn't in Shakespeare, it's from Danny Hupfer—

Miss Violet of the Very Spiky Heels figured we had way too many altos, and she told me to move forward to sing the melody with the sopranos.

"Me?" I said.

"You have a lovely, clear voice, Holling."

"I can't sing soprano."

"Of course you can," said Miss Violet. "Just reach for the high notes."

I gave my music—my tenor music—to Danny Hupfer. "You have a lovely, clear voice, Holling," he said.

"Pied ninny," I said.

Meryl Lee made room for me on her music stand. "You didn't know you could sing like a girl, did you?" she said.

"Blind mole, a wicked dew from unwholesome fen drop you," I said. I was getting good at making combinations.

Meryl Lee grabbed my arm. "What did you say?"

Miss Violet of the Very Spiky Heels tapped her baton for silence. Then she raised her hands and waved them grandly, and we began a medley of American folk songs—which are supposed to make your heart swell patriotically. I tried to look like I cared a whole lot about reaching for the high notes, of which there were more than enough.

Meryl Lee still held my arm. "What did you say?" she asked again.

"I'm just a poor wayfaring stranger . . ."

"That's not what you said," she said.

"A-trav'ling through this world of woe. . ."

Meryl Lee moved her hand up toward my throat.

Then Miss Violet of the Very Spiky Heels tapped her baton again.

Everyone went quiet.

"Meryl Lee?" Miss Violet said.

Meryl Lee dropped her hand and looked at Miss Violet. Her cheeks flushed into a color you only see in television cartoons.

"Meryl Lee," said Miss Violet, "I didn't send Holling up there so that you could flirt with him."

Well, the look that came over Meryl Lee's face was the look you'd have if you wanted the earth to open up so that you could jump in and no one would see you again forever and ever. Her mouth opened, and her eyes opened, and her nostrils opened. Even the freckles across her nose got a whole lot bigger.

Miss Violet tapped the baton again, and we started to sing.

"Yes, we're all dodging, dodging, dodging, dodging,
Yes, we're all dodging a way through the world."

I tried not to show anything when Meryl Lee put her foot on top of mine and pushed down as hard as she could, which, let me tell you, teaches you something about a world of woe, and dodging, too.

The next hour was Gym, where we ran laps around the track along with the eighth-grade class, who all smelled smoky—especially Doug Swieteck's brother.

"Hoodhood," called Coach Quatrini, "you call that running?"

The quality of mercy doesn't drop much from Gym teachers.

The reason I wasn't running well was because Meryl Lee had

kept pushing down on my foot for all of "Goin' Down the Road
Feeling Bad" and almost all of "Worried Man Blues," and if it's possible for there to be internal bleeding in a foot, then that's what
mine was doing.

"Pied ninny," I said, not loud enough for Coach Quatrini to
hear me.

But loud enough for Doug Swieteck's brother, who was running just behind me, to hear.

"What does that mean?" he said, coming up beside me.

"What?"

He slowed down to match my limp. "'Pied ninny.' What does
that mean?"

"Uh . . ."

"C'mon," said Doug Swieteck's brother.

"It means . . . uh . . ."

"You don't know."

"It means someone who's so stupid that he's eaten all these pies
and gotten really sick—sick like he's going to throw up all over himself. That sick."

It was the best I could do while limping along with internal
bleeding.

"That's it?" he said.

"That's it," I said.

"Thanks," he said, and ran ahead, the scent of cigarette smoke
lingering in the air.

That afternoon, after everyone had left for Temple Beth-El or Saint
Adelbert's, Mrs. Baker handed me a 150-question test on *The Tempest*. One hundred and fifty questions! Let me tell you, Shakespeare
himself couldn't have answered half of these questions.

"Show me what you've read and understood," said Mrs. Baker.

I sat down at my desk and picked up my pencil.

"And Mr. Hoodhood," she said, "there isn't a single question there about Caliban's curses—presuming, as I do, that you have mastered those already."

That's the Teacher Gene at work, giving its bearer an extra sense. It's a little frightening. Maybe that's how people decide to become teachers. They have that extra sense, and once they have it, and know that they have it, they don't have any choice except to become a teacher.

I got down to work. Overhead, the scurrying sounds of Caliban and Sycorax across the asbestos tiles accompanied the scratching of my pencil.

I handed the test in five minutes before the end of the day. Mrs. Baker took it calmly, then reached into her bottom drawer for an enormous red pen with a wide felt tip. "Stand here and we'll see how you've done," she said, which is sort of like a dentist handing you a mirror and saying, "Sit here and watch while I drill a hole in your tooth." The first four were wrong, and she slashed through my answers with a broad swathe of bright red ink. It looked like my test was bleeding to death.

"Not such a good beginning," she said.

"The quality of mercy is not strained," I said.

She looked up at me and almost smiled a real smile. Not a teacher smile. Think of it! Mrs. Baker almost smiling a real smile.

"Nothing so much as a pound of flesh is at stake."

You could have fooled me.

Maybe it was mercy, or maybe I just needed to get into the rhythm of the thing, but after the first four wrong, the rest went pretty well, and the gushing blood slowed to a trickle, and then, for the last thirty questions in a row, a complete stop.

"You've coagulated, Mr. Hoodhood," Mrs. Baker said, which I think is a Caliban curse that I missed. "For next week, we'll review what you missed. And read *The Tempest* again."

"Read *The Tempest* again?" I said. I mean, you can understand reading *Treasure Island* four times, but no matter how good a Shakespeare play is, no one reads it twice.

"You'll find that there is a lot more to *The Tempest* than a list of colorful curses."

"Read *The Tempest* again?" I said.

"Repetition is not always a rhetorical virtue," said Mrs. Baker. "Yes, read it again. From the start."

So.

It had turned out to be an all-right Wednesday afternoon after all. Except for the internal bleeding. And except for the 150-question test. And except for having to read *The Tempest* again. From the start.

But as I limped on home, I figured that if I read an act that night, and another on Thursday, and Sunday, Monday, and Tuesday, I could have it all finished pretty painlessly. And each one would probably go a lot quicker, since I had already read them all once.

Life got brighter, and somehow, the world suddenly got brighter, too. You know how this is? You're walking along, and then the sun comes out from behind a cloud, and the birds start to sing, and the air is suddenly warm, and it's like the whole world is happy because you're happy.

It's a great feeling.

But never trust it. Especially in November on Long Island.

Because as I limped past Goldman's Best Bakery, the front window was filled with cream puffs. Brown, light, perfect cream puffs. And I remembered the death threats hanging over me like Shylock's knife hanging over Antonio's chest.

I decided that to be safe I'd better get the cream puffs—even if it meant asking for an advance on my allowance.

Which I had about as much chance of getting as Shylock had of getting his ducats back.

Still, I thought I might have a little chance when Dad got home that evening and let out the great news: Hoodhood and Associates had won the Baker Sporting Emporium contract! They were going to design a new main store and redesign every single one of the chain stores—and there were plenty of them, one in almost every town on Long Island. He grabbed my mother and twirled her around, and they danced beneath the newly plastered ceiling of the living room. Can you believe it? They went into the Perfect Living Room! Then they danced through the kitchen, back into the Perfect Living Room, out onto the front stoop, down the stairs, and past the embarrassed azaleas.

Let me tell you, when Presbyterians start to dance on the front stoop, you know that something big has happened.

"We got the contract, we got the contract, we got the contract, we got the contract," my father sang. It sounded like he was waiting for a full string orchestra to come in, something out of *The Sound of Music*.

When he swept back inside, pirouetting my mother, it seemed the perfect moment to ask.

"Dad, could I have an advance on my allowance next week?"

"We got the contract, we got the contract, not on your sweet life, we got the contract."

That night, I dreamed that Caliban sat at the foot of my bed, looking a lot like Danny Hupfer and telling me how I was going to end up all scurvy and blistered if I didn't get the cream puffs next week—the end of the three weeks I had promised. "Beware, beware," he said, and I decided I should.

So on Friday, I went to Goldman's Best Bakery and put two dollars and forty-five cents on the counter—all the money I had in the world.

"Two dollars and forty-five cents can buy a great deal," said Mr. Goldman. "So what is it you want to buy?"

"Twenty-two cream puffs," I said.

Mr. Goldman added up twenty-two cream puffs in his head.

"For that you need two more dollars and eighty cents."

"I need the cream puffs by next week."

"You still need two more dollars and eighty cents."

"I can work. I can wash dishes and stuff."

"I should need you to wash dishes? I have two good hands. They can wash dishes, too—and I don't have to pay them."

"I could sweep and clean up."

Mr. Goldman held up his two good hands.

I sighed. "You don't need anything done around here?"

"What I should really need," he said, "is a boy who knows Shakespeare. But is there a boy who knows Shakespeare these days? No. Not one. You would think that they should teach Shakespeare in school. But do they? No."

Okay, I'm not kidding here. Mr. Goldman really said that: "What I should really need is a boy who knows Shakespeare." Those words came right out of his mouth.

"I know Shakespeare," I said.

"Sure you do," Mr. Goldman said. "You still need two more dollars and eighty cents."

"I do."

Mr. Goldman put his hands on his hips. "Show me some Shakespeare, then."

I went back to *The Tempest,* and not just the Caliban curses, either—which is all that Mrs. Baker thought I knew. I spread my arms out wide.

> *Now does my project gather to a head.*
> *My charms crack not, my spirits obey, and Time*
> *Goes upright with his carriage. How's the day?*

Mr. Goldman clapped his hands—really!—and then he leaped upon a stool behind the counter—and Mr. Goldman is not someone whose size encourages leaping. He clapped his hands again above his head, and a fine, light flouring flew into the air—sort of like chalk dust—and a haze shimmered about his face. His voice changed, and when he spoke, it was as though he was chanting a high and faraway music.

> *On the sixth hour, at which time, my lord,*
> *You said our work should cease.*

I spread my arms out even wider, and tried to imagine long robes with sleeves that flowed down along the arms of Prospero.

> *I did say so*
> *When first I raised the tempest. Say, my spirit,*
> *How fares the king and 's followers?*

The "and 's" is not easy to say, but it came off pretty well, with about as much spit as "beetles."

Mr. Goldman clapped his hands again, and another shimmering of flour fell.

Confined together
In the same fashion as you gave in charge,
Just as you left them.

Mr. Goldman climbed down from the stool and held out his still floury hand. His smile pushed his cheeks into round lumps.

And that was how I got to be part of the Long Island Shakespeare Company's Holiday Extravaganza, which was opening next month.

And how I got twenty-two cream puffs for two dollars and eighty cents less than I should have—plus two more free, since they come cheaper by the dozen.

And it was a good thing.

When Monday came and I walked into the classroom carrying a long box of cream puffs, it was pretty clear that Danny Hupfer and Meryl Lee and Doug Swieteck and Mai Thi would have been at me with daggers, looking for a pound of flesh, if I had failed them. I set the box on the shelf by the window and opened it up. Twenty-four cream puffs—brown, light, perfect cream puffs—waiting to be eaten after lunch.

Mrs. Baker didn't say anything. But all through *English for You and Me,* the buttery vanilla smell of the cream puffs wafted around the room with the circulating air, and even Mrs. Baker couldn't help but look at them. I saw her nostrils grow wide. Danny Hupfer kept turning around and grinning at me. Meryl Lee pretended like she didn't care much, but she's a terrible liar.

If lunchtime hadn't come when it did, we might have all gone wild. Even Mrs. Baker. But finally, finally, *finally* the school clock clicked to noon, and we crammed our sandwiches down our throats, and then Danny Hupfer stood up and approached the brown, light, perfect cream puffs sort of reverently.

"Not just yet, Mr. Hupfer," said Mrs. Baker.

Danny Hupfer looked at her like he'd just missed an easy goal.

Meryl Lee looked at me like it was my fault.

"If you are going to eat cream puffs," said Mrs. Baker, "you are going to do it on your own time. Go out for lunch recess and come back a few minutes early. Then you may gorge yourselves as you please."

"I bet she's going to take three for herself," whispered Doug Swieteck.

"No, Mr. Swieteck, she is not going to take three for herself," said Mrs. Baker. "She is going to Saint Adelbert's quickly to light a candle, and she will be back in time for your gorging. Now, out, all of you."

We went out.

It was, of course, a cold November day on Long Island, and everything was, of course, gray—the sky, the air, the grass, the drizzle misting down. Gray everywhere. We stood around in huddled groups, a little bit damp, and still hungry because we'd eaten so fast and there were twenty-four cream puffs waiting for everyone back in the classroom. Twenty-four brown, light, perfect cream puffs.

"They better be good," said Meryl Lee.

"They'll be good," I said.

"They better be really good," said Danny Hupfer.

"They'll be really good," I said.

When there were only seven minutes left in recess, Danny Hupfer declared that we had served our time, and even if Mrs. Baker hadn't come back yet, we deserved our cream puffs. So like an unstoppable mob, like a tidal wave, like an avalanche, we rushed into Camillo Junior High, up two flights of stairs, and to the doorway of our classroom.

And stopped.

On the shelf, the long box of cream puffs lay ripped apart, and in the middle of the buttery, brown, light, perfect cream puffs stood Sycorax and Caliban, up on their hind legs, their paws holding shreds of crust to their mouths. Their faces were covered with yellow vanilla filling and powdered sugar. Their naked tails were thick with it. Their scabby skin was slathered with it.

Then Mrs. Baker came behind us and peered in. The rats opened their snouts and clacked their yellow teeth at her.

And Mrs. Baker screamed, "Strange stuff, the dropsy drown you! The red plague rid you, thrice double-ass!"

That last one I knew about, but I wasn't going to tell you I knew it, because of what you'd think of me.

Sycorax and Caliban understood the meaning of all those, I guess. They scurried out of the box, skidding in the vanilla cream, and leaped into the radiators. We heard them climb up inside the walls, then scamper across the asbestos tiles.

There was a long and absolute silence.

Then Meryl Lee turned to me. "You still owe us cream puffs," she said.

"Ten day," said Mai Thi.

"Ten days!" I said.

"We gave you three weeks already," said Danny Hupfer. "Now you have ten days."

"Ten days!" I said.

"Here is another situation where repetition is not a rhetorical virtue. Clean up the mess, Mr. Hoodhood," said Mrs. Baker.

And I did.

But I wasn't happy.

Usually, the last week before Thanksgiving was pretty easy. Every-one is thinking about two days off from school, grandparents coming for dinner, the Syosset-Farmingdale football rivalry, and all that.

But it wasn't an easy week this year. Not for me.

It was a long week.

First, it somehow became my fault that Sycorax and Caliban ate the cream puffs. I think this was because of Meryl Lee. For three days, things were whispered about me that I hope I never have to hear.

Then second, on Wednesday afternoon, when I went to get the script for the Long Island Shakespeare Company's Holiday Extravaganza from Mr. Goldman, I found out that I was going to play Ariel from *The Tempest*. Ariel is a fairy. A fairy! Let me tell you, it is not a good thing for a boy from Camillo Junior High to play a fairy. Especially a boy who has been singing soprano for Miss Violet of the Very Spiky Heels.

"I don't think I can play Ariel," I told Mr. Goldman.

"Here's your costume," he said, and handed me a pair of bright yellow tights with white feathers on the . . . well, I'll let you guess what part the white feathers were attached to.

Third, now that I needed another set of cream puffs, I asked my father if he might ever, ever, ever imagine a three-week advance on my allowance, since he had clinched the deal with the Baker Sporting Emporium, and he just laughed out loud. "You ought to be a comedian," he said. "You and Bob Hope. You could travel to Saigon together and do troop shows."

"I wasn't trying to be funny," I said.

"You *must* have been trying to be funny, since no kid of mine in his right mind would ever ask for a three-week advance on his allowance," he said.

"I was trying to be funny," I said.

"I thought so," he said.

Fourth, when I told Meryl Lee that I might not be able to get the cream puffs by next Wednesday ("I wouldn't spread that around if I were you," she said) and that my father was a cheapskate since he'd just landed this big deal with the Baker Sporting Emporium and he wouldn't give me a dime, she started to cry.

Really.

"Meryl Lee," I said, "it's not all that bad. I'll find a way to get the cream puffs. I mean . . ."

"You jerk," said Meryl Lee, "you don't understand anything," and she wouldn't speak to me or anyone else the rest of the day.

Fifth, on the Tuesday before the Wednesday of the cream puffs deadline, Mr. Guareschi came in and asked Mrs. Baker if she knew what "pied ninny" meant. She asked him why he needed to know that, and he told her that Doug Swieteck's brother was in his office at that very moment for having called Mr. Ludema a pied ninny.

Mrs. Baker stared straight at me.

And sixth, when Wednesday morning came around and I walked in with a bag of five cream puffs—which was as far as a one-week allowance stretches—it was pretty clear that I was doomed. With five cream puffs, almost everyone could have one quarter of a cream puff, I pointed out. It was better than nothing.

Meryl Lee shook her head.

"You're dead," said Danny Hupfer.

And I supposed I was. At least I wouldn't have to wear the yellow tights with the white feathers attached you can guess where.

But you know that stuff about the darkest nights turning into the brightest dawns? That can sometimes come true. Even when you least expect it.

Because when we came back in from recess, on the shelf was a long box from Goldman's Best Bakery . . . filled with twenty-four cream puffs! Twenty-four brown, light, perfect cream puffs! Twenty-four buttery vanilla cream puffs!

"Mr. Hoodhood was simply playing a joke on you all," said Mrs. Baker. "Now, enjoy."

And we did.

That afternoon, Mrs. Baker asked me if I thought that the ending to *The Tempest* was happy or not. Maybe because I had just had my own happy ending, I told her that I figured it was.

"How about for Caliban?" she asked. "Does he deserve a happy ending?"

"No. He's the monster. If there's going to be a happy ending, it means he has to be defeated. You can't end *Godzilla* without killing Godzilla. And you can't end *The Tempest* without Caliban getting . . ."

"Getting what, Mr. Hoodhood?"

"He can't win."

"No, he can't win. But sometimes I wonder if perhaps Shakespeare might have let something happen that would at least have allowed a happy ending even for a monster—some way for him to grow beyond what Prospero thought of him. There is a part of us that can be so awful. And Shakespeare shows it to us in Caliban. But there's another part of us, too—a part that uses defeat to grow. I wish we could have seen that by the end of the play." She closed her book.

"Defeat doesn't help you to grow," I said. "It's just defeat."

Mrs. Baker smiled. "Two weeks ago, the Saturn V lunar rocket passed its first flight test. It's been less than ten months since we lost three astronauts, but we're still testing the next rocket, so that some day we can go to the moon and make our world a great deal bigger." She held her hands up to her face. "Wouldn't Shakespeare have admired that happy ending?" she whispered.

Then she put the book away in her lower desk drawer.

It was quiet and still in the room. You could hear the soft rain on the windows.

"Thank you for the cream puffs," I said.

"The quality of mercy is not strained," she said.

Mrs. Baker looked up and almost smiled a real smile. Again.

And that was when Mrs. Bigio came into the classroom. Actually, she didn't quite come in. She opened the door and stood leaning against the doorway, one hand up to her mouth, the other trembling on the doorknob.

Mrs. Baker stood. "Oh, Edna, did they find him?"

Mrs. Bigio nodded.

"And is he . . ."

Mrs. Bigio opened her mouth, but the only sounds that came out were the sounds of sadness. I can't tell you what they sounded like. But you know them when you hear them.

Mrs. Baker sprinted out from behind her desk and gathered Mrs. Bigio in her arms. She helped Mrs. Bigio to her own chair, where she slumped down like someone who had nothing left in her.

"Mr. Hoodhood, you may go home now," Mrs. Baker said.

I did.

But I will never forget those sounds.

☾☽

I found out the next day that Mrs. Bigio's husband had died on a small hill with no name, in a small part of Vietnam. He had died at night, on a reconnaissance mission. Afterward, the army decided the hill was not a significant military target, and abandoned it.

Three weeks later, the body of First Sergeant Anthony Bigio of the United States Marine Corps was brought back home and buried in the cemetery beside Saint Adelbert's, the church he had been christened and married in. The *Home Town Chronicle* showed a picture of Mrs. Bigio on the front page, holding in one hand the American flag that had been draped over his casket, now folded into a triangle. The other hand was over her face.

Two nights after that, the *Home Town Chronicle* showed a different picture—the home of the Catholic Relief Agency where Mai Thi lived, which had been attacked by unknown vandals. Across its front was scrawled these words in broad black letters: GO HOME VIET CONG.

At the happy ending of *The Tempest,* Prospero brings the king back together with his son, and finds Miranda's true love, and punishes the bad duke, and frees Ariel, and becomes a duke himself again. Everyone—except for Caliban—is happy, and everyone is forgiven, and everyone is fine, and they all sail away on calm seas. Happy endings.

That's how it is in Shakespeare.

But Shakespeare was wrong.

Sometimes there isn't a Prospero to make everything fine again.

And sometimes the quality of mercy *is* strained.

december

On the first Wednesday of December, Mr. Guareschi announced over the P.A. that in January every junior and senior high school in the state would be taking the New York State Standardized Achievement Tests and that we should plan on taking practice exams at home during the holiday break. The reputation of the school was at stake, he told us, and he was very, very, very confident that we would not let Camillo Junior High down.

I'm not sure, but I think Mrs. Baker may have rolled her eyes.

The rest of the Morning Announcements were as exciting as December drizzles, and maybe Mr. Guareschi knew that, because he said he wanted to conclude by reading a lovely note, from Mrs. Sidman. She wished us all a happy holiday spirit at this very special time of year and hoped that, even in a time of war, we might be able to use these holidays to reflect on the virtues of peace and good will. She hoped all of this very sincerely.

The letter, Mr. Guareschi told us, was written from Connecticut, where Mrs. Sidman was taking "a retreat in seclusion."

Actually, the whole school was in a happy holiday spirit, even before Mrs. Sidman's letter. On one side of the main lobby, Mr. Vendleri had put up a huge fir tree and wound it with silver garlands. Balls as big as grapefruits hung from each branch—plastic

73

ones, because last Christmas Mr. Vendleri had seen what Doug Swieteck's brother did to glass ones. Wherever there wasn't a Christmas ball, tinsel hung down, except when the lobby doors opened and it blew straight out. And then, I guess because Mr. Vendleri believed that no Christmas tree should show any green at all, he had sprayed quick-drying foam snow over the whole thing, as though there really might be snow on Long Island on Christmas Day—which hadn't happened since before there was a Christmas Day.

On the other side of the main lobby was the menorah. It was heavy and old, and had belonged in Mr. Samowitz's family for a whole lot longer than two hundred years. Some of the white wax that clung to the sides of the bronze cups came from candles that had been lit in Russia. We looked at it, standing on its white linen cloth as huge as History, and could almost smell the sweet wax in the darkness of a long time ago.

That first week, the second graders made red-and-green construction paper chains that they hung the length of the elementary and junior high school halls. The fourth graders cut menorahs from cardboard and covered them with glittering aluminum foil. The first graders cut out the flames for each of the nine candles, and together they put a menorah on every classroom door. The fifth graders had Charles, who could not only collect erasers but also write exquisite calligraphy—which made every girl in his grade (and some in the sixth grade) fall in love with him. Just because he could write "Merry Christmas" and "Happy Hanukkah" with loopy swirls. His signs appeared all over the halls, and gushing fifth-grade girls colored in the loops secretly to show their eternal love and devotion to the artist.

Danny Hupfer said it just about made him throw up.

All through Camillo Junior High, there were signs of the season. The windows on the classroom doors became crepe paper–stained glass. Mr. Petrelli put flashing colored lights around his door and a menorah with orange light bulbs on his window shelf. Mr. Ludema, who was from Holland, put wooden shoes on his window shelf and filled them with straw and coal—probably because he was Doug Swieteck's brother's teacher.

Mrs. Baker didn't put anything up. Nothing at all. She took down the aluminum-foil menorah the first graders had put on her door, and she wouldn't let any of Charles's signs into the room. When Mrs. Kabakoff came in carrying a crock of apple cider left over from the second-grade Pilgrim Feast, offering a special holiday drink for lunch, Mrs. Baker smiled one of those smiles that isn't really a smile, then had Danny Hupfer take the crock and shove it back on the high shelf in the Coat Room above the moldering lunches.

Mrs. Baker was not in a happy holiday spirit.

And to be really honest, neither was I—all because of Mr. Goldman and the Long Island Shakespeare Company's Holiday Extravaganza. In which I was going to play Ariel.

Ariel the Fairy.

And nothing I said to Mr. Goldman helped.

"Every boy should be so lucky as you, to play in a Shakespeare Company's Holiday Extravaganza, and with such a part!" he said. "I should have been lucky as you at your age."

But let me tell you, wearing yellow tights wasn't making me feel lucky. Not if I wanted to keep living in this town.

So I showed the tights to my mother, who I figured would have some concern for her only son's reputation.

"They're very yellow," she said.

"And they have white feathers all over the—"

"Yes," she said. "But it will be cute. They'll sort of wave in the breeze when you walk. I still can't get over it—my son playing Shakespeare."

"They're yellow tights. I'm playing a fairy. If this gets out, I'll never be able to go back to school."

"No one from Camillo Junior High will be there. And even if they were, everyone will think it's cute."

I tried my father.

I handed him the tights while Walter Cronkite was announcing new bombing in Vietnam. I thought they might catch his eye, even though the *CBS Evening News* was on.

They did.

"You're going to wear these?" he said.

"That's what they want."

"Yellow tights with white feathers on the—"

"Yup."

"Whose idea is this?"

"Mr. Goldman's idea."

My father tried looking away from the yellow tights—which wasn't easy, since they were the brightest thing in the room and tended to draw the eye.

"Mr. Goldman?" he said.

I think you've heard the rest of this conversation before.

"Yes," I said.

"The Benjamin Goldman who belongs to Goldman's Best Bakery?"

"I guess that's the one," I said.

My father looked at the yellow tights again, sort of shielding his eyes, and considered. "The day might come," he said finally, "when

Goldman thinks about expanding his business. And then he'd need to hire an architect."

"Dad."

"Maybe one that he remembers doing him a favor."

"I can't wear these," I said.

He handed the tights back to me. "Wear them. Just hope that no one from your school sees you."

I didn't try my sister, but she came to my room anyway.

"Mom told me about the tights," she said. "Let me see them."

I showed her.

"When this gets around school . . ."

"It won't get around school," I said.

"Sure it won't," she said. "Keep telling yourself that, and maybe it will come true. But if it ever gets over to the high school, you'd better pray that no one knows I'm your sister." She shut the door.

"That sure doesn't sound like a flower child who doesn't do harm to anyone," I hollered after her. But she didn't answer.

It didn't help that on the night of the first dress rehearsal (I wore my blue jeans over the yellow tights until the last minute), the entire cast of the Long Island Shakespeare Company's Holiday Extravaganza clapped when I came onstage.

Which they did because they had to do something when they saw where the feathers were, and what they really wanted to do was laugh out loud, but they knew what I would do and it was too late to find another kid to play Ariel the Fairy. I mean, who else was going to wander into Goldman's Best Bakery and be $2.80 short on an order of cream puffs?

"Mr. Goldman," I said after the applause, "I can't wear these."

"Of course you can wear these. You are wearing these now."

"I look like a fairy."

"And this isn't the point? You should look like a fairy. You are a fairy."

"Do you know what will happen if someone from school sees me?"

"They will say, 'There is Holling Hoodhood, onstage, playing one of Shakespeare's greatest scenes from one of his greatest plays.' This is what will happen."

"Mr. Goldman, it's been a long time since you were in seventh grade."

"I never went to seventh grade. Where I come from, no boy went to seventh grade. We were all working in fields, digging and hoeing and digging and hoeing. But you—you go to school, then you go home and play. Then you come onstage to be a famous Shakespeare character. There is more that a boy could want?"

Without even trying, it wouldn't be hard to come up with a list of 410 things more that a boy could want. But it's hard to keep complaining after the "When I Was a Boy, Life Was So Hard" card is played on you.

So I did it. I got through the whole dress rehearsal playing Ariel the Fairy while wearing bright yellow tights with white feathers on the . . . well, I might as well say it—butt. There. On my butt! White feathers waving on my butt!

Let me tell you, this did not put me in a happy holiday spirit.

The whole of December could have been ruined because of the yellow tights—except for one thing. One glorious, amazing, unbelievable, spectacular thing. The one thing that kept us going in the bare, holiday-less classroom of Mrs. Baker. The one thing that brought back meaning to Hanukkah and Christmas.

Mickey Mantle.

The greatest player to put on Yankee pinstripes since Babe Ruth.

Mickey Mantle.

And it was Mrs. Baker who announced his advent.

"I suppose it will be of some interest to some of you," she said, "that Mickey Mantle is coming to town next week."

The class went as quiet as if Sycorax and Caliban—the rats, not the monsters—had appeared before us, clacking their appalling yellow teeth.

"Some interest!" said Danny Hupfer.

"To some of us!" I said.

"Who's Mickey Mantle?" asked Meryl Lee.

"Who Mickey Mantle?" asked Mai Thi.

"He is a baseball player," said Mrs. Baker.

"He is *the* baseball player," said Danny Hupfer.

"He had a batting average of .245 this year," said Doug Swieteck.

We all turned to look at him.

"Down from .288 last year," Doug Swieteck said.

Danny Hupfer turned to look at me. "How does he know that?"

"What is a batting average?" asked Meryl Lee.

"My brother-in-law," said Mrs. Baker loudly, "has developed strong ties to the Yankee organization, and he has arranged for Mickey Mantle to come to the Baker Sporting Emporium. I am told that in addition to strutting around swinging baseball bats as if it were a worthy vocation, he will sign baseballs for anyone willing to bring one to him."

A cheer from the class, as if the happy holidays were already here.

"This is not an occasion to clamber onto your desk, Mr.

Hupfer. You should tell your parents that he is coming a week from this Saturday night, and that he will be swinging bats and signing baseballs from eight o'clock until nine thirty. You should all take note that had he been swinging bats and signing baseballs on a school night, I never would have agreed to make this announcement."

Another cheer, wild and extravagant.

"Who's Mickey Mantle?" asked Meryl Lee again.

We all ignored her.

Mickey Mantle!

Now, things would have been fine if Mrs. Baker had just left it there. I mean, Mickey Mantle coming to the Baker Sporting Emporium and all. But she didn't.

"I have a second announcement," said Mrs. Baker.

We all got quiet again.

"Is someone else coming to the Emporium, too?" asked Danny Hupfer.

"Maybe someone I know?" asked Meryl Lee.

"No one else is coming, unless you want to say that someone is 'up and coming.'"

That was a teacher joke. No one laughed, even though we were all supposed to. No one ever laughs at teacher jokes.

"I have been informed by Mr. Goldman, who is the president of the Long Island Shakespeare Company, that one of the students in our class will be performing in the company's Holiday Extravaganza. He will be playing a part from *The Tempest*."

I knew what was coming next. For a while, I had wondered if Mrs. Baker had stopped hating my guts. Now I figured she hadn't.

"As the corresponding secretary of the company, I invite you all to come see Mr. Holling Hoodhood in his Shakespeare debut. It will be a week from this Saturday—the very same night that the eminent Mr. Mantle will be at the Emporium swinging bats. The performance should be finished thirty minutes before Mr. Mantle makes his exit, so you will all have time for both."

Toads, beetles, bats. The only thing worse would have been if she found a way to bribe them to come. Maybe with cream puffs.

"And for those who attend," said Mrs. Baker, "your ticket stub will bring you extra credit for your next *English for You and Me* assignment."

It *was* worse.

Mrs. Baker looked at me and smiled. It was like the smile she had before Doug Swieteck's brother's assassination attempt. And shouldn't someone have told me that Mrs. Baker was the corresponding secretary?

This is the part where, if we lived in a just world, some natural disaster would occur right then, or maybe an atomic bomb attack to obliterate the news of the Long Island Shakespeare Company's Holiday Extravaganza and so save me from my undeserved humiliation.

Still, even though there wasn't a natural disaster or atomic bomb attack, Mickey Mantle was almost enough. After all, with Mickey Mantle coming, no one really cared about my Shakespeare debut. No one except Meryl Lee, who didn't know who Mickey Mantle was, and Mai Thi, who also didn't know who Mickey Mantle was, and Danny Hupfer, who did know who Mickey Mantle was—and they all cornered me after lunch.

"Why so sneaky?" asked Meryl Lee. "Are you playing a girl's part?"

"No, I'm not playing a girl's part. It's a part from *The Tempest,*" I said.

"Gee, so when Mrs. Baker said you were playing a part from *The Tempest,* she meant that you were really playing a part from *The Tempest,*" said Danny Hupfer. "We know a whole lot more now than we did before."

"Ariel. I'm going to play Ariel."

"That's a girl's name," said Meryl Lee. "Isn't it a girl's name?"

"Suspicion is an unbecoming passion," I said. "Ariel is a warrior."

I know. That sounds like a lie. But Presbyterians know that every so often a lie isn't all that bad, and I figured that this was about the best place it could happen.

"Who does the warrior fight?"

"The rebels who usurped Prospero's kingdom and who want to murder him and his daughter."

"That sounds all right," said Danny Hupfer. "So you get to fight for them, like a knight who's their champion."

"Yes."

"And you get to wear armor and stuff like that," said Danny Hupfer.

"Stuff like that," I said.

"Maybe I'll come then, to see the armor," he said. "But it'd better be over in time for Mickey Mantle."

"It still sounds like a girl's name to me," said Meryl Lee.

We ignored her again and headed back into the classroom.

But just before we got in the door, Mai Thi stopped me with a hand on my chest. She looked at me for a long moment and then whispered, "Not good to be warrior." I looked at her, I guess kind of startled, and she went in to her desk before I could say a thing.

But what did she know?

༙༙

At the next rehearsal, I asked Mr. Goldman if Ariel could wear armor instead of yellow tights.

"Armor? We have no armor," said Mr. Goldman.

"You have no armor? What do you do in a play if you need it?"

"We don't put those plays on. We should buy armor just to do *Julius Caesar*? No. And why should Ariel wear armor?"

"Because he's Prospero's champion. He's fighting, like a jousting knight."

Mr. Goldman shook his head. "Like a jousting knight? Holling, you are a fairy. Go put on your tights. We have a dress rehearsal."

I didn't get to wear any armor.

The next Wednesday, as soon as everyone left for Temple Beth-El and Saint Adelbert's, Mrs. Baker took out her copy of Shakespeare from the lower drawer in her desk. "Mr. Goldman says that you are doing very well, though you need some practice on interpretation."

"He said that?"

"He did. Open your book to the fourth act. I'll be Prospero. We'll start with 'What would my potent master' and continue through to the end. Begin."

"He really said I was doing very well?"

"And that you need some practice. Begin."

"What would my potent master?" I said.

"No, no, Mr. Hoodhood. You are an enslaved magical creature about to be given your freedom if you perform well these last few moments. You, however, sound as if you're waiting for the crosstown bus. You're almost free, but not quite."

"What would my potent master?" I said.

Mrs. Baker crossed her arms. "There is supposed to be a passion in your face that works you strongly. You're on a knife's edge."

"What would my potent master?" I said.

"Indeed, there you are," said Mrs. Baker. "Stay on the knife's edge. And now Prospero . . ."

I stayed on the knife's edge, because I couldn't help it. When Mrs. Baker read Prospero's part, it was like Prospero himself had come into the classroom, with his flowing cloak and magical hands. She *was* Prospero and I *was* Ariel, and when she gave me my last command and said, "Be free, and fare thou well!" I suddenly knew what Ariel felt. The whole world had just opened out in front of me, and I could go wherever I wished, and be whatever I wanted. Absolutely free.

I could decide my own happy ending for myself.

"That," said Mrs. Baker, "should please Mr. Goldman."

And it did. When we finished rehearsal that night, I could almost imagine myself leaping out into the airy elements and dropping the insubstantial pageant of life behind me.

At least, that's what it felt like on the stage.

It didn't feel like that in Camillo Junior High, where Mrs. Baker reminded the class to purchase tickets in advance, and where I dropped hints almost every day that the Long Island Shakespeare Company's Holiday Extravaganza was going to run really, *really* long, and that there was no chance in creation that anyone could go see the Extravaganza and make it to Mickey Mantle, too.

I know. Another lie. But just a Presbyterian lie.

So the days passed, and the Hanukkah and Christmas decorations in Camillo Junior High started to look a little shabby, and the dress rehearsals were over, and Saturday night came, and I put on my bright yellow tights with the white feathers on the butt, and I put on my jeans over them, and I found the newest baseball I had, and my father dropped me off at the Festival Theater—"Don't mess it up"—and the Long Island Shakespeare Company's Holiday Extravaganza began.

And while Mr. Goldman played Falstaff from *Henry IV,* I looked out through the peephole in the wings, and I could see almost every face—and there weren't many, since anyone with any sense was over at the Sporting Emporium. I found Mrs. Baker right away. She was in the center of the third row, sitting next to Mrs. Bigio and wearing that teacher look that makes it seem as if she is about to start slashing at something with her red felt pen. (I suppose teachers just get that way. They can't help it.)

Behind Mrs. Baker and Mrs. Bigio were Danny Hupfer's parents.

Really.

I guess Danny must have told them about the Extravaganza, and they had come to see me play the part of Ariel the Warrior. I guess it didn't matter to them that the Bing Crosby Christmas special was on television tonight, the way it mattered to my parents, who would never, ever miss it. I guess the Hupfers thought that a Shakespeare debut was a whole lot more important than hearing "I'm dreaming of a white Christmas" one more time—even though Mr. Hupfer was loosening his tie and holding his hand over a yawn.

And I guess you can't look out stage peepholes very long, because your eyes start to water, and the stuff in your nose gets drippy, and you have to wipe at them both, and there goes all your makeup.

There wasn't anyone else from Camillo Junior High that I

could see. No one. And except for the very front row I could see every seat in the theater.

Let me tell you, when it was my turn to go on, not seeing anyone from Camillo Junior High made leaping out onto the stage hollering "What would my potent master?" and wearing yellow tights with white feathers waving on my butt a whole lot easier.

I stayed on the knife's edge, and when Mr. Goldman, who was really Prospero, sent me to fetch the traitors, or terrorize Caliban, or grieve the king, I did it as though all, all was at stake. When I reminded him that he had promised me my freedom on the sixth hour, I wanted it as badly as Mickey Mantle's signature on a baseball. And when I drew the boatmen into the island, I thrilled at Prospero's line: "Thou shalt be free." And when at last it was done and Prospero stepped to the edge of the stage to beg the audience to send its gentle breath to fill the sails of our freedom, I could hardly keep myself from trembling.

Suppose they wouldn't fill the sails?

"Our revels now are ended," Prospero had said. But when I walked onstage with the rest of the company for curtain calls, the revels felt like they had not ended; they were still ringing in the hands of the audience—who were all standing.

Still ringing in the hands of Mrs. Baker—who was smiling at me. Really.

Still ringing in the hands of Mr. and Mrs. Hupfer—who were waving at me.

Still ringing in the hands of Danny Hupfer and Meryl Lee and Mai Thi—who were standing in the very front row!

Danny Hupfer and Meryl Lee and Mai Thi!

I looked down at them looking up at the bright yellow tights with white feathers on the butt.

But they weren't looking at the yellow tights. Because they were all three crying. They stood in the light from the foot lamps, and their cheeks glistened with tears.

Shakespeare can do that to you.

They clapped and clapped, and clapped and clapped, and Meryl Lee wiped at her eyes, and then suddenly in Danny Hupfer's eyes came this startled look, and there was a passion in his face that seemed to work him strongly—and it was Mickey Mantle.

He pointed to his watch.

"Nine fifteen," he mouthed, and he turned and waved desperately to his parents.

And when the curtain came down and I could be free, I didn't wait for the audience's breath to fill my sails after all. I careened back behind the stage and around to the men's dressing room.

And found that it was locked.

Locked!

I pounded on the door. No one answered.

I heard my name for another curtain call.

I pounded on the dressing room door again. No one answered.

I ran back into the wings, desperate. Mr. Goldman was still onstage, bowing. It looked like he would be bowing for a while.

But he had left Prospero's blue floral cape behind in the stage wings.

I grabbed it, flung it around my shoulders, and made for the elements, where my father would be waiting for what I hoped would be an illegally fast drive to the Baker Sporting Emporium. I ran out the back stage door—and let me tell you, it had gotten a whole lot colder, and a cape when you're just wearing yellow tights doesn't help much—and sprinted around to the front of the Festival Theater.

My father wasn't there.

I guess the Bing Crosby Christmas special wasn't over yet.

Standing on the street in front of the Festival Theater in bright yellow tights and a blue floral cape covering white feathers on his butt—this was not an Ariel in a happy holiday spirit.

I looked up and down the street.

Not a single car was moving—except one speeding away: Danny Hupfer's parents. I decided I would wait for my father for five minutes. So I counted three hundred Mississippis.

No car.

People started to come out of the theater and point at me.

And then, the scent of diesel fumes came in on the breeze—which was cutting right through my floral cape—and the crosstown bus lumbered around the corner, gritty and grimy and the most beautiful thing I'd ever seen. It even had plastic Christmas balls hanging from its rearview mirror.

I sprinted across the street—which probably looked pretty impressive with the blue cape flowing behind me—and stood at the Festival Theater bus stop.

But I wasn't sure the bus was going to stop when the driver saw me. He went two or three bus lengths beyond the sign, and even after he stopped and I ran up, he didn't open the doors at first. The plastic Christmas balls rocked back and forth while he looked at me like I had escaped from someplace I shouldn't have escaped from.

I counted another fifteen Mississippis before he opened the doors.

"Who are you supposed to be, kid?"

"John Wayne."

"John Wayne never wore tights his whole life."

"I need to get to the Baker Sporting Emporium."

"Well, John Wayne, do you have thirty cents?"

I reached into my pocket, which wasn't there.

"I didn't think so," said the bus driver.

"Please," I said. "I need to get to the Baker Sporting Emporium."

"Since Mickey Mantle is signing baseballs, right?"

"Yes."

"He looked at his watch. "You might make it. If you had thirty cents."

"The quality of mercy is not strained," I said.

He looked at me like I had just spoken a foreign language.

"Please," I said.

The driver shook his head. "Okay, John Wayne. But this is the kind of stuff that gets bus drivers fired, giving free rides. And if it wasn't so cold out there, I'd close the door on you. Did you know that when that cape is blowing out, people can see that you have white feathers on your—"

"Yes," I said, and took a seat.

It was mercy alone that there was no one else on the bus.

We drove through the cold night, well under the speed limit. The driver slowed down properly at every light—even if it was still green. He looked both ways twice at every stop sign.

"Do you think—" I began.

"Look, I'm missing the Bing Crosby Christmas special, and I'm putting my job on the line for you, kid. It's not a great night. So do you want to be quiet, or do you want to get out?"

I was quiet. I wrapped the blue floral cape around me.

By the time we reached the bus stop a block away from the

Baker Sporting Emporium, I was about as frantic as a fairy warrior being very quiet can ever get. The bus driver looked at his watch. "Nine thirty-seven," he said. "You'd better giddyup, John Wayne."

He opened the door, and I started down the steps.

"You do have a baseball somewhere under that cape, right?" the bus driver asked.

I stopped. Dead. My baseball was back at the Festival Theater, in the locked men's dressing room.

I almost cried. Almost. But I didn't, because if you're in seventh grade and you cry while wearing a blue floral cape and yellow tights with white feathers on the butt, you just have to curl up and die somewhere in a dark alley.

The bus driver shook his head. "John Wayne is always prepared for whatever happens," he said. "Me, too." He reached under the dashboard and pulled out a cardboard box filled with stuff. "You can't believe what people leave behind on their bus seats," he said. He reached into the box and pulled out—I am not making this up—a perfect new white baseball. Every seam tight and clean, like it had never even been thrown before.

"You got no clothes that any decent person would wear," he said. "No bus fare. And no baseball. How're you going to make it in this world, kid?"

At that moment, I truly did not care. I stared at the baseball. Its perfect whiteness filled my whole vision.

The bus driver shook his head. "You'd better meet a whole lot of people who are really kind to you, kid." Then he handed the baseball to me. The perfect new white baseball.

"Merry Christmas," he said.

Again I almost cried.

I sprinted to the Baker Sporting Emporium, the blue cape straight out behind me, the baseball in hand. Who knows what the white feathers were doing.

And I made it. I really did. I slammed through the door, and there he was—Mickey Mantle.

He was sitting at a table, dressed in his street clothes. Behind him, Mr. Mercutio Baker, who owned the Emporium, had put up a bulletin board full of Yankee photographs, most of Mickey Mantle swinging away. Above them was a jersey with Number 7. Mickey Mantle had signed his name below it.

He was bigger than he looked on television. He had hands as large as shovels, and the forearms that came from his sleeves were strong as stone. His legs stuck out from beneath the table, and they looked like they could run down a train on the Long Island Rail Road. He yawned a couple of times, big yawns that he didn't even try to hide. He must have had a long day.

In front of me, standing at the table all by themselves with Mickey Mantle, were Danny Hupfer and his father. Mickey Mantle was just handing a baseball back, and Danny was just taking it into his hands. It was sort of a holy moment, and the light that shone around them seemed to glow softly, like something you'd see in one of the stained glass windows at Saint Andrew's.

"Thanks," said Danny. He said it in awe and worship.

"Yeah, kid," said Mickey Mantle.

Then I came up.

I held out the new perfect white baseball and whispered, "Can I please have your autograph?" And he took the ball from my hand and held his pen over it. And then Mickey Mantle looked at me. Mickey Mantle, he looked at me!

And he spoke.

"What are you supposed to be?" he said.

I froze. What was I supposed to say?

"You look like a fairy," he said.

I coughed once. "I'm Ariel," I said.

"Who?"

"Ariel."

"Sounds like a girl's name."

"He's a warrior," I said.

Mickey Mantle looked me up and down. "Sure he is. Listen, I don't sign baseballs for kids in yellow tights." Mickey Mantle looked at his watch and turned to Mr. Baker. "It's past nine thirty. I'm done." He tossed my new perfect white baseball onto the floor. It rolled past my feet and into the folds of my blue cape.

The world should split in two. The world should split in two, and I should fall into the crack and never be heard from again.

Holling Hoodhood. Me. The boy in yellow tights with white feathers on the butt and a blue floral cape.

The boy Mickey Mantle wouldn't sign a baseball for.

And Danny Hupfer had seen it all. The yellow tights. The cape. The ball. Everything.

Danny Hupfer, who stepped to the table and slowly placed his baseball—his baseball signed by Mickey Mantle—back in front of the greatest player to put on Yankee pinstripes since Babe Ruth. "I guess I don't need this after all," Danny said. He lifted his hand from it, and I could tell it wasn't easy.

"What's the matter, kid?" said Mickey Mantle.

"You are a pied ninny," said Danny Hupfer. "C'mon, Holling."

I picked up the bus driver's baseball and handed it to Danny. We turned, and left Mickey Mantle behind us.

We didn't say anything.

❧

When gods die, they die hard. It's not like they fade away, or grow old, or fall asleep. They die in fire and pain, and when they come out of you, they leave your guts burned. It hurts more than anything you can talk about. And maybe worst of all is, you're not sure if there will ever be another god to fill their place. Or if you'd ever want another god to fill their place. You don't want fire to go out inside you twice.

The Hupfers drove me back to the Festival Theater. I went in to see if the men's dressing room was unlocked. It was, and Mr. Goldman was holding forth.

"My dainty Ariel!" he called, and threw his arms out wide, and the company—the men, that is, for the record—all clapped. "Where have you been? You, the star of the Extravaganza? Something should be wrong?"

I shook my head. How could you tell Mr. Goldman that the gods had died, when they lived so strongly in him? "Was 't well done?" I asked.

"Bravely, my diligence. Thou shalt be free."

And I was. I changed, and left the yellow tights with the feathers on the butt in a locker. Mr. Goldman told me I should stop by the bakery for some cream puffs "which will cost you not a thing," and I left. That was it. Outside, it was the first really cold night of winter, and the only fire in sight was the stars high above us and far away, glittering like ice.

The Hupfers were waiting, and drove me home.

We still didn't talk. Not the whole way.

When I got back, my parents were in the den watching television. It was so cold, the furnace was on high. The hot air tinkled the silver bells that decorated the white artificial Christmas tree that never dropped a single pine needle in the Perfect House.

"You're done earlier than I thought," my father said. "Bing Crosby is just about to start 'White Christmas,' as soon as this commercial is over."

"How did it go, Holling?" said my mother.

"Fine."

"I hope Mr. Goldman was happy with what you did," said my father.

"He said it was just swell."

"Good."

I went upstairs. The crooning notes of Bing Crosby's treetops glistening and children listening and sleigh bells in the snow followed me.

Just swell.

Happy holidays.

When we got back to school on Monday, there were only three more days before the holiday break. They were supposed to be a relaxed three days. Most teachers coasted through them, figuring that no one was going to learn all that much just before vacation. And they had to leave time for holiday parties on the last day, and making presents for each other, and for looking out the window, hoping for the miracle of snow on Long Island.

Even the lunches were supposed to have something special to them, like some kind of cake with thick white frosting, or pizza that actually had some cheese on it, or hamburgers that hadn't been cooked as thin as a record. Maybe something chocolate on the side. But Mrs. Bigio wasn't interested in chocolate these days. It

could have been the last holidays the planet was ever going to celebrate, and you wouldn't have known it from what Mrs. Bigio
cooked for Camillo Junior High's lunch. It was Something Surprise every day, except that after the first day it wasn't Something
Surprise anymore, because we knew what was coming. It was just
Something.

But I didn't complain. I remembered the Wednesday afternoon Mrs. Bigio had come into Mrs. Baker's classroom and the
sound of her sadness, and I knew what burned guts felt like.

Everyone else didn't complain because they were afraid to. You
don't complain when Mrs. Bigio stares at you as you're going
through the lunch line, with her hands on her hips and her hairnet
pulled tight. You don't complain.

Not even when she spreads around her own happy holiday
greetings.

"Take it and eat it," she said to Danny Hupfer when his hand
hesitated over the Something.

"You're not supposed to examine it," she said to Meryl Lee, who
was trying to figure out the Surprise part.

"You waiting for another cream puff?" she said to me. "Don't
count on it this millennium."

And, on the last day before the holiday break, to Mai Thi: "Pick
it up and be glad you're getting it. You shouldn't even be here, sitting like a queen in a refugee home while American boys are sitting
in swamps on Christmas Day. They're the ones who should be here.
Not you."

Mai Thi took her Something. She looked down, and kept
going.

She probably didn't see that Mrs. Bigio was pulling her hairnet
down lower over her face, because she was almost crying.

And probably Mrs. Bigio didn't see that Mai Thi was almost crying, too.

But I did. I saw them. And I wondered how many gods were dying in both of them right then, and whether any of them could be saved.

You'd think that Mrs. Baker would try to make up for the holiday disappointments of the Camillo Junior High kitchen over those three days. But she didn't. We went back to diagramming sentences, focusing on the imperfect tenses. She convinced Mr. Samowitz to start some pre-algebra equations in *Mathematics for You and Me* that Albert Einstein couldn't have figured out. She even bullied Mr. Petrelli into buckling down and making us present our "Mississippi River and You" projects out loud to the class.

Mr. Petrelli had us finish in a day and a half, but Mrs. Baker didn't let up all three days, and we were the only class in Camillo Junior High who sweated behind a closed decoration-less door, in a hot decoration-less classroom. And did we complain? No, because at the first hint of a complaint, Mrs. Baker folded her arms across her chest and stood still, staring at whoever had started to rebel until all rebellion died. That's how it was as we came up to the happy holidays—all the way until that last Wednesday afternoon.

As everyone got ready to leave for Temple Beth-El or Saint Adelbert's, I figured I'd probably be diagramming sentences for the next hour and a half, since we hadn't started another Shakespeare play yet.

Just swell.

But I was wrong.

"Mr. Hupfer and Mr. Swieteck," said Mrs. Baker, "I've arranged with your parents for you to stay in school this afternoon."

Danny and Doug looked at me, then at each other, then back at Mrs. Baker. "Okay by me," Danny said.

"I'm so pleased to have your approval," said Mrs. Baker. "Now, the rest of you . . . ," and there was the usual hubbub of leaving, while Danny and Doug sat back at their desks.

"What's it about?" Danny asked.

I shrugged. "Erasers or sentence diagramming. Maybe Shakespeare," I said.

We looked over at Doug Swieteck. "You didn't do Number 166?" I said.

He shook his head.

"You're sure?" said Danny.

"Don't you think I'd know?" said Doug Swieteck.

We weren't so sure. But actually, he hadn't.

After everyone left, Mrs. Baker went to her desk and opened her lower desk drawer. She took out three—no, not books of Shakespeare, like you might think—three brand-new baseballs, their covers as white as snow, their threads tight and ready for fingers to grip into a curve. And then she reached in again and took out three mitts. Their leathery smell filled the room. She handed them to us. The leather was soft and supple. We slipped our hands in and pushed the new baseballs into their deep pockets.

"My brother-in-law, whom I believe Mr. Hupfer and Mr. Hoodhood both saw the other night following the Extravaganza, has asked me to give you these as holiday gifts, compliments of the Baker Sporting Emporium," said Mrs. Baker. "And after telling me what happened during your time there, he and I made some arrangements for you to break the mitts in. So take them down to the gymnasium—and don't throw balls in the hall. And dropping one's jaw in surprise happens only in cartoons and bad plays, gentlemen."

Danny grinned as we went out. "The gym is empty last period. She's giving us the afternoon off."

But he was wrong, too.

The gym wasn't empty.

Joe Pepitone and Horace Clarke were waiting for us in the bleachers. In their Yankee uniforms. Number 25 and Number 20. The two greatest players to put on Yankee pinstripes since Babe Ruth.

Joe Pepitone and Horace Clarke.

Can you believe it?

"Which one of you is Holling?" said Horace Clarke.

I pointed to my chest.

"And Doug?"

Doug Swieteck slowly raised his hand.

"So you're Danny," said Joe Pepitone.

Danny nodded.

Horace Clarke held up his mitt. "Let's see your arm, Holling," he said.

I threw with Horace Clarke, and Danny and Doug threw with Joe Pepitone. Then we switched, and Danny threw with Horace Clarke, and Doug and I threw with Joe Pepitone. Then we went outside, and under a warm sun and on a diamond that hadn't been used since October, Horace Clarke crouched behind the plate and I threw fastballs to him, and even, once, a knuckleball. Really. And then Danny got up and Horace Clarke pitched and Joe Pepitone and I shagged balls in the outfield. And then Joe Pepitone got up and Doug and I shagged balls in the outfield. And then we took some infield practice from Horace

Clarke. And then we stood around the diamond—Joe Pepitone at home, Danny at first, Horace Clarke at second, Doug at deep shortstop, me at third—and we whipped the ball to each other around and around and around, as fast as we could, while Horace Clarke chanted, "Out of there, out of there, out of there," and the balls struck soft and deep in the pockets of the gloves, and the smack of them, and the smell of the gloves, filled the bright yellow air, while a breeze drew across us the whole time, as soft as feathers.

Afterward, they signed our baseballs and signed our mitts. They gave us each two tickets for Opening Day next April. And they gave Doug and Danny their caps.

And for me? Joe Pepitone gave me his jacket.

Can you believe it?

His jacket.

When they drove off, it felt like a place inside me had filled again. Our revels were *not* ended.

Danny and Doug and I ran up to the third floor to find Mrs. Baker. Mr. Vendleri was already taking down the Christmas and Hanukkah decorations. The halls were ghostly dark, and the classroom doors shut with the lights out behind them.

Mrs. Baker was gone, but she had left a note on the door.

"Mr. Hoodhood," it said, "read *The Tragedy of Macbeth* for the first Wednesday of January."

"Too bad," said Danny.

But Doug went on in, and he came back out carrying the cardboard box for Number 166 from the Coat Room. He looked at us, shrugged, and hauled it away down the hall, staggering under its clumsy weight.

We never saw it again.

༄

The next day, President Johnson declared a Christmas ceasefire in Vietnam, and the bombs stopped dropping.

And so the happy holidays finally began.

January

On New Year's Day, the *Home Town Chronicle* devoted itself proudly to celebrating the many accomplishments of those, young and old, who had made outstanding contributions to the life and culture of our town in the past year. It wasn't a very big issue. Most of the stories were about librarians and the Kiwanis Club officers and the Veterans of Foreign Wars and Mr. Guareschi for something and even about my father for the enormous success of Hoodhood and Associates and how he had been voted the Chamber of Commerce Businessman of 1967. The paper printed grainy headshots of people looking distinguished—like they were already thinking about their next outstanding contribution to the life and culture of the town.

There was one action shot, though.

Of Ariel the Fairy, flying high in the air, across the stage of the Festival Theater, his legs splayed out as though he really *was* flying.

The picture covered almost half of the front page.

And the story told the whole world that the tights were yellow!

And that they had white feathers on the butt!

"No one is going to see it," said my mother. "It's New Year's Day. Who looks at the newspaper on New Year's Day?"

It turned out that Doug Swieteck's brother did. Probably he looked at the picture on the front page. He saw who it was and what he was doing. And there was a flash of inspiration and ambition—which was, according to Shakespeare, what Macbeth was feeling a day or so before he murdered Duncan.

Maybe for a second, Doug Swieteck's brother thought that, since I had told him about "pied ninny," he shouldn't do anything about what his inspiration and ambition were telling him to do. But probably only for a second. In the end, he was Doug Swieteck's brother, and he couldn't help himself. It's like there's a Doug Swieteck's Brother Gene that switches on, too.

Some of what happened after that we found out from Doug Swieteck, who came back to Camillo Junior High with a black eye—which is not how you're supposed to come back to school after the happy holidays. The shiner had been a whole lot bigger and blacker a couple of days earlier, he said. But it was still pretty impressive. It's hard to believe that parts of you can turn green and purple at the same time, but they can.

At first he wouldn't tell anyone what had happened—not even when Danny threatened to give him a matching set of black, green, and purple eyes. But when I promised him one of my free cream puffs from Goldman's Best Bakery, he gave in. (People will do just about anything for one of Mr. Goldman's cream puffs, I guess.)

So here's what happened.

It was still early in the morning when his brother found the newspaper, Doug told us. Since it was the day after people had stayed up to watch the New Year's ball drop in Times Square, his brother figured everyone was sleeping late. He put his coat on, went out into the neighborhood, and stole the front page of the *Home Town Chronicle* from every stoop he could find. And there were plenty. Then he came back home, carried them up to his lair, and cut out the Ariel the Fairy picture from each one, careful to include the headline, which was this:

> *Holling Hoodhood as Ariel the Fairy Soars Onstage*
> *to Rescue His Potent Master*

This isn't at all what was happening in the play, but that was the least thing to fuss about.

After he finished cutting out the pictures, he took them all to the basement and found the bright yellow oil paint left over from a go-cart he had made to run kids down with. Then he went to get Doug—probably because he didn't know how to paint inside the lines.

Doug wouldn't tell us what he said when he saw the pictures and the can of yellow paint. All I know is that he wouldn't help, and so took a black eye. His brother probably promised a whole lot more if he said anything about the pictures—or the black eye. Then he found a brush and got to work himself.

Whatever it means to be a friend, taking a black eye for someone has to be in it.

The rest of what happened I figured out myself.

On the morning that school started again, Doug Swieteck's brother got to Camillo Junior High early. This should have warned somebody. If Mr. Guareschi had been in the halls trying to track down Sycorax and Caliban, he might have intercepted him. But he was probably supervising the unloading of multiple boxes of the New York State Standardized Achievement Tests—which I hadn't been preparing for because Mrs. Baker refused to give us practice exams to do during the holiday break. So Mr. Guareschi never saw him, and Doug Swieteck's brother was free to change his inspiration and ambition into reality.

He went up and down the halls taping up pictures of Holling Hoodhood as Ariel the Fairy Soaring Onstage—all in bright, vivid, living, impossible-to-take-your-eyes-away-from color—even though a lot of it wasn't in the lines. He stuffed some in the eighth-grade lockers. He taped some to the asbestos tiles on classroom ceilings. He put them in all the stalls of the boys' restroom, and in all the stalls in the girls' restroom, too. (I heard that from Meryl Lee.) He put them over the drinking fountains, and on every classroom door, and on the fire escape doors, and on the walls of the stairwells. He put them on the arches over the doors of the main lobby (no one figured out how he got that high without a ladder), and on the backboards of the basketball hoops in the gym. He even got them on all the trophies in the locked glass cases by the Main Administrative Office, and found a way to tape them to the Administrative Office counter, so that they were the first thing you saw when you walked in.

By the time he was done, every place you looked was bright yellow. It was high noon in the halls. The only thing that could have been worse was if the pictures had shown the white feathers on my butt. If they had, I would have had to leave the country.

As it was, when I walked into school, I figured this would be my last day at Camillo Junior High.

Maybe I'd try the Alabama Military Institute.

Can you imagine what it's like to walk down the halls of your junior high and just about every single person you meet looks at you and starts to grin, and it's not because they're glad to see you? Can you imagine what it's like to walk into the boys' restroom before the eighth graders have cleared out? Can you imagine what it's like to go to Gym and have Coach Quatrini, the pied ninny, announce that morning exercises will be stretches so that we can all practice soaring like Ariel the Fairy?

No, you cannot imagine this. But let me tell you, it was a long first Wednesday back.

And to top it off, Mrs. Baker gave me a 150-question test on *The Tragedy of Macbeth*.

"Let's keep you on your toes," she said cheerfully.

Sometimes I still think that she hates my guts.

By the next morning, Mr. Vendleri had torn down almost all of the pictures. He hadn't gotten to the ones in the trophy case yet, or the ones in the main lobby. Meryl Lee took care of the ones in the girls' restroom.

Good old Meryl Lee.

But Doug Swieteck's brother had an ample supply. They showed up in the halls again that Friday. On Monday in the cafeteria. On Tuesday across the stage front in the auditorium. Mr. Vendleri could hardly keep up.

And when Tuesday was over and I walked home, figuring that I would be free of the picture for at least the evening, my sister was waiting for me at the front door of the Perfect House, and she was holding one in her hand, complete with yellow oil paint.

"This," she said, "was taped to my locker."

So it had migrated to the high school, too.

"Do you want to tell me why this was taped to my locker?" she said.

"Because someone wanted to be a jerk," I said.

"Someone?" She looked at the picture, then held it out to me again. "Who looks like a jerk in this picture, Holling?"

"I didn't take it," I said.

"You're the one wearing the yellow tights! I told you this would happen. I didn't care as long as it was just you. But it's not just you now, is it? This was taped to my locker. And now I'm the one who has a baby brother who wears yellow tights."

"I'm not your baby brother."

"No, you're right. You're my brother who is all grown up and wearing yellow tights." She shoved the picture into my chest. "Fix this or you die," she said.

I never thought being in seventh grade would mean so many death threats.

I considered my options. Cream puffs were not going to work again. The Alabama Military Institute was looking pretty good. Maybe Dad would even like the idea.

That hope lasted until suppertime, when my father announced that the town had decided to build a new junior high school, and that Hoodhood and Associates had been invited to bid to become the architect.

He looked at my sister after making the announcement. "You see what being named Chamber of Commerce Businessman of 1967 can do for you?"

"Gee," she said, "I thought it was getting the nifty magnetic sign for the side of your car that was the big deal." She smiled.

My father looked at me.

"Just swell," I said.

"That's right," he said. "And having a kid in the school is a big plus in making a bid like this. It makes the board members think that we have a deep commitment already. And if Hoodhood and Associates gets this contract, we'll really be going places."

"I've been thinking of military school," I said.

Dad took a sip of his coffee.

"I'm not sure Kowalski will even bother to put in a bid," he said.

"I'm thinking of military school," I said again. "In Alabama."

"You don't have to say ridiculous things twice, Holling. Once is more than enough."

"Why is military school ridiculous?" asked my sister.

"Today the Mets decided to pay Buddy Harrelson eighteen thousand dollars a year to play baseball. Can you imagine that? Eighteen thousand dollars a year . . . just to play baseball. This for a player who can't hit the ball out of the infield. Holling going to military school isn't quite as ridiculous as that, but I'll give him this—it's pretty close."

"It's not any more ridiculous than going to our high school," said my sister.

My father closed his eyes. He took another sip of coffee. I think he was fortifying himself.

"Girls can't wear their hair too short, boys can't wear their hair too long," my sister said. "We can't wear skirts that are too short, or slacks that are too long, or sweaters that are too tight, or jeans that are too—and I'm not making this up—too blue. We can't even wear a turtleneck because it's too something—no one knows what, but it's something. Now, that's ridiculous. That a principal even cares about this stuff while bombs are dropping on people who hardly have any clothes is even more ridiculous."

"You don't wear those things because you're not a hippie," said my father. His eyes were still closed.

"What's all that got to do with education? Why can a principal just make all those rules up?"

My father opened his eyes. "Because he can," he said, and put down his cup of coffee. "Eighteen thousand dollars. They are out of their minds."

The Alabama Military Institute faded right away.

After supper, my sister came into my room.

"So you don't think you need to knock?" I said.

"Holling, going to military school is a ridiculous idea."

"That's not what you said at supper."

"It's not a ridiculous idea because of why Dad thinks it's a ridiculous idea. It's a ridiculous idea because it's military school, and because the next stop after military school is Saigon."

"So?"

She put her hands on her hips. "Sometimes I wonder if you're even worth trying to save," she said. "There's a war going on in Vietnam, Holling. Have you noticed? A war. Two hundred soldiers die every week. They come back home in black body bags stacked into planes. And after they're buried in the ground, their families get a new American flag with fancy folds. And that's it."

She stopped.

"And I couldn't stand it if . . ."

She stopped again.

"It's a ridiculous idea, Holling," she said, and left.

Pete Seeger began to play loudly in her room.

The next afternoon, after everyone had left for Temple Beth-El or Saint Adelbert's, and after Doug Swieteck and Danny had waited around until the last minute in case Mrs. Baker had arranged for Whitey Ford to show up, Mrs. Baker handed me back my *Macbeth* test.

"Macbeth and Malcolm are not the same person, though their names share an initial consonant," she said.

"I know," I said.

"Nor are Duncan and Donalbain, who also share an initial and, for that matter, concluding, consonant, the same person."

"I guess not," I said.

"Malcolm and Donalbain are the king's sons, not . . ."

"You know," I said, "it's not so easy to read Shakespeare—especially when he can't come up with names that you can tell apart."

Mrs. Baker rolled her eyes. This time I was sure.

"Shakespeare did not write for your ease of reading," she said.

No kidding, I thought.

"He wrote to express something about what it means to be a human being in words more beautiful than had ever yet been written."

"So in *Macbeth,* when he wasn't trying to find names that sound alike, what did he want to express in words more beautiful than had ever yet been written?"

Mrs. Baker looked at me for a long moment. Then she went and sat back down at her desk. "That we are made for more than power," she said softly. "That we are made for more than our desires. That pride combined with stubbornness can be disaster. And that compared with love, malice is a small and petty thing."

We were both quiet.

"Malice is not always small and petty," I said. "Have you seen what Doug Swieteck's brother put up in the halls?"

"I have," said Mrs. Baker. "A wonderful picture of you playing a wonderful part."

"In yellow tights," I said.

"Well," she said, "you may chance have some odd quirks and remnants of wit broken on you."

"That doesn't sound like it's from *Macbeth.*"

"It's not. But I promise you, people will soon forget about Ariel."

I sighed. "It's a whole lot easier saying that than seeing yourself in that picture."

"I suppose that would be true," she said.

"It's not like it's *your* picture in the halls, or that you have all that much to worry about," I said.

I know. Dumb.

Mrs. Baker's face went suddenly white. She opened her lower desk drawer, put her copy of Shakespeare into it, and closed it. Loudly. "Go sit down and fix the errors on your *Macbeth* exam," she said.

I did.

We said nothing else to each other that whole afternoon. Not even when I left.

I walked home under gray clouds whose undersides had been shredded. They hung in tatters, and a cold mist leaked out of them. The cold got colder, and the mist got mistier all through the afternoon, so that by suppertime a drizzle was making everything wet and everyone miserable—especially my sister, who believed that she had hair that belonged in southern California, where it would be springy and bouncy all the time, instead of in gray, cold, misty Long Island, where it just hung.

So dumb.

Lying in bed that night, I listened as the drizzle turned to a rain, and then the rain started to spatter thickly on the window, and then all sounds of it faded away, and my room began to grow cold. I got up and looked out, but the glass was covered with a sheet of thin ice, and the only thing I could see was the crazed pattern of the streetlight outside.

In the morning, ice covered the town. If the sun had been shining, it would have been a spectacle, like something Prospero might conjure up. But as it was, the tattered gray clouds hung even lower, and the mist was leaking out of them again, and the town looked more like the kind of foul heath where Macbeth's Three Weird Sisters lived.

As I walked to school that morning, the mist laid down a fine, light coating of water on last night's ice, and by the time I got to the library, I could stand on the sidewalk, give a little push, and slide. By the time I got to Goldman's Best Bakery, I didn't even need to push: The last block and a half was all downhill, so I pointed my feet, leaned down a bit, bent my knees, and let myself go. Since there wasn't a single car anywhere, I didn't even stop at the corners. By the time I reached Camillo Junior High, I had enough speed to take out Doug Swieteck's brother—if he'd been anywhere in sight.

And then, suddenly, there he was—just like the Three Weird Sisters appearing because Macbeth had thought of them—Doug Swieteck's brother, on the other side of Camillo Junior High, waiting for a school bus to turn the corner so that he could grab on to its bumper and have it pull him along on the icy roads.

It was what eighth graders whose career goal was the state penitentiary did.

The school buses were driving around town even though no cars were because Mr. Guareschi was principal of Camillo Junior High, and Mr. Guareschi wouldn't have let the school close right before the New York State Standardized Achievement Tests even if the Soviet Union had started raining atomic bombs on the entire east coast of the United States. I heard that from Mr. Petrelli himself, and it's probably true.

So the buses were driving on ice, and they all pulled in late, and you only had to look at the drivers' faces to see they were all mad at Mr. Guareschi, and Mrs. Baker was mad because we straggled in throughout the morning because the buses were late. I figured that the only one who was happy in the whole school was Mr. Ludema, Doug Swieteck's brother's teacher, because Doug Swieteck's brother stayed out until the last bus came in.

"It's the dictator-of-a-small-country thing," Danny said when he finally got to class—he was on the last bus. "Mr. Guareschi thinks he can control the weather! He tells us to come to school in the ice, and we come. He tells bus drivers to drive in the ice, and they drive! He controls all the school buses of the world!" He held his hands up high in the air. "He controls us all!"

Danny Hupfer can get carried away.

But even if Mr. Guareschi could control the school buses like the dictator of a small country, he couldn't control the Long Island Power Company, which that morning was spending its time not giving electricity to most of its customers—including Camillo Junior High. You couldn't have raised a spark of electricity anywhere. Any light that came into the classrooms was from the windows, and on a day of gray tattered clouds, that wasn't much.

So we sat in the half-dark, in our coats, in the cold. We could hear Sycorax and Caliban scurrying in the walls, climbing down from the ceiling to find someplace warm to burrow in. Like a human body. I figured they probably could sense us, and soon the walls would start to shred, and we'd see claws and nails, and there would be clacking yellow teeth, and before Birnam Wood could come to Dunsinane, we'd all run screaming out of the room into the misty cold.

That's how we spent our day preparing for the New York State Standardized Achievement Tests. In Mrs. Baker's class, we drilled on sentence diagramming. In Mr. Samowitz's class, we drilled on mathematical sets. (We didn't tell his homeroom class, who were coming into our room for sentence diagramming, about Sycorax and Caliban. We figured we'd hear if anything happened.) In Mr. Petrelli's class, we recited European borders and exports. And as we drilled, our hands got colder and colder, so that by noon it was hard to feel our pencils with our fingers.

But at lunch, Mrs. Bigio came into the classroom carrying a tray of thick paper cups, steaming with the hot scent of chocolate—probably because she felt guilty about the Something Surprise from before the holidays. "Don't ask how I got them hot," she said to Mrs. Baker. "But if Mr. Guareschi is looking for his desk, he might have a hard time finding it."

Can you believe it? Hot chocolate!

Mrs. Baker laughed—a real laugh, not a teacher laugh—and sat down behind her desk with the cup Mrs. Bigio gave her. She held both her hands around it to warm them.

Mrs. Bigio walked down the aisles, and we each took a cup from her tray. Doug Swieteck tried to take two, but when Mrs. Bigio put her heavy and sensible shoe on his sneaker, he put the extra cup back.

Mai Thi did not reach for the chocolate when Mrs. Bigio came beside her. She did not raise her head.

And Mrs. Bigio did not pause. She finished the rest of the aisles, and left with one cup still steaming on her tray.

"Let's begin the next sentences," said Mrs. Baker.

We groaned.

"Now," said Mrs. Baker, "while the sugar is coursing through your veins."

She walked up and down the aisles to watch us work. I don't know if anyone else saw her put her cup of hot chocolate on Mai Thi's desk.

Not that she had suddenly become filled with the milk of human kindness. (That's from *The Tragedy of Macbeth*, by the way.) Mrs. Baker did not even let us outside after lunch. We kept drilling.

In midafternoon, the clouds pulled up their tatters and started to thicken. Then they began to billow out toward the ground, as though they were carrying some heavy load and were about to split. They billowed further and further, until a few minutes before we finished school they finally did split, and huge wet snowflakes fell from them onto the icy roads—just as the bus drivers were pulling into the parking lot, probably watching for signs of Doug Swieteck's brother.

Before we left, Mrs. Baker read a memo that Mr. Guareschi had sent around to all the classrooms. "Since the New York State Standardized Achievement Tests are to be administered tomorrow throughout the entire state, plan on attending school. No student will be excused without permission from the principal. Weather will not be a factor. The school will be open for the administration of the tests."

Mrs. Baker put the memo on the desk. She looked outside at the snow that was already gathering on top of the ice. "I will see you all tomorrow," she said.

It was like Mr. Petrelli had said: Even if atomic bombs had started raining down.

When I left, I realized that for the whole day Mrs. Baker had not said a word to me.

So dumb.

Through the late afternoon and evening, the wind sculpted the snow first into low mounds and then into strange, sharp shapes. And when the wind was finished with the snow, it threw itself against our house, wailed under the eaves, and looked for any chink it could push through. At times the Long Island Power Company would muster up some electricity and send it out, and suddenly all the lights in the house would flick on, along with my sister's radio turned up to full volume, and the light over the stoop would show how deep the snow had become. But then the electricity would flit away again, and we were left in the candlelight and cold.

If you think the four of us huddled together under blankets like the pioneers and told stories and sang old western songs in front of a roaring fire, you're wrong. And not just because houses on Long Island don't have fireplaces—at least, none that give off heat.

It was more like this:

Every half-hour when the shows switched, my mother walked over to the television and tried the on-off button several times. Then she turned the channel and tried the on-off button again. "You'd think that at least this would work," she said. Then she turned the channel and tried again. When nothing happened, she went out to the kitchen and opened the windows so we couldn't tell that she was smoking. We tried to ignore the cold billows that swept through the house and made us clutch the blankets around us even tighter.

My father raged by the phone. He couldn't believe that employees of Hoodhood and Associates were already calling, wondering if the firm was going to be closed the next day. "Don't they know we have a contract to compete for? And they're going to let a little snow get in the way? They must not want to work for me much longer," he said. "It's not like I'm the Mets and I can pay Ed Kranepool twenty-four thousand dollars next season. Twenty-four thousand dollars! For Ed Kranepool! Next thing you know, they'll be paying Tom Seaver twenty-four thousand dollars too. Are they out of their minds?"

My sister was tormented, absolutely tormented, absolutely, positively tormented by three things. First, she could never hope to put on her makeup without lights, and she'd die before she went out anywhere without her makeup. Second (and these are supposed to be getting worse as we go along), the Beatles television special, which was at eight o'clock, was starting right now—Right Now!— and was being seen by every single person in the country except for her, and somehow Ringo would find out about that and never, ever forgive her. And third, because the New York State Standardized Achievement Tests would take an hour longer at the high school, she would be walking home at the same time as her brother—the one who wore yellow tights—who, if he knew what was good for him, would walk home on the far side of the road, far enough away from her that no one would ever suspect any sort of family connection.

So it wasn't pioneer songs by firelight.

It snowed all night, and in the morning we looked like Alaska. Northern Alaska.

But it didn't matter. A whole new Ice Age could have started, and it wouldn't have mattered. Because Mr. Guareschi was as good as his word. My sister's transistor radio announced that all the schools would be open, this despite more snow overnight than we had seen the last three winters combined. Students were advised to leave early, as travel might be slowed by the snow—like this was the most astonishing observation of the century.

So I did leave early, and I hiked through knee-deep drifts to school, the wind still wailing and throwing itself against me, three sharpened Number 2 pencils for the New York State Standardized Achievement Tests in my pocket. Since the power was still off at the school, I wore thermal underwear—top and bottom—plus an extra T-shirt, a sweatshirt, and two pairs of heavy socks. I was sweating by the time I reached Camillo Junior High, but I figured that I would be warm and cozy through the tests, even if I couldn't move my toes in my boots.

None of the roads had been plowed yet, but enough buses had come down Lee Avenue that it was packed hard and slick. And Doug Swieteck's brother was riding the bumpers again, heading for the state penitentiary, all happy, as if he hadn't spent the last week with newspaper pictures and a jar of yellow oil paint, ruining my life.

When I saw him riding by, holding on with just one hand, something in me snapped. I'm not sure what it was. I guess Presbyterians would call it sin, but I don't think it was sin. It was more like the human need for revenge—sort of what Malcolm and Donalbain were thinking. (Please note that I *do* know the names of the king's two sons.) By the time I saw Doug Swieteck's brother come by again, my plan was fully formed. A snowball had appeared before me, a fatal vision. I dug down into the snow and pulled up some of the slush underneath. I packed the snowball tight. I rounded it so that it would fly straight. Then I spit on it a few times to give it a frozen overcoating.

The next bus started to come down Lee Avenue.

In my mind I could see it all: I pull back my arm, plant my left foot, Doug Swieteck's brother comes sliding into sight, I release the fastball, his face turns toward me at the last moment, and the snow-ice-slush-spitball splatters against his nose. Perfect.

I didn't really think it would happen that way. The snowball would hit the bus. Or I'd miss entirely. Or it would hit someplace that he'd hardly feel. Or maybe he wouldn't even be holding the bumper. Or maybe I wouldn't even throw it.

But I did.

And it all happened exactly as I'd imagined it.

Really.

By the time he could get the snow and slush and ice-spit out of his eyes and look for who'd thrown it, I was hanging up my coat in the Coat Room, feeling like Jim Hawkins aboard the *Hispaniola,* putting her before the wind and so paying back all the wicked pirates of Flint's crew.

Vengeance is sweet. Vengeance taken when the vengee isn't sure who the venger is, is sweeter still.

I went into the New York State Standardized Achievement Tests happy.

I stayed that way through the morning, filling in bubbles with my three sharpened Number 2 pencils like you wouldn't believe, working through Parts of Speech like I was Robert Louis Stevenson, and making decimals look like playground stuff. I had the Falkland Islands down pat, and when there was a long Reading-Comprehension passage about the Mississippi River, I thanked the good Mr. Petrelli, who had made me get to know it personally.

Then at lunch recess—during which we all sharpened our three Number 2 pencils again—the power came on. This brought as many cheers as Mickey Mantle. Right away the radiators began to clank and pound as if Mr. Vendleri was going at them with a wrench, and the room started to grow warmer. Pretty soon we couldn't see our breath anymore. Even Sycorax and Caliban scampered back up to their asbestos ceiling tiles.

We took off our coats and hats and gloves and scarves and settled in for the second half of the achievement tests. Vocabulary first—mostly words that even William Shakespeare wouldn't have known.

Halfway through the afternoon test, I took off my sweatshirt.

The radiators were giving off that hot iron smell, sort of like a southwest wind that blisters you all o'er.

Then Spelling. The parts of the radiators that rust had worn down began to glow softly. They took on a color that you can usually see only in sunsets.

I kicked off my boots and one of the pairs of thick socks. (Danny was already barefoot.) It felt good to be able to move my toes again.

Then a short section on Roman numerals, and on to fractions. The room was now downright tropical. And I had on thermal underwear—thermal underwear that was supposed to keep me warm in minus-ten-degree temperatures. I was starting to sweat everywhere—even my fingernails—and I think that I was probably turning the color of the rusted radiators.

On to Imperfect Verb Forms—which I had down, let me tell you.

But I thought I was going to pass out. My fingers were sliding on my sharpened Number 2 pencil. And I could hardly see the little bubbles anymore. I think my eyes were sweating.

I raised my hand and asked Mrs. Baker if I could go to the boys' restroom.

She picked up the instruction booklet for the New York State Standardized Achievement Tests. "No student is permitted to leave his seat for any reason other than a dramatic health concern once a section of the achievement tests has begun. There are no exceptions." She set the instructions back on the desk and turned her face to the radiators, which by now were putting out so much heat that they were probably giving her a tan.

It seemed to me that we were in dramatic-health-concern territory, but you can't exactly raise your hand in class and announce that you have to go take off what I had to go take off.

When we got to Sentence Diagramming—a section that Mrs. Baker began without even giving anyone a chance for a moment of release—most of the water component of my body had been sucked into the little cotton compartments of my thermal underwear. Everything felt squishy, and the answer sheet for my test had turned soggy, sort of like how cornflakes left overnight in half a bowl of milk look, with about the same smell.

By 2:30, when we finally handed our answer sheets in, I was afraid that mine was going to dissolve into some sort of pulp.

Meryl Lee's answer sheet looked white and starched.

"That wasn't so bad, was it?" she said.

"Nope," said Danny. He was putting on his socks again.

"Not bad at all," said Doug Swieteck. Even Doug Swieteck!

"Are you all right?" asked Meryl Lee.

"Anyone who needs to, may now go to the restroom," said Mrs. Baker.

I was the first one out of the room. I squished my soggy self down the hall as fast as I could, glad that there weren't any radiators there. I ran the last twenty yards or so, even though running in the halls is one of the deadly sins at Camillo Junior High, right up there with pride, envy, wrath. I burst through the door into the boys' restroom, pulling at my top T-shirt, imagining the sensation of tearing off the thermal underwear.

The boys' restroom was filled with eighth graders. All smoking.

And Doug Swieteck's brother was leaning against one of the sinks.

"That's him," said one of the eighth graders. He was pointing at me.

"Him?" said Doug Swieteck's brother. He threw his cigarette to the floor and smashed it. I think he was trying to send me a message.

He walked over to me, stuck his finger out, and poked it into my thermal underweared chest. "Did you throw that snowball at me?"

"When?" I said. This is called a delaying tactic, and is sometimes more strategic than denial all by itself.

"You"—he poked his finger into me—"are"—he poked again—"dead"—he poked again. The he wiped his wet finger off on his shirt.

This is getting familiar, isn't it? Another death threat. I could sort of understand how it must have been for Banquo, and for a moment, in my heated, sweaty brain, I could almost see him there in the boys' restroom, covered with stab wounds, looking sort of lost and shaking his head like he wanted to warn me.

"Dead," said Doug Swieteck's brother again.

I backed out. Doug Swieteck's brother's little rat eyes followed me all the way.

I went back to Mrs. Baker's classroom and sat down squishily.

Toads, beetles, bats.

"Are you feeling better?" asked Meryl Lee.

"Just swell," I said.

Outside it was still snowing, but the temperature had come up, and the flakes that were coming down were the kind that really wanted to be rain but couldn't quite get there. When they hit the snow that had already fallen, they froze into a thin crust and coated everything in sight. Mrs. Baker was looking out the window and frowning, and I knew she was wondering how the school buses would ever drive on roads with a frozen crust, and snow beneath that, and ice beneath that.

She was probably also wondering how she would drive home

herself on roads with a frozen crust, and snow beneath that, and ice beneath that.

In every other class at Camillo Junior High, the last half-hour after a day of the New York State Standardized Achievement Tests was Free Reading Time or Snacks or Story Hour or something. A lot of teachers brought in brown, light, perfect cream puffs for their classes.

But Mrs. Baker—the holiday-hating Mrs. Baker—had us open *English for You and Me* and start in on a new unit: "Strong Verb Systems." It was hard to concentrate, fresh from Doug Swieteck's brother's rat eyes and sitting in squishy thermal underwear. But Mrs. Baker never called on me. Not even when I raised my hand. Not even when I hollered out that I could tell her why "to write" was a strong verb.

And so the clock clicked down to the end of the school day.

I headed outside, watching, watching, watching for Doug Swieteck's brother, his words hovering like the snow in the air: "You . . . are . . . dead." Nowhere in the halls. I left through the main lobby doors, under a picture of Ariel that Mr. Vendleri hadn't reached. Looking up at it, I felt again the thrill of the venger. But I kept looking for the vengee. Still nowhere in sight. And now the cold air struck me, and I held my coat open to it, and down below my two T-shirts, my thermal underwear suddenly chilled, and I felt the temperature of my body drop and my face cool.

"Are you all right?" asked Danny Hupfer.

"Just swell," I said, and I really meant it.

I crossed the schoolyard—Doug Swieteck's brother must have already gone—and came out onto Lee Avenue, where the school buses were spinning their wheels on the ice while Mr. Guareschi stood by the fence with his arms crossed—I suppose to prevent the state penitentiary crowd from riding the bumpers. But none of them were in sight, either.

Which I'm sure that Mr. Guareschi was glad for, since on the other side of the street a *Home Town Chronicle* photographer was taking pictures of the buses turning onto the ice, finding a little traction for a moment, and then losing it and sliding sideways, flinging down snow from their yellow roofs.

By the time I got to the corner opposite Camillo Junior High, one of the buses was gunning its engine frantically, trying to get some momentum and, at the same time, trying to ease around Mrs. Baker's very, very slowly moving car. And that's what made the rest of what happened happen.

It took only about three seconds.

And I didn't see much of it, since the wet flakes were coming down hard again.

But here's what happened, as near as I can tell:

When I got to the corner, Doug Swieteck's brother and the state penitentiary crowd were waiting for me on the other side. They stood in line like a platoon, and each one lifted up his left arm and pointed at me. In their right hands they held snowballs as big as bowling balls. The streetlights were already on in the gray darkness, and their light glittered yellow off the snowballs' icy coating.

At least, I hoped that's why the snowballs looked yellow.

I needed about a second to take that in, I guess.

In the next second, the school bus gunned its ancient engine and then started to slide across the intersection—slide sideways, that is, and through the red light. I watched as the bus's back end went by me, moving in a couple of different directions. I could see Danny's face out the back window. He was looking kind of startled but happy. The next day, he told me that he'd never heard a school-bus driver scream that way before.

Which I can vouch for. I heard her, too.

And that leaves the third second, when I started to turn back from the bus to see what Doug Swieteck's brother and the penitentiary crowd were going to do when the bus slid across the intersection and onto their corner, but I never got to them. Because walking across Lee Avenue, in the middle of the road, her head down and her scarf pulled over her ears because she didn't want the wet snow to dampen her southern California hair, was my sister.

Walking back home an hour late because of the New York State Standardized Achievement Tests.

I took off.

I remember hearing the air brakes, and someone yelling "Mr. Hoodhood," and the "Oh" that came out of my sister when I hit her just ahead of the sliding school bus.

I remember seeing her rolling out of the way and into a snowbank by the curb—which I saw from a sort of aerial view, because the right rear bumper of the bus caught me where I had worn my white feathers, and so I was crossing the rest of the Lee Avenue intersection at a height of about five feet.

I landed in the snowbank by Goldman's Best Bakery.

When I opened my eyes, my sister was looking down at me. Mr. Goldman was looking down at me. Doug Swieteck's brother and the state penitentiary crowd were looking down at me. The bus driver was looking down at me. Danny was looking down at me. Mr. Guareschi was looking down at me. And Mrs. Baker was holding my head in her hands.

"Holling," she said, "are you hurt?"

"Not the part you're holding," I said.

My sister was crying.

Really.

"Holling," she said, "you saved my life."

"High drama does not help us right now," said Mrs. Baker. "Hold his head out of the snow, and I'll get my car."

I shifted myself around. I was starting to get cold, since the sweat in the little cotton compartments of my thermal underwear was turning to ice. "I think I'm all right," I said.

"You'll have to go to the emergency room," said Mr. Guareschi. "Mrs. Baker is going to drive us. Can you move your toes?"

Of course I couldn't move my toes. I still had on my thick socks. "No. But I think I'm really all right."

Mrs. Baker pulled up in her car. "Help him in," she said to Doug Swieteck's brother. "And you help, too," she said to the state penitentiary crowd.

They gathered around me.

"Mrs. Baker," I said.

"Be quiet," she said. And Doug Swieteck's brother and the state penitentiary crowd lifted me up out of the snowbank and hefted me across the icy crust and handed me into Mrs. Baker's back seat. Mr. Guareschi got in beside me and held my head still—though that wasn't the part of me that was hurting. My sister got in the front seat, and we careened down Lee Avenue, stopping only to let my sister off at our house so that she could tell my mother where we were going. Mrs. Baker held her hand down on the horn at every intersection, fishtailed through most of her turns, and pretty much hit the entrance to the emergency room in one long sideways slide.

When we got inside—I was limping a little, but Mr. Guareschi held on to my right arm the whole way—Mrs. Baker couldn't find the word she needed to describe the location of the injury. Shakespeare doesn't give you everything. She finally settled on "his buttocks," which the nurse understood.

"Are you his father?" the nurse asked Mr. Guareschi.

"His principal."

"Then you must be his mother," said the nurse.

"I am his teacher," said Mrs. Baker. "Perhaps a diagnostic hip x-ray would be in order."

"I'll inform the doctor of your intended procedure," said the nurse, which was a nurse joke, which is worse than a teacher joke. "I'll need to speak to one of the boy's parents before we do anything."

Mr. Guareschi helped me back to the waiting room, and Mrs. Baker made me lie down on three of the chairs—"Stay on your side and be still"—while she called my father. Mr. Guareschi took off my boots so that I could move my toes, and then found a blanket— who knows where—to stretch over me.

When Mrs. Baker came back, her face was set and hard. "Your father has spoken over the phone with the nurse at the front desk. He has given approval for any necessary procedure, and says that, since everything seems under control, he will be along as soon as may be convenient." She adjusted the blanket, and sat down next to Mr. Guareschi.

We waited, and waited, and waited, since apparently being hit on the buttocks isn't that big a deal in this emergency room. Outside it grew dark, and still we waited. A nurse came in to turn on a portable television in the corner, and after a few horizontal blips, there was Robert Kennedy confirming that he was considering a run against President Johnson because of the government's war policy, and then Walter Cronkite looking about as serious as a human being

can look and reporting the news from Vietnam. There were pictures
of soldiers cutting through a jungle path. There were pictures of soldiers capturing a Vietcong POW. There were pictures of soldiers
standing around supply caches.

It was warm in the waiting room, and close, and the blanket
was heavy, and my thermal underwear had thawed and was starting
to heat up again. I yawned. "I think I could fall asleep," I said to
Mrs. Baker.

But she didn't answer. When I turned to see why—and this wasn't
easy, since I was still lying down and wasn't supposed to move my
buttocks—she was standing with her hands up to her face, watching the pictures from Vietnam like she was watching for someone
she knew.

Actually, like she was watching for someone she was worrying
about.

Someone she loved.

Mr. Guareschi and I left her alone.

The nurse came for me soon afterward, and my buttocks
were x-rayed—and let me tell you, it's embarrassing to hold your
buttocks the way I had to hold my buttocks so that they could be
x-rayed. Then we waited again until the doctor came out and told
us everything was fine, that I would be sore for a week or so and
have a bruise that would turn purple and green, but it didn't matter
since it was where it was. Then Mrs. Baker signed some papers
while Mr. Guareschi put my boots back on and helped me outside
to the car and settled me in the back seat—he took the blanket with
us so I would be warm. When Mrs. Baker came, he got in the front
seat with her, and Mrs. Baker drove me to the Perfect House.
Together they walked me to the door—"Thank you so much for
bringing him home on such a terrible night to drive," said my

mother—and I limped out to the kitchen to eat supper standing.

On the counter was the late edition of the *Home Town Chronicle*.

And on the front page, there was an action shot—of me, Holling Hoodhood, flying high in the air across the intersection of Lee Avenue and Main Street, my legs splayed out as though I really *was* flying—which I guess I was. Underneath was the headline, which was this:

*Local Hero Holling Hoodhood Soars Across Intersection
to Rescue Sister*

You could see her in the picture, too, but mostly just her buttocks.

The doctor was right about being sore. I'm not sure about the bruise, since it hurt to stretch around that far to see. But it didn't matter all that much, because when I got to school on Monday, someone had gone up and down the halls of Camillo Junior High taping up pictures of Local Hero Holling Hoodhood soaring across the intersection. They were on the eighth-grade lockers, on the asbestos tiles on the ceiling, on the stalls of the boys' restroom and the girls' restroom, too, over the drinking fountains, on the classroom doors, on the fire escape doors, on the walls of the stairwells, over the doors of the main lobby, and on the backboards of the basketball hoops in the gym.

Can you imagine what it's like to walk down the halls of your junior high and just about every single person you meet looks at you and starts to grin, and it's because they're glad to see you?

It's sort of like Macduff walking in with Macbeth's head in his hand and showing it to Malcolm—who, as we all know, is one of the king's sons—and everyone starts to celebrate because Malcolm will finally be king. But all that Malcolm is thinking is that now he has no more need for vengeance.

Let me tell you, it was a great day back.

And Tom Seaver had a pretty good day, too. The Mets announced that they were going to pay him twenty-four thousand dollars next season, just like Ed Kranepool.

Can you believe it?

February

On the first Friday of February, my father missed Walter Cronkite and the *CBS Evening News* because he was spending almost the whole day getting ready for the formal presentation of the Chamber of Commerce Businessman of 1967 Award at the Kiwanis Club that night. Actually, we were *all* spending a lot of time getting ready for the Kiwanis Club, because my mother and sister were wearing long gowns, and my father and I were wearing tuxedos, which are uncomfortable and don't fit right and come with shoes made for people with very wide feet.

My sister had used most of the getting-ready time to complain, especially about the stupid purple orchid that the Kiwanis Club had sent and which she had to pin to her shoulder. It didn't help when I pointed out that I had to wear a white carnation in my lapel and that wearing a purple orchid wasn't nearly as bad. And it really didn't help when I pointed out that I had had to wear white feathers on my butt and that wearing a purple orchid really wasn't as bad as that.

And it really, *really* didn't help when my father pointed out that she had wanted to be a flower child, and so here was her chance.

"You don't take anything I believe seriously, do you?" she said to him.

"Tie your hair back from your face," he said.

She went upstairs to the bathroom to tie her hair back from her face.

I went up after her. "You should take the orchid and flush it down the toilet," I said.

She looked at me. "Why don't you take your carnation and flush *it* down the toilet?"

"Maybe I will."

She pointed toward the toilet. "Go ahead."

But I didn't have to flush my carnation down the toilet, because right then a whole series of low chords sounded from the piano in the Perfect Living Room below us, followed by a roar and crash as the entire newly plastered ceiling fell, smashing down the top of the baby grand piano, ripping the plastic seat cushions, flattening the fake tropical flowers, tearing the gleaming mirror from the wall, and spreading its glittering shards onto the floor, where they mixed with the dank, wet plaster that immediately began to settle into the carpet to stain it forever.

All four of us stood in the hall, the sickly smell of mold in our nostrils.

If the committee that chose the Chamber of Commerce Businessman of 1967 had heard what my father had to say about the carpenters and plasterers who had come to fix our living room ceiling, they might not have given him the award, since one of the requirements was that the nominee had to support the general business atmosphere of the town, and my red-faced father was hollering and swearing about how he was going to decrease the number of the town's businesses by two—and he was shredding his white carnation as he said this, which is probably what Shylock would have done if he had been wearing a white carnation after being cheated out of his ducats.

It was a good thing that neither the carpenters nor the plasterers were at the Kiwanis Club that night.

We drove there in silence, and just before we walked into the club, I took off my carnation and handed it to my father. He took it without a word, and while my mother pinned it to his lapel, I held my flowerless lapel out to my sister and smirked.

She smiled back very sweetly. Then, as soon as we had gotten inside, she excused herself, went into the ladies' room, and came back without her orchid. She was still smiling sweetly when she leaned down to me and whispered, "Down the toilet, you little jerk."

So we were both flowerless as we went into the reception hall, but no one would have seen the flowers anyway, since the hall was so dark. The only light came from the candles on the tables, the lit ends of cigarettes, and the lamps at the head table, which shone off the fake paneling on the wall behind. My father sat up there, and the rest of us sat below him at a center table with the wives of the Kiwanis Club officers. My mother refused an offered cigarette—I could tell this wasn't easy—and then she chattered to the Kiwanis wives while my sister and I sat silently through the dinner—roast beef and mashed potatoes and buttered lima beans—and through dessert—lemon meringue pie with a whole lot more meringue than lemon—and through the opening greetings and speeches, and then through my father's speech of grateful acceptance.

He was still red in the face when he got up to speak, and you could tell he was looking out at the audience for the carpenters and plasterers. But he made it through without any hollering and swearing, and everyone clapped when he talked about the growing business opportunities of the town, and how he was glad to be a part of it all, and how someday he hoped to leave a thriving and prosperous business in a thriving and prosperous town to his son to carry on the good name of Hoodhood and Associates. Lots of clapping at this. When everyone at the head table looked down at me, I smiled and nodded like I was supposed to, since I'm the Son Who Is Going to Inherit Hoodhood and Associates.

My sister kicked me under our table.

Toads, beetles, bats.

When we got home that night, my father phoned the carpenters and the plasterers. He told them that he didn't care that it was late on a Friday night. And he didn't care that tomorrow was a Saturday. They had better be at the house first thing in the morning, ready to fix the ceiling permanently and to offer restitution for the property damage their carelessness had caused.

They were there, first thing in the morning.

If I had had anything to say about it—which, of course, I didn't—I would have had the carpenters and plasterers head over to Camillo Junior High as soon as they were done with the Perfect Living Room, because the ceiling in our classroom was getting to be a bigger and bigger problem as the weeks went by and Mr. Guareschi and Mr. Vendleri couldn't trap, poison, snag, snare, net, corner, maim, coax, or convince the rats to give themselves up. Eight asbestos ceiling tiles had started to bulge down, which meant that either Sycorax and Caliban were getting fatter or the ceiling was getting weaker. Every morning, Mrs. Baker looked up at the bulges to inspect them. And every morning she looked a little more nervous.

"So suppose she looks up there and sees that they've chewed a hole in the tiles and they're looking back down at her. What happens then?" I said to Danny.

"You know that sound the bus driver made just before she hit you?"

I remembered the sound.

"It wasn't anything compared to what Mrs. Baker would do."

We waited hopefully, but the eight bulging tiles stayed intact.

At the beginning of February, Mrs. Baker had assigned me *Romeo and Juliet*. I read it in three nights.

Let me tell you, these two wouldn't make it very far in Camillo Junior High. Never mind that Romeo wears tights—at least according to the pictures—but he just isn't very smart. And Juliet isn't too strong in that department, either. I mean, a potion to *almost* kill you? She drinks a potion to *almost* kill you? Who would drink a potion to *almost* kill you? Then Romeo goes ahead and drinks a potion that *will* kill you because he can't figure out that she's only had a potion that *almost* kills you? And then Juliet, who at least is smart enough to figure out that Romeo really is dead, makes sure that she uses a knife this time, which is not *almost* going to kill you, but really *will* kill you?

Doesn't this sound like something that two people who can't find their way around the block would get themselves into?

Of course it does.

Mrs. Baker couldn't see this problem at all. Because she's a teacher, and no teacher ever does. "Didn't you find it tragic and beautiful and lovely?" she asked me when I told her I'd finished reading it.

See?

"Not really," I said.

"What did you find it then?"

"Stupid."

"There we have an opinion that overturns three hundred and seventy-five years of critical appreciation. Is there a particular reason that you find it 'stupid'?"

"Because they never would have done what they did."

"Fall in love?"

"All the stuff at the end."

"The poison and the knife," she said.

"Yes. They never would have done that."

Mrs. Baker considered this for a moment. "What would they have done?"

"Gone to Mantua together."

"And their parents?"

"Ignored them."

"I'm not sure that life is quite as simple as that. These are star-crossed lovers. Their fate is not in their own hands. They have to do what has already been decided for them. That's why it's so tragic and beautiful and lovely."

You see? Tragic and beautiful and lovely again. Why not just stupid and dumb?

Meryl Lee thought it was wonderful that I was reading *Romeo and Juliet,* since, having been inspired by the Long Island Shakespeare Company's Holiday Extravaganza, she was reading it, too. "Don't you think it's romantic, Holling?"

"I guess so."

"And you're reading it just before Valentine's Day."

"Yeah."

"The most romantic day of the year. Don't you love the balcony scene?" She clasped her hands and held them beneath her chin. "O Romeo, Romeo! Wherefore art thou Romeo?"

"Meryl Lee, let's go somewhere together for Valentine's Day."

I turned around to look behind me, because someone else must have said what just popped out of my mouth.

"What?" said Meryl Lee.

I was still trying to figure out how that popped out. I think it must have been because of Mrs. Baker and her "Shakespeare is expressing something about what it means to be a human being" and the "tragic and beautiful and lovely" routine. It all had gotten into the air and mixed together, and the first thing you know after you start breathing that stuff, you say things like what I said to Meryl Lee.

But what could I do now? So I said it again: "Let's go somewhere together for Valentine's Day."

She put her hand on her hip and thought for a moment. Then, "No," she said.

This, in case you're missing it, is the tragic part.

"Why not?" I said.

"Because you called me a blind mole, and then you acted like a jerk about your father winning the Baker Sporting Emporium contract."

"That was three months ago, and I did not act like a jerk."

"You still called me a blind mole and hoped—let me see if I can get this right—you hoped that an unwholesome dew from a wicked fen would drop on me."

It was actually a wicked dew from an unwholesome fen, but I'm a lot smarter than Romeo, and I know when to shut up.

Now, here comes the lovely part.

"Meryl Lee," I said, "there lies more peril in thine eye than twenty of their swords. Look thou but sweet."

"Twenty of whose swords?"

"It's Shakespeare," I said. "It doesn't have to make sense. They just have to be words more beautiful than have ever yet been written."

"So *mole* and *blind* are two words more beautiful than have ever yet been written?"

"Had I it written, I would tear the word."

Meryl Lee smiled. "All right," she said. "I'll go."

I told you it was the lovely part.

Even though I still can't figure out how those words popped out of my mouth.

That night, I sat through supper trying to decide where I could take Meryl Lee on an allowance that I had to string together for three weeks just to get some cream puffs. There was a moment— this will tell you how desperate I was—when I thought I might ask Mr. Goldman about another play. But it might be *Romeo and Juliet,* and that would mean more tights. And not for the whole wide world was I going to wear tights again.

So I asked my mother, "Where could I take someone with $3.78?"

The supper table quieted.

"Well," she said, "I suppose for an ice cream cone."

"It's February," I said.

"Then, maybe to Woolworth's for a hamburger and a Coke."

"Woolworth's."

She shrugged. "And then to a movie afterward."

My mother was not powerful at arithmetic.

"Who are you taking?" asked my father.

"Meryl Lee."

"Meryl Lee who?"

"Meryl Lee Kowalski."

"Meryl Lee Kowalski, the daughter of Paul Kowalski, of Kowalski and Associates?"

"I guess," I said.

He laughed. "You'd better hurry."

"Why hurry?"

"If Hoodhood and Associates get the junior high school con-tract—and we intend to—then Kowalski and Associates may very well be no more." He laughed again.

"Take her to Woolworth's," said my sister.

"Really?"

"Really. Then she'll know you're a cheapskate and dump you after the first date."

If you think that saving someone's life is all it's cracked up to be, and that the savee should swear eternal loyalty and gratitude to the saver, you don't know the part about how the savee, if she has a pic-ture of her buttocks published in the *Home Town Chronicle,* has no further obligations to the saver.

If my father was sounding more arrogant than usual, it's because he had brought home a scale model of his design for the new junior high school, and he figured it was a winner. And look-ing at it sitting on the dining room sideboard, where all the silver had been pushed to the edges to make room for it, I thought he might be right. No pillars, he pointed out. No brickwork. No sym-metrical layout. Everything was to be new and modern. So there were curved corners and curved walls. The roof was a string of domes all made out of glass. They arched over the main lobby, the gym, and clusters of science and art classrooms. When I pointed out that the building wasn't square, he pointed out that this was 1968 after all, and times were changing. Architecture should change, too. He pushed back his chair, walked over to the model, and took off its top half. "Look at this interior," he said. "Open hall-ways that rise three stories to the domes. Every classroom looks out into sunlit space. No one's ever come up with that concept for a junior high school before."

Like I told you, it was a winner.

But it didn't help me plan a $3.78 evening for Valentine's Day with Meryl Lee.

And after supper, while my sister washed and I dried, she was even more helpful than she had been before.

"What are you going to give Meryl Lee before you go out on your date?" she asked.

"It's not a date, so why should I give her something before we go out?"

"Of course it's a date. You have to give her something, like flowers or candy. Don't you know anything? It's Valentine's Day."

"I have $3.78."

"Then buy a rose. Have the florist put a ribbon on it or something. Meryl Lee will figure out you're a cheapskate soon enough anyway."

"I'm not a cheapskate. I just don't have any money."

My sister shrugged. "It's the same thing," she said.

The next day, I asked Danny where he would take someone if he were going somewhere for Valentine's Day.

"I *am* going somewhere for Valentine's Day," he said.

"You are?"

"I'm going out with Mai Thi."

"You are?" I said again.

He nodded.

"Where are you going?"

"To Milleridge Inn."

"Milleridge Inn?"

You have to know that this is the most expensive place to eat you can go to on the eastern seaboard.

"And afterward, my dad is going to drive us to see *Camelot*."

"He is?"

Danny nodded again.

"Just swell," I said.

You know how it's sometimes possible to hate your best friend's guts? I figured that by the time Danny was done, he'd spend $17 or $18. And he'd probably buy her a rose, too.

Toads, beetles, bats.

The Wednesday before Valentine's Day for the cheapskate, Mrs. Baker and I read aloud the last two acts of *Romeo and Juliet*. It was okay, but Romeo still was a jerk.

> *Come, bitter conduct, come, unsavory guide!*
> *Thou desperate pilot, now at once run on*
> *The dashing rocks thy seasick weary bark.*

Sure. If I was about to die for love, I think I could come up with something better than that. But I guess the rest was all right, down in the tombs with torches and swords and stuff. Shakespeare needed to get more of that in.

By the time we were done, Mrs. Baker was almost in tears, it was all so tragic and beautiful and lovely. "You need to see this on stage, Mr. Hoodhood. It's playing at the Festival Theater on Valentine's Day. Go see it."

Now, aren't you glad I didn't ask Mr. Goldman about another play? I told you the next one would be *Romeo and Juliet*—in tights. This is called foresight, and it probably saved me from more white feathers on my butt.

"I'm already taking Meryl Lee someplace on Valentine's Day," I told Mrs. Baker.

"Are you? Where are you taking her?"

"Someplace that costs less than what's left over from $3.78 after you buy a rose with a ribbon on it."

"That limits you somewhat." ·

"My sister says that Meryl Lee will think I'm a cheapskate."

"It's not how much you spend on a lady," said Mrs. Baker. "It's how much you give her of yourself."

"Like Romeo."

She nodded. "Like Romeo."

"He didn't end up too well," I pointed out.

"No," she said. "But Juliet never asked for anything but him."

"So is that what Shakespeare wanted to express about being a human being?"

"That," said Mrs. Baker, "may well be a question for your essay examination on *Romeo and Juliet*. Next Wednesday we'll review, and you'll write it the week after that. No—no more one-hundred-and-fifty-question tests. You are ready to do more than that."

I guess that was good news.

On Valentine's Day, Mr. Guareschi announced over the P.A. that Mrs. Bigio had baked Valentine's Day cupcakes for the junior high, and each class should send down a representative to pick up the class's allotted number of cupcakes at 1:00. I know this doesn't sound like a big deal, but let me tell you, Mrs. Bigio can bake cupcakes. You never want to turn down a Mrs. Bigio cupcake—even if it is all pastel pink with little hearts in the frosting.

We thought about the cupcakes all day. We even smelled them baking, their beautiful and lovely cake-y aroma wafting down the halls. When the clock clicked to 1:05, Danny gently reminded Mrs. Baker about the cupcakes. He said that he hoped that she hadn't forgotten them.

"Mr. Hupfer, has it been your experience that I have ever forgotten anything?" asked Mrs. Baker.

Danny had to admit that she never forgot anything.

Mrs. Baker looked at her watch. "I'm sure that Mrs. Bigio will have made a sufficient number." She went back to reading aloud a tragic love poem by Alfred, Lord Tennyson—who, I guess, couldn't figure out how to punctuate his own name.

1:14. Still waiting for Mrs. Baker to send down a representative for the cupcakes. Up above the asbestos ceiling tiles, Caliban and Sycorax are stirring, probably since the smell of pink icing is now filling the hallways.

1:17. Still waiting. The bulging asbestos ceiling tiles are vibrating.

1:18. Mrs. Baker finally sends me down to Mrs. Bigio. Danny tells me to hurry, since he is always hungry.

1:18½. I run in the hallways.

Mrs. Bigio was waiting for me with the last tray of Valentine's Day cupcakes. She slid them along the kitchen table toward me, and then slid an envelope across as well.

"Open it," she said. "You'll want it for tonight."

I opened it. Inside were two tickets for *Romeo and Juliet* at the Festival Theater.

"Mrs. Bigio," I said.

"They're season tickets, and I won't be using them tonight. So they'll just go to waste if you don't take them—and the gossip I've picked up is that you can use them—unless you want to be known as a cheapskate."

"Thank you," I said. "I can use them."

That night, Mr. Kowalski drove Meryl Lee and me to the Festival Theater to see a production of *Romeo and Juliet* by William Shakespeare for Valentine's Day. We sat in two seats in the center of the third row. Meryl Lee held the red rose with a ribbon I had bought her. Mr. Goldman played Friar Laurence, and winked at me once from the stage. The poisoning and stabbing scene was okay, but I still think that Romeo is a jerk. They needed the ghost of Banquo up there to tell them to lay off the stabbing. Or maybe Caliban.

But Meryl Lee loved it all. She was sobbing by the time it was over. "Wasn't it beautiful?" she said as the lights came up.

"So tragic," I said.

"That's just the word," she said.

We walked through the evening light to Woolworth's, where we sat at the lunch counter and I ordered two Cokes.

Let me tell you, it was just swell.

We did the balcony scene together as nearly as we could—until the guy behind the counter began to look like he wanted us gone. So we ordered two more Cokes to make him happy—I still had $1.37 left, and I didn't want Meryl Lee to think I was a cheapskate.

"Are you going to play a part in another Shakespeare play?" Meryl Lee asked.

I thought of her sobbing at the end of *Romeo and Juliet*.

"Of course," I said.

That wasn't even a Presbyterian lie; it was a flat-out lie. But after doing the balcony scene with Meryl Lee, I wasn't going to tell her what a jerk Romeo was and how the only way I was going back onto the Festival Theater stage was—well, there wasn't any way.

Meryl Lee looked at her watch. "My father will be here soon," she said. "I hope he remembers."

I sipped my Coke. I hoped he forgot.

"All he does is work on the model for the new junior high school. He goes over and over it. He moves a pillar here, then another one there. 'It's not classical enough,' he says. 'It needs to look like the Capitol building. Classical.'"

When Meryl Lee imitated her father, her eyes got large, and her hands went up, and she spoke low. She should be on the Festival Theater stage.

"Classical, classical, classical," said Meryl Lee. "There's hardly another word that comes out of his mouth."

"My dad doesn't have any pillars," I said. "He's got his model all modern."

"Modern."

I nodded. "No pillars, no straight walls, so much glass that they'll need three Mr. Vendleris to keep it all clean. That kind of modern." I asked the guy behind the counter for his pencil—he hesitated a second, since I guess he wasn't so sure about us. But he handed it over and made me promise to give it back, and then I drew the glass domes over the main lobby and gym and the science and art classrooms, and the curved corners and walls, and the clusters of classrooms looking out into sunlit space, all over my white paper placemat. "No one's ever come up with that concept for a junior high school before," I said.

Meryl Lee stared at my drawing, then went back to sipping her Coke. Her hair is auburn. Did I tell you that? In the lights of Woolworth's, it shimmered.

Mr. Kowalski did remember to come. We finished our Cokes, and I handed back the pencil to the guy behind the counter, and Meryl Lee took my placemat as a souvenir, and we walked to the car, hand in hand. Mr. Kowalski dropped me off at my house, and I wasn't sure, sitting in the back seat, how to say goodbye to Meryl

Lee. But she saved the day: "'Tis almost morning," she said. "I would have thee gone."

"Sleep dwell upon thine eyes," I said.

I didn't have to look at Mr. Kowalski to know that his eyes were rolling in his head.

So that was Valentine's Day.

The following week, the school board met to decide on the model for the new junior high school—which was probably why Mr. Kowalski had been spending all his time muttering "classical, classical, classical." The meeting was to be at four o'clock in the high school administration building. Mr. Kowalski would present his plan and model, and then my father would present his plan and model, and then the school board would meet in private session to decide whether Kowalski and Associates or Hoodhood and Associates would be the architect for the new junior high school.

I know all of this because my father was making me come. It was time I started to learn the business, he said. I needed to see firsthand how competitive bidding worked. I needed to experience architectural presentations. I needed to see architecture as the blood sport that it truly was.

Which makes architecture sound like a profession that Macbeth could have done pretty well in.

The meeting was in the public conference room, and when I got there after school, the school board members were all sitting at the head table, studying the folders with the architectural bids. Mr. Kowalski and my father were sitting at two of the high school desks—which made the whole thing seem a little weirder than it needed to be. In front of them was a long table with the two models for the new junior high school, each one covered with a white sheet, like they were some sort of national secret.

I sat behind my father.

There was a whole lot of Preliminary Agenda stuff, and Old Business, and procedural decisions, and all that. My father sat through it coolly, occasionally looking at his watch or squaring the edges of his presentation notes. Mr. Kowalski was more nervous. I'm not sure that his cigarette was out of his mouth for more than three seconds at a time.

"Mr. Kowalski, we're ready for your presentation now," said Mr. Bradbrook, who was the chairman of the school board. He sat at the head of the table, sort of like God would sit if God wore a suit. He was smoking, too, but he wasn't working at it as hard as Mr. Kowalski was. "You have eight minutes," he said.

Mr. Kowalski picked up his presentation notes and angled out of his seat. He went up to the table with the models and stood there for a moment. Then he turned and looked at—no, not my father. At me!

Really.

My father looked at him. Then he turned and looked at me like I should know what was going on.

But I didn't. I just shrugged.

"Seven minutes," said Mr. Bradbrook.

Mr. Kowalski cleared his throat. Twice. He looked at his design papers. He cleared his throat again. Then he looked back at me once more, and began.

"Gentlemen," he said, "though this is irregular, I have made some significant design changes for the interior of the new junior high since my original submission. In fact, the entire concept has changed markedly. So the plans that you studied for this afternoon's presentation have also changed. I have copies of the new interior plans, and ask the board's patience as I show you the concept. This may take slightly longer than the allotted time, but I'm sure that the Chamber of Commerce Businessman of 1967 won't begrudge Kowalski and Associates a few extra minutes in order to clarify the proposal, and to promote the general business atmosphere of the town."

"This is irregular," said Mr. Bradbrook. "Has the new concept affected the cost estimates?"

"Not significantly," said Mr. Kowalski.

Mr. Bradbrook considered. "Well," he said, "if Mr. Hoodhood will agree, then I see nothing wrong with your presentation going slightly longer. Mr. Hoodhood?"

What could the Chamber of Commerce Businessman of 1967 do? He shrugged and nodded. But the back of his neck grew as red as boiling sin, and I knew he *did* begrudge the extra time. He begrudged it a whole lot.

Mr. Kowalski pulled off the sheet from his model of the new junior high school. He cleared his throat again. "As you can see, gentlemen," said Mr. Kowalski, "the design is quite classical, in the best traditions of our national architecture, for a time when our children desperately need to be reminded of our great American traditions."

And it was. It looked like the Capitol in Washington, D.C. Wide steps swooped up past a line of pillars and up to the central doors. Above that rose a steep dome, with thin windows cut all around it. On either side of the dome, the building spread graceful wings—all with thin windows again—and behind, the long gymnasium formed the tail, whose rows of bright windows faced south and north to let in as much light as any gymnasium could ever have.

"But we live in 1968, gentlemen," Mr. Kowalski said. "Just as our children need to be reminded of our great traditions, so, too, do they need to enjoy the advantages of contemporary technology. I think you'll find the new interior design both modern and innovative, a perfect blend of where we have been and where we are going as a nation." He handed out copies of the plans for the new design to all the school board members, keeping his back to my father and me the whole time. Then he took us all through the new interior. Slowly.

No pillars, no straight walls. The roof a series of glass plates above the science and art rooms. The central dome three stories high over the main lobby and clusters of classrooms all looking out into the sunlit space. All as modern as could be.

"I don't believe that anyone has ever come up with this blended concept for a junior high school before," said Mr. Kowalski. Then he sat back down. He did not look over at us. Instead, he lit another cigarette and began pulling at it. He shuffled all of his papers into a folder.

The school board was astounded. Three of them applauded— not Mr. Bradbrook, since God doesn't applaud.

My father turned and looked at me again. His face was very red, and I could tell he was fighting for some kind of control. "Holling, there's something you should have told me, isn't there?" he whispered slowly.

I looked at him.

"Do you think this is a game? This is the future of Hoodhood and Associates. Everything rides on this. My future *and* your future. So what did you do?"

He used the kind of voice that, in my family, means that a voice a whole lot louder is about to come along in a minute or two, so you'd better start preparing.

But let me tell you, I didn't really care all that much about what he would say or how loudly he would say it. I really didn't.

Because suddenly I knew something a whole lot worse.

Romeo was a genius compared to me.

I hadn't seen at all what Meryl Lee was doing on Valentine's Day, while we were sipping Cokes at the lunch counter at Woolworth's. I hadn't realized how easily she had gotten what she wanted from me: my father's design for the new junior high.

Run me on the dashing rocks and hand me a vial of poison. I'm such a jerk, I'd probably drink it. I'm a bigger jerk even than Mickey Mantle.

I got up before I began to bawl like a first grader.

"Holling," warned my father—a slightly louder slow whisper.

I left the conference room.

My red father never did tell me what he did for his presentation. Probably it began with him demanding to see Mr. Kowalski's plans, and then suggesting that he took these from Hoodhood and Associates—not saying it outright, but just suggesting it, like he knew it was the truth but wouldn't say it—and then arguing that Mr. Kowalski should withdraw his proposal because it wasn't the same one he had submitted and that's not how honest businessmen worked. It would have been something like that, with him getting redder and redder all the time.

I bet if you were watching it, you sure would have seen that architecture is a blood sport, and Macbeth couldn't have played it any bloodier than my father.

February is a can't-decide-what-it-wants-to-be month on Long Island. What's left of any snow has melted into brown slush and runs in dirty ridges alongside the street gutters. The grass is dank and dark. Everything is damp, as if the whole island had been dipped under dark water and is only starting to dry out. Mornings are always gray and cold.

That's what it was like between Meryl Lee and me the next day at school. Slushy, damp, dirty, dark, gray, and cold. We didn't look at each other. At lunch, we ate about as far away from each other as we could, and she went outside early—even though Meryl Lee hardly ever went outside. She didn't come to Chorus, so I sang the soprano part for Miss Violet of the Very Spiky Heels alone at our stand. When Mrs. Baker asked if I'd like to partner with Meryl Lee on the sentence diagramming exercise in the afternoon, I told her I'd rather do it with Doug Swieteck.

On Friday, things were still slushy, damp, dirty, dark, and cold. Meryl Lee wore sunglasses to school, even though it was gray like always. When Mrs. Baker asked her to remove them for class, she said that her doctor had asked her to keep them on. That she was supposed to keep them on for, maybe, the rest of the school year.

I was the only one in class who didn't laugh at that.

I looked out the window.

For the next Wednesday, I wrote an essay for Mrs. Baker about what Shakespeare wanted to express about being a human being in *Romeo and Juliet*. Here is the first sentence in my essay:

What Shakespeare wanted to express about being a human being in Romeo and Juliet *is that you better be careful who you trust.*

Here is the last sentence:

If Romeo had never met Juliet, he would have been all right. But because he was star-crossed, he did meet her, and because she came up with all sorts of plans that she didn't bother telling him about,

he ended up taking poison and dying, which is an important les-
son for us to learn in life.

I had Meryl Lee to thank for this, you know. If she hadn't done what she did, I never would have figured out what Shakespeare was trying to express in Romeo and Juliet about what it means to be a human being.

When I handed the essay in, Mrs. Baker read it through. Twice. "So," she said slowly, "do you think Juliet was right to stab herself at the end of the play?"

"Yes," I said.

"I see," she said, and she put the essay in a manila folder and left it on top of her desk.

But unlike Juliet, Meryl Lee didn't stab herself. In fact, that afternoon she was waiting for me outside the gates of Camillo Junior High, standing beside a ridge of crusted snow that she had stamped down flat.

"It wasn't my fault," she said.

"Aren't you supposed to be at Saint Adelbert's?"

"I just showed him your drawing, because it was so good. I didn't know he would use the same design."

"Sure, Meryl Lee."

"It's true," she said.

"All right, it's true. Whatever you say, Meryl Lee. You told him everything about my father's design. Everything. And then a few days later, he draws up new plans so that the inside of his school is just like the inside of my father's school. You had nothing to do with it."

"I didn't say I had nothing to do with it," said Meryl Lee. "I said I didn't know he would use the same design."

"I'd keep the dark glasses on, Meryl Lee. It's easier to lie to someone if they can't see your eyes."

A long moment went by. Then Meryl Lee took off the glasses and threw them past my head.

I think she was trying to throw them *at* my head.

Then she turned and walked away—but not before I saw why she'd been wearing them.

I picked up the glasses and put them in my pocket.

That night, I saw those glasses flying past my head again and again and again. And I saw Meryl Lee's red eyes. Again and again and again.

Meryl Lee wasn't in school the next day. I kept looking over at her empty desk.

At lunch recess, I wrote a new *Romeo and Juliet* essay in the library. Here is the first sentence of the essay:

What Shakespeare wanted to express about being a human being in Romeo and Juliet *is that it's hard to care about two things at the same time—like caring about the Montague family and caring about Juliet, too.*

Here is the last sentence:

If Romeo had never met Juliet, maybe they both would have still been alive, but what would they have been alive for is the question that Shakespeare wants us to answer.

I handed the essay in to Mrs. Baker at the end of the day. She read it through. Twice. Then she took my old essay out of the manila folder—which was still on top of her desk—and put in the new essay.

She dropped the old essay into the trash, put the folder with the new essay into her desk, and then she looked up at me. "So what will you do now?" she said.

That night, with 79 cents left over from Valentine's Day and $1 from Monday's allowance, I bought two Cokes and a rose with a ribbon. I took them over to Meryl Lee's house and rang the doorbell. Mr. Kowalski answered it.

"You're the Hoodhood boy," he said.

"Is Meryl Lee home?" I said.

He opened the door further and I came in. He hesitated. Then, "Her room is the one at the top of the stairs," he said.

I went up the stairs slowly. I felt his eyes on my back, but I didn't want to turn around to let him know that I felt his eyes on my back.

I knocked at Meryl Lee's door.

"Go away," she said.

I knocked again. I heard her chair scrape against the floor, and her footsteps stomping across the room. Her door opened. "I told you—" Then she stopped. Her mouth was open.

"I thought you might be thirsty," I said.

Her mouth was still open.

"Are you?"

"Am I what?"

"Thirsty."

She looked at the Cokes in my hand. "Yes," she said.

I handed her a bottle and pulled the opener out of my pocket. I love the sound of a brand-new bottle of Coke when you pry the lid off and it starts to fizz. Whenever I hear that sound, I think of roses, and of sitting together with someone you care about, and of Romeo and Juliet waking up somewhere and saying to each other, Weren't we jerks? And then having all that be over. That's what I think of when I hear the sound of a brand-new bottle of Coke being opened.

On Thursday, before the school board met to decide on its new architect, Kowalski and Associates withdrew its bid for the new junior high school. Hoodhood and Associates was given the contract.

"What chumps," said my father. "They were going to win hands down. What chumps." He shook his head. "They're bound to go under now, but if you can't play for keeps, you shouldn't be in the business in the first place. And Kowalski never could play for keeps. And Hoodhood and Associates can." He rubbed his hands together like Shylock onstage.

And that's when something changed. I suddenly wondered if my father was really like Shylock. Not because he loved ducats, but because maybe he had become the person that everyone expected him to become. I wondered if he had ever had a choice, or if he had ever felt trapped. Or if he had ever imagined a different life.

With this new contract, he was a sure bet for the Chamber of Commerce Businessman of 1968. It's probably what everyone expected.

For the first time, I wondered if it was what he wanted—or if there was a time when he might have wanted something else.

Or if I wanted something else.

Or if we were both only Fortune's fools—like Romeo.

Meryl Lee and I were partners on Friday for sentence diagramming. We ate together at lunch. And we decided to be partners for Mr. Petrelli's next geography assignment, which was on "The California Gold Rush and You." "Make it relevant," said Mr. Petrelli. We sang together in Chorus for Miss Violet of the Very Spiky Heels, and when it came time at the end of the day to clean the board, we did that together, too.

And that's why we were at the board together when Mr. Guareschi came into the classroom to give Mrs. Baker a yellow telegram—a telegram that she took out of the envelope, then read, then dropped onto the floor as she rushed out, leaving Mr. Guareschi standing in front of the class without any idea what to do.

When we picked up the telegram to put on her desk, Meryl Lee and I could hardly not read it ourselves. Or at least the words that mattered:

DOWNED HELICOPTER TRANSPORT STOP KHESANH STOP
LT T BAKER MISSING IN ACTION STOP

march

The news from Khesanh that Walter Cronkite reported each night kept getting grimmer. The five thousand marines there were cut off and could get supplies only by air, even though any helicopter that flew over took a lot of enemy fire from the twenty thousand surrounding Vietcong troops. Meanwhile, the marines were dug into bunkers covered with three feet of earth to protect them from the mortar shells that the Vietcong were lobbing into the camp—about five hundred mortar shells a day. And when they weren't lobbing shells, the Vietcong were digging tunnels that they could use to put explosives beneath the marines. Some reports said that the tunnels were only a hundred yards away from the barbed wire around the Khesanh base. The marines had started to use stethoscopes and divining rods to see if they could find them.

You know things are bad when the United States Marine Corps is using stethoscopes and divining rods.

Still, the White House announced that the enemy offensive was running out of steam, that casualties at Khesanh were light, that we would never give up the marine base there.

We watched Walter Cronkite together every night after supper now—even my sister. We were all quiet, and not just because my father would have hollered if anyone had interrupted Walter

Cronkite. Sometimes, though, my father himself would shake his head and whisper, "Five thousand boys trapped. Good Lord. Five thousand." We'd watch the pictures of the marines in their zigzagging trenches, or deep in their bunkers, holding their hands over their ears inside their helmets because of the thunder of the mortar shells. Then my father would reach for my mother's hand, and they would look at each other.

My sister sat rigid—with anger, I guess. She probably wanted to say something like "I told you so" or "If President Johnson had listened and gotten us out of there in time" or "No one in Washington knows what he's doing," but she didn't. When five hundred mortar shells are coming in every day on top of soldiers huddled in holes with their hands over their ears, even a flower child who wanted nothing but world peace could only watch and hope.

I also was watching the newscasts and hoping for a sign, any sign, of Lieutenant Tybalt Baker. There never was one—not in any of the films of the mortars or the trenches or the downed and burning helicopters or the wounded. Walter Cronkite didn't read off the names of the missing in action, so Lieutenant Baker was never mentioned. But I still watched anyway, holding my breath, hoping.

Which is what I think the whole town was doing.

Which is certainly what Mrs. Baker was doing.

But you would never have been able to tell that she was holding her breath at Camillo Junior High. She moved through our classroom as coolly as if Khesanh were just a proper noun in a sentence that needed to be diagrammed. It was early spring and we were her garden, and she was starting to see the bulbs and seeds that she had planted in us last fall coming up. She raked away our dead leaves, spaded new soil around us, and watered and fertilized.

And we grew fast and green, let me tell you. Especially Mai Thi, who was now the best sentence diagrammer in the seventh grade—which may not sound like much, but with Mrs. Baker, it was a big deal.

During class, it didn't seem as if anything was bothering Mrs. Baker at all.

Except maybe the eight bulging asbestos ceiling tiles, which now had about as much bulge as asbestos ceiling tiles can take. They looked like sails in a full breeze.

We still didn't know exactly what was making them so heavy. Maybe the rats were hoarding supplies for the summer drought up there. Maybe Sycorax and Caliban were just getting bigger and bigger and bigger. But whatever it was, no one wanted those tiles to come down with whatever was bulging them out. Not even Danny Hupfer.

Which was why on the first Wednesday afternoon in March, while Mrs. Baker was grading and I was at my desk starting in on *Julius Caesar*—who, let me tell you, was a whole lot smarter than Romeo, even though he ended up pretty badly, too—Mr. Vendleri came in with a ladder, eight new asbestos ceiling tiles, and a heavy mallet.

Mrs. Baker looked at him.

"A mallet?" she said.

He brandished it in the air, like *Julius Caesar* himself. "You don't know how big a rat on the loose can get in five months," he said.

Mrs. Baker looked up at the bulging ceiling tiles. "I have some idea," she said.

Mr. Vendleri set his ladder under one of the bulges. He steadied it, and grabbed his mallet tightly in his right hand. He took three steps up the ladder. Then, with his left hand, he slowly reached up to one of the bulging tiles. He tapped it a couple of times, and we listened.

Nothing.

He pushed against it.

Nothing.

He hit it lightly with the mallet.

Still nothing.

He came back down the ladder and went over to the corner of the room. He picked up the trash can and came back to the foot of the ladder. "I'll need someone to hold this underneath the tile when I take it off, just in case stuff comes out," he said.

"'Just in case stuff comes out?'" said Mrs. Baker.

"That's right," said Mr. Vendleri.

Mrs. Baker looked over at me.

Sometimes, I think she still hates my guts.

So there I was, holding this trash can underneath the eight bulging asbestos ceiling tiles, and Mr. Vendleri started to push up on one of them with his mallet. "You won't catch the stuff standing over there," he said to me. I moved a little closer. "Right here," he said, pointing to the target area. Then he turned and lifted one of the ceiling tiles with his mallet. We listened for the scrambling of two large rats.

Nothing.

So Mr. Vendleri tilted the tile to get it out . . . and Shredded Everything came pouring down: homework announcements, PTA letters home, blue dittos, Bazooka bubblegum wrappers (these were from Danny), chewed up Number 2 pencils, red and green and blue and yellow construction paper, napkins from the cafeteria, part of a black sneaker (this was from Doug Swieteck, who had been looking for it for a couple of months), a gnawed picture of me leaping across stage in yellow tights, and scraps of Meryl Lee's "Mississippi River and You" project. It all came down like wet snow.

"Hold the trash can under it!" hollered Mr. Vendleri.

Which is exactly what I was doing, except that the stuff was also falling into my eyes and hair and down the back of my shirt, and I think I must have started screaming because Mrs. Baker came and took the trash can from me. "Maybe you should find a different way to collect the refuse," she said to Mr. Vendleri, brushing the rat-chewed stuff off me.

By the time Mr. Vendleri brought back a tarp, I had pretty much gotten my shaking under control.

He handed me that mallet. "What am I supposed to do with this?" I asked.

"Swing at anything that has yellow teeth," he said.

"Oh," I said quietly. I wasn't sure if that was better than having the rat-chewed stuff come down on my head.

But even though I started to shake again, I held the mallet over my shoulder ready to strike, which you have to admit is not only brave and courageous and true and blue and worthy of Jim Hawkins himself, but also pretty remarkable, considering I still had rat-chewed stuff in my hair and down my back.

But we never saw Sycorax or Caliban. Mr. Vendleri replaced the bulging ceiling tiles with eight new ones, then stepped from the ladder and stood back. "Good as new," he said.

"Are you sure?" asked Mrs. Baker.

"I'm sure," I willed him to say. "I'm sure. I'm sure. I'm sure."

"I'm sure," said Mr. Vendleri.

"Then," said Mrs. Baker to me, "you may return to *Julius Caesar.*"

But let me tell you, it's not easy to read a Shakespeare play when you've just been holding a mallet over your shoulder, ready to swing at anything that has yellow teeth, and Mr. Vendleri is still poking at the other tiles to see if they were bulging, too, and knowing that any tile could come crashing to the floor along with Sycorax and Caliban, and they would not be happy, let me tell you.

I wanted to read *Julius Caesar* standing on my desk, but that would definitely not have been worthy of Jim Hawkins.

When he finally left, Mr. Vendleri told us he'd come check on the new asbestos ceiling tiles tomorrow. "Thank you," said Mrs. Baker. Then she went back to her grading. I wondered if she had wanted to stand on her desk, too.

Grading, by the way, is also something that makes it hard to read Shakespeare. When your teacher is covering papers with red ink a few desks away from you, and you know that yours is in the stack and it's probably coming up soon, and that your grasp of non-restrictive clauses might not be all that it should be, it's hard to read anything. Even though there was some good stuff in *Julius Caesar*: "You blocks, you stones, you worse than senseless things!" It doesn't have the cut of a Caliban curse, but it's all right.

It also didn't help that Mrs. Baker kept wiping at her eyes during her grading. She'd told us that she had a terrible cold, but she hardly needed to tell us. Her eyes were mostly red all the time, and the way she blew her nose could be pretty impressive. Sometimes while sitting at her desk, she'd just stop doing whatever she was doing and look somewhere far away, like she wasn't even in the classroom anymore.

It was a terrible cold, and day after day it kept on, and even seemed to be getting worse. Meryl Lee said that she was up to half a box of Kleenex per class, which has got to be some kind of world record.

So when she announced on Friday that members of the school board were coming to our room to observe and evaluate classroom performance by both students and their teacher, she told us in a soggy voice that drowned at the end. But drowning or not, she kept going.

She was Mrs. Baker.

"I will expect you all to be polite to the school board members. I will expect you to be on your very best behavior. I will expect you to show in an appropriate manner what you have been studying this school year."

"When are they coming?" asked Meryl Lee.

Before I tell you what Mrs. Baker said, I have something else to tell you, because you won't believe what happened otherwise if I don't. When Julius Caesar is coming into Rome—which is a place where very bad things will happen to him—this soothsayer comes up to him to tell him what's going to happen. And this is what he says to Julius Caesar:

Beware the ides of March.

So now I'll tell you what happened after Meryl Lee asked, "When are they coming?"

"Beware the ides of March," I said.

And Mrs. Baker looked at me, and her eyes opened a little bit, and without looking away from me, she said to Meryl Lee, "A week from today, Miss Kowalski."

Which was the ides of March!

"You are a soothsayer, Mr. Hoodhood," said Mrs. Baker.

"Sometimes I scare even myself," I said.

"Prophecy is not an unalloyed gift," she said. "Be careful how you use it." Which is a teacher strategy to get you to look up the word "unalloyed," which I did, and it still didn't make much sense.

But what happened later that day was even weirder.

In Gym, Coach Quatrini announced that he was planning to form the Camillo Junior High School cross-country team. It wouldn't be a regular team, since cross-country was a fall sport. But he wanted to start the seventh and eighth graders now so that he could choose a varsity team and have them run over the summer and be ready to begin real competition by September. He expected everybody to try out—everybody—and to get us started in our training, we would be running two miles at tempo.

"What's 'at tempo'?" I asked.

"Race pace," he said.

"How bad could that be?" I said to Danny.

"Bad," Danny said.

Coach Quatrini had us stretch for three minutes, then do four short sprints down the length of the gym, and then stretch for another two minutes. Afterward, he took us outside to the track— where there was a pretty brisk March wind that cut right through my T-shirt. He put us at the starting line, held up his stopwatch, and blew his whistle.

Danny was right. Race pace could be bad.

I don't know how many times Coach Quatrini used the word "faster," but if a word can get worn out and die, this one died like Julius Caesar. He liked to add words to the front of "faster," words like "a whole lot" and "can't you go any" and "you'd better get" and "dang it." He also added words after "faster," like "you wimps" and "you slugs" and "you dang slugs" toward the end. It wouldn't have taken much for him to be able to play Caliban on the Festival Theater stage.

Afterward, when we all had our hands on our knees and were trying to suck some air into wherever it wasn't that it needed to get, he reminded us that we all had to try out for the varsity team and promised that tryouts would be a whole lot harder than what we'd just done.

Toads, beetles, bats.

Now here's where the weird part comes.

Into my head jumped this sentence: Tryouts will be in a week, on the ides of March.

And as soon as I thought it, Coach Quatrini said, "Tryouts will be in a week, and you better be a whole lot faster than this, you dang wimpy slugs."

I wondered if somewhere down deep within me, I really was a soothsayer—even if only the first parts of the sentences were the same.

I ran over the weekend, not because I was worried that Coach Quatrini would think I was a dang wimpy slug, but because I was pretty sure that if I didn't, I might have something awful happen to me after running at tryout pace on the ides of March. I ran three miles on Saturday, and then four miles on Sunday afternoon, even though it was the Sabbath and I deserved some time off.

And actually, there was another reason for running over the weekend. An even better reason.

My father was mad at my sister, which meant somehow that he was mad at me, too, and it was better to be running with my lungs screaming for air than be in a house with my father screaming at me.

And let me tell you, it wasn't for anything I'd done.

Now that he had the new junior high school contract, my father needed to hire someone else in his office as a receptionist for weekday afternoons and Saturday mornings, and since he didn't want to pay anyone much for this, he decided that my sister should do it, and he would pay her $1.35 an hour, and not take out any taxes.

He announced this at supper on Friday night.

"I can't," said my sister, while passing the lima beans and not taking any.

"Of course you can," said my father. "It's about time you started a real job."

"I'm already working," said my sister.

We looked at her.

"Who for?" my father asked.

"For Bobby Kennedy," she said.

"For Bobby Kennedy?" said my father.

"Mr. Goldman is letting us use the back of his bakery for campaign headquarters."

"Bobby Kennedy?" said my father again. "Bobby Kennedy is a rich kid from Cape Cod who's never done anything on his own his whole life."

"Bobby Kennedy will end the war, end the discrimination that's splitting our country in two, and end the control of the government by a handful of fat old men."

My father—who was not fat and old yet, but who could probably imagine himself that way—started to get a little louder. Not a good sign. "You might as well go work for that Martin Luther King."

"Maybe I will. He and Bobby Kennedy are the only ones who care that this country is about to explode."

"He's a Communist."

"Oh, *there's* deep political analysis. He's leading a demonstration for striking sanitation workers, so he must be a Communist."

"Now you've got it," said my father. "You start work Monday afternoon."

I think you can figure out how the rest of that conversation went, and how my mother and I didn't say much, and how we never did make it to dessert, and why it was a healthy thing for me to be running over the weekend.

Even though I hadn't done a thing.

Still, I was glad that Bobby Kennedy was running for president. It was hard every night hearing President Johnson and all of his generals with medals spread over their chests say how well the war was going and how the enemy was about to give up, and then having CBS News cut to pictures of soldiers who were wading through rice paddies and holding their rifles high above the water, or who were carrying out a buddy whose face was covered with dried blood, or who were huddled in holes and covering their heads as the mortars came over in Khesanh. After that, you just wanted someone to say the plain truth, and maybe Bobby Kennedy would be that someone.

I was glad he was running for president.

And so maybe, after all, I had done something to make my father mad. Just not out loud.

At Gym on Monday, Coach Quatrini had us run three miles, all at tempo. Let me tell you, after running for two miles and hearing "Can't you go any faster, you dang wimpy slug?" in your ears for most of it, you start to wonder if life is worth living. You still have four more times around the track, and the sky is turning darker, and the air is thinner, and you can't feel the ends of your fingers, and your legs are rock heavy, and there's something hurting deep down in your guts—probably your liver is about to explode—but that doesn't matter so much because your lungs are drying out, and that hurts so much that nothing else can get your attention.

"It'll be five miles on Friday," said Coach Quatrini when we were finished.

Five miles on the ides of March!

On Wednesday afternoon, Mrs. Baker asked how my cross-country preparation was going.

"Death, a necessary end," I said, "will come when it will come."

Mrs. Baker smiled. "Do you think that death is coming for you on the cross-country course, Mr. Hoodhood?"

"You know what happened to Julius Caesar on the ides of March?" I said. "Cross-country tryouts will make that look like Opening Day at Yankee Stadium."

"It's because you run so straight up," she said.

"Because I run so straight up?"

"And tight. You run so tight. I've watched you. It looks as if you're digging your fingernails into your palms."

Which is exactly what I always did.

"Are you saying I could run better?"

She put down her copy of *Julius Caesar*. From her lower desk drawer she took out a pair of bright white sneakers and put them on. "Caesar shall go forth," she said.

"Where?" I asked.

"Out to the track."

"The two of us?"

"Are you embarrassed that I might be faster than you?" she asked.

"I'm not really worried about that, Mrs. Baker," I said.

"Perhaps you should be," she said. "Look what happened to Julius Caesar when he underestimated those around him."

So we went out to the track, with Mrs. Baker wearing bright white sneakers.

Really.

"Let's start with your stance," she said. "Let's lean you forward a little bit, so that you can always be moving into the next stride, instead of holding yourself back on each stride. Lean this way."

I did.

"Run fifty paces and come back."

I did.

"Again."

I did.

"At tempo," she said.

I did.

"That's fine. One could only wish that you took as easily to diagramming sentences. Now, your arm position, and then your head position, and then we'll get to breathing patterns."

By the end of the afternoon, Mrs. Baker had remade the way that I ran. "I look like a jerk," I said. "If Romeo was a runner, he would run like this."

"What you look like," she said, "is Jesse Owens, who won four gold medals at the 1936 Olympics running like that."

So, figuring that you can't argue with four gold medals, that night I ran like Jesse Owens through the dark March streets. Leaning forward. Arms and legs like pistons. Head straight and still. Hands loose. Breathing controlled.

And then I ran like Jesse Owens in Gym on Thursday, and came in before Danny. And in front of a whole lot of eighth graders. And I heard only one "Faster, you wimp!" Just one.

Running like Jesse Owens really worked!

So that afternoon, at the very end of the day, after everyone else had left, I went up to Mrs. Baker's desk.

"A big day for us both tomorrow," said Mrs. Baker.

"The ides of March," I said.

"Let's hope we both emerge unscathed." Which, in case you missed it, was the teacher strategy again to make me look up the word "unscathed."

"Mrs. Baker," I said, "you helped a lot with my running."

"Thank you, Mr. Hoodhood."

"So I thought I would try to pay you back."

"Pay me back."

"Yes. To help you get ready for tomorrow, when the school board comes."

"You want to coach me in teaching, Mr. Hoodhood?"

"Yes."

"Have you ever been a seventh-grade English teacher?"

"No, but you've never been a track runner."

Mrs. Baker raised a single eyebrow. "So what do you suggest, coach?"

"No teacher jokes," I said. "No one ever laughs at teacher jokes."

"All right. . . . No teacher jokes."

"And no folding your arms like this." I folded my arms across my chest. "It makes it look like you're about to shoot us if we don't do what you say."

"That is the point," said Mrs. Baker.

"And no rolling your eyes, even if someone says something really stupid."

"I never roll my eyes," said Mrs. Baker.

I looked at her.

"All right," she said. "No rolling my eyes. Anything else, coach?"

"When someone does something good, I think you should let them know, with some sort of code."

"I think you mean that when someone does something *well*—as in obeying the rules of proper diction—we should use a code. What do you suggest?"

"Well, maybe 'Azalea' for something good, and 'Chrysanthemum' for something really good."

"Thank you, Mr. Hoodhood. We'll dispense with the code, and I'll simply use the unvarnished English language to tell you when you've done something well. But as to teacher jokes, folding of arms, and rolling of eyes, I'll consider your advice."

I nodded.

"And, coach, one more thing before you leave," said Mrs. Baker. She reached into her lower desk drawer again and pulled out a wooden box. "Open it," she said.

I did. Inside was a round silver disk on a velvet dark red ribbon. "XVIth Olympiad—Melbourne—1956," it said.

Mrs. Baker leaned back in her chair. "It was for the women's four-by-one hundred relay. Don't look so surprised. You didn't think I'd spent my whole life behind this desk, did you?"

And I suddenly realized that, well, I guess I had. Weren't all teachers born behind their desks, fully grown, with a red pen in their hand and ready to grade?

"Go home now, Mr. Hoodhood," said Mrs. Baker. "And tomorrow, run like Jesse Owens."

The ides of March dawned on Friday with a green and brown sky, the color of the water in a dying pond. All morning, the sky hung low, and sometimes the green and brown clouds would roll up and rumble a bit, and then settle back down like a layer of unhappiness over everything.

We all talked in whispers, and we waited for something to happen up in heaven.

Or maybe up in the asbestos ceiling tiles.

And since waiting gets boring really quickly, I decided that in the pause between nonrestrictive clauses and weak verb systems, I would tell Danny about the scene where Julius Caesar gets stabbed—which is a lot better than the scene where Juliet gets stabbed—and act it out with appropriate sound effects—which I do pretty well, since I have some experience acting out Shakespeare onstage, as you might remember.

I don't know if it was because of the green and brown sky or because of her cold or because of something else, but Mrs. Baker came over like Brutus himself to do Julius Caesar in.

"Mr. Hoodhood," she said, "I have not taught you the plays of William Shakespeare for the last five months for you to demean them by acting as though they were all about people stabbing each other."

I thought that was unfair.

"But they are," I said. "They do it all the time. Macbeth kills Duncan, Macduff kills Macbeth, Brutus kills Julius Caesar, then Brutus kills himself, like when Juliet kills herself after Romeo kills himself, but not before Romeo kills Tybalt—"

"And is that all you've learned from Shakespeare?"

I thought that was unfair, too.

Mrs. Baker held out her hand. "Give me the book," she said.

I opened up my desk.

"Shakespeare is all about the power of goodness and honesty

and faithfulness," she said. "It is about the abundance of love. It is about the weakness of armies and battles and guns and . . ." She stopped. Her mouth worked back and forth. "It is about the endurance of love," she whispered. "Give me the book."

I handed it to her—at the same moment that the classroom door opened and Mr. Guareschi walked in, accompanied by Mr. Bradbrook and two other members of the school board.

"Mrs. Baker," said Mr. Guareschi.

Mrs. Baker looked at him. Both of our hands were still on Shakespeare.

"Mrs. Baker, you know Mr. Bradbrook, of course, the chairman of the school board. And Mr. Smilzo. And you know Mrs. Sidman, who has just returned from Connecticut and been appointed to our school board."

Mrs. Baker nodded to each one. "How good to have you back, Mrs. Sidman," she said.

Mrs. Sidman smiled. Her eyes darted around a little bit, like she was expecting something awful to happen but didn't want to show that she was expecting it.

"Mrs. Baker is one of our very finest teachers," said Mr. Guareschi.

"She will have a chance to show that to be true," said Mr. Bradbrook. He pointed to the book that Mrs. Baker and I were still holding. "What are you giving to that young mind?" he asked.

Mrs. Baker looked at me, then back at Mr. Bradbrook. "This is a volume of Shakespeare's plays," she said a little weakly. She let go of the book.

Mr. Bradbrook came over to my desk and peered at the book. Then he took it from me and weighed it in his hands. He looked at the gilt edges, and fingered the red ribbon tied at the spine. "This seems like an awfully expensive volume for our schools to be purchasing," he said.

"It is my own copy," said Mrs. Baker.

Mr. Bradbrook was relieved. He looked down at me. "Young man, do you think you'll enjoy reading the Master's plays?"

"I already do," I said.

"When I was a boy your age," said Mr. Bradbrook, "I would memorize long passages and recite them whenever I was called upon to do so. When you read the Master's lines, perhaps you, too, will be moved to memorize some. Perhaps one day you may even enact some."

"I already have," I said.

"Or perhaps Mrs. Baker will assign selected lines to you. Do you think that you might enjoy learning a line or two?" He patted the top of my head. Really. He reached out and patted the top of my head.

Danny Hupfer nearly fell out of his chair.

"He has already memorized quite a bit," said Mrs. Baker.

"Has he?" said Mr. Bradbrook. He seemed sort of surprised. "Well, let's hear some from the boy."

Mrs. Baker looked down at me. I couldn't really tell what was in her eyes. I thought at first that there might be a death threat, but either I'm getting used to them or that wasn't what was there.

"Holling Hood, do you know any lines or not?" That was from Mr. Guareschi.

And I almost said, "You block, you stone, you worse than senseless thing" to him. But whatever it was in Mrs. Baker's eyes, it told me that that might not be the right thing to say.

Probably a Caliban curse wouldn't work, either.

So I tried something else.

> *"This was the noblest Roman of them all.*
> *All the conspirators, save only he,*
> *Did that they did in envy of great Caesar.*
> *He only, in a general honest thought*
> *And common good to all, made one of them.*
> *His life was gentle, and the elements*
> *So mix'd in him that Nature might stand up*
> *And say to all the world, 'This was a man.'"*

Meryl Lee clapped.

Even Doug Swieteck clapped.

I looked at Mrs. Baker's eyes.

"Azalea," she said quietly.

"What was all that about?" said Mr. Bradbrook.

"The power of goodness and honesty and faithfulness," said Mrs. Baker. "Now, if Mr. Guareschi will show you your seats, the class will work through the day's lesson." She went up to the board.

"This is the sentence you'll be diagramming," she said to us all, and wrote it out:

> *You blocks, you stones, you worse than senseless things!*

Then she turned to us. "Who can identify the implied verb?" she asked.

For the next hour, we did pretty well by Mrs. Baker. We answered everything she threw at us, and even Doug Swieteck helped out. (He answered the implied-verb question.) And Mrs. Baker did her part, too. There were no teacher jokes. She never crossed her arms. And when Doug Swieteck, who I guess thought he was in the rhythm after he got the implied-verb question right, called Alfred, Lord Tennyson—and you have to admit, it is a bizarre name—Alfred, Lord Tennis, Mrs. Baker did not roll her eyes. Not even a little.

It was an hour of pretty spectacular stuff. Let me tell you, we could have been America's Model Classroom of 1968. Mrs. Baker was so pleased that she even let me act out the stabbing scene from *Julius Caesar* after all—probably because she had forgotten all about the soothsayer business, which she shouldn't have, since when I got to the "*Et tu, Bruté*? Then fall, Caesar!*" part, an asbestos ceiling tile over Mrs. Sidman's head that wasn't even bulging suddenly gave way, and it wasn't Julius Caesar who fell. It was Sycorax and Caliban who plummeted onto Mrs. Sidman's lap.

I think that she was the only one in the classroom who did not scream—and I'm including Mr. Bradbrook and Mr. Guareschi in that. We all crashed over chairs and tables and desks to the sides of the classroom, so that Mrs. Sidman was left completely alone, at her student desk, with two huge rats in her lap, who were shaking their heads and trying to get some idea of what had just happened to them.

Then they pulled up their snouts and clacked their yellow teeth.

Okay, so I panicked, too. After living with the bulging ceiling tiles for all this time, we had gotten to believe they would never come down. But now we were face to face with huge, scabby, yellow-toothed, angry rats, looking at us with eyes reddened with anger. And all we could think about was putting distance between us and them. And I want to point out, for the record, that it was members of the school board who were up on Mrs. Baker's desk first. Just about everyone else climbed the bookshelves and window shelf and radiators after throwing aside anything that got in our way.

Except for two people.

One was Mai Thi, who took off one of her shoes and stood beside her desk, ready to swing at anything that had yellow teeth. She looked as fierce as all get-out.

And the other was Mrs. Sidman, who I guess had determined that nothing more was going to happen to her at Camillo Junior High School without her say-so.

She grabbed the rats by the back of their necks—which was not easy, since they were so fat—pulled them off her lap, and hoisted them into the air. Their paws scrambled, their mouths hissed, their yellow teeth clicked, but Mrs. Sidman didn't care. She stood and held them up, like Macduff holding Macbeth's head.

By now, the screams—which had been increasing in volume— had brought Mr. Vendleri.

"Where do you want them?" asked the triumphant Mrs. Sidman.

"I've got a cage in the basement," he said.

"Lead the way," said Mrs. Sidman.

And he went ahead of her, closing all of the classroom doors as he went. But I wish that everyone in Camillo Junior High could have seen her, the noblest school board member of them all, Mrs. Sidman with her vanquished enemies still squirming in her hands, marching to the basement to dispatch them.

While the school board members went to have an emergency meeting in Mr. Guareschi's office, we tried to put Mrs. Baker's classroom back together, since absolutely all of the desks had been knocked over. It took us most of the day to get everything right. Someone—I think it was Mr. Bradbrook—had knocked the globe of the world off Mrs. Baker's desk, and there was now a deep valley where the Himalaya Mountains had once been. The red *Thorndike* dictionaries were going to need some help; most of their covers had come off when we stepped onto them to climb higher up the bookshelves. And at least two of our desks were gone for good, since all of their legs had splayed out.

Julius Caesar's army wouldn't have left such a mess after crossing the Rubicon.

That afternoon, Coach Quatrini held his cross-country tryouts. By then, the story of Sycorax and Caliban was all over school, and so we figured that tryouts might be delayed. And it might be that some coaches somewhere *would* delay a tryout on an afternoon when some of the tryoutees have just been traumatized by two gigantic rats falling out of their classroom ceiling. But Coach Quatrini thought it would give us motivation.

"The Big M," he said. "*Motivation*. You won't run fast unless you really want to run fast, and really wanting to run fast is what gives you Motivation. The Big M."

He had set out a course for us that stretched to someplace beyond human endurance. We were supposed to start at the gym doors and go around the parking lot (where Sycorax and Caliban were hissing in their cage, waiting for the exterminator to come put them in his truck), past the fence that enclosed the tennis courts, out onto Lee Avenue, down past Goldman's Best Bakery, around in front of the school by the main lobby, behind the elementary school wing, and so back to the gym doors.

"Four times," Coach Quatrini said, holding up four fingers. "You do that route four times. At tempo. Top seven will be varsity—that'll be all eighth graders, I expect. The rest of you will be junior varsity—if you're good enough to make that, you dang slugs."

And with that encouragement, Coach Quatrini blew his whistle and we began.

The sky had not improved during the day. The green and brown had swirled together, and the clouds had lowered themselves further and further, and they had dropped a kind of vapor from them that made it seem that we were running through the jungles of Vietnam, and breathing more water than air. I leaned forward, and I kept my arms low and my hands loose. I didn't rush it. But even so, by the time I passed Sycorax and Caliban—who hissed and threw themselves against the bars toward me when I kicked their cage to say goodbye—I was already feeling the wet air welling inside me. By the time I came around for the second time, things were slowing down considerably, and every eighth grader—and a whole lot of the seventh graders—were far ahead of me.

It's hard to run like Jesse Owens when you're feeling like you're drowning.

The third lap was better. Meryl Lee was standing by the main lobby, and when I ran past, she held up a dried rose with a ribbon on it.

When a girl holds a rose up to you, you run better, let me tell you.

By the time I came around for the fourth lap, I was up to Danny. I had even passed some of the eighth graders, and I could see the leaders in front of me again. I ran past the gym doors— "Can't you go any faster?" from Coach Quatrini—and out into the parking lot, where the exterminator truck had pulled up to unload Sycorax and Caliban into their new cage.

The sky had lowered itself even more, and everything looked like we were seeing it from underwater in a greenish haze. Even sounds were muffled, so that my footsteps seemed to come from far away.

But what wasn't muffled was the cry that came from the exterminator behind me, the sound of a large cage dropping, a scream, and the clicking of clacking teeth. I looked back, and there were the demon rats, racing with their scabby paws toward me, their eyes filled with the Big M—Murder!—and their pointy heads bobbing up and down with each leap. I couldn't scream; I couldn't get enough air into my lungs for screaming. I could only run. But the faster I ran, the more their yellow hatred grew, and every time I looked back—which was a lot—they were flat out after me, their scabby whiskers swept back by their speed, their yellow teeth clacking. I could imagine those teeth sinking into my heels like the assassins' daggers sinking into Caesar, and I ran faster.

I'd be running still if the tennis courts hadn't been there. Since they were, I sprinted into the courts and kicked the wire gate closed behind me. Sycorax and Caliban smashed into the gate and poked their yellow scabby snouts through.

Then they started to climb the fence. Really. They started to climb up the fence, never taking their red eyes off me.

Fear can bring out the Big M. I ran across the courts, and I was up and over the far-side fence before they were up and over the near-side one.

By that time, Mr. Guareschi, who had heard all the screaming, was trying to get the exterminator to go inside the tennis courts to catch the rats. But the exterminator wouldn't go near them. "Did you see those teeth?" he said. He got into his truck and drove a safe distance away.

Meanwhile, Sycorax and Caliban were climbing up the far-side fence after me. Before they reached the ground outside, the entire schoolyard had emptied—me last, when Danny Hupfer grabbed me from where I'd been standing in paralyzed horror.

So what happened after that is all a guess.

At the same time that Sycorax and Caliban hit the bottom of the fence and ran into the parking lot looking for me, a school bus was coming back in for the late-afternoon run. The driver later said that she saw the rats and tried to swerve but that they leaped onto their hind legs and jumped in front of her. She slammed down on her brakes, but the rats stood their ground, their paws up, their snouts pulled back, their yellow teeth clacking, their demon eyes flashing—none of which you'd have been able to recognize among the squashed bits when the bus, after skidding on the suddenly slick asphalt, finally came to a stop.

And as the exterminator drove away, since there was nothing more for him to do, the green and brown sky finally opened, and the rain came down in torrents, so fast it blew sideways, and when it had raged for about the time it takes to run two laps around Camillo Junior High, it stopped, and the green sky evaporated, and it was the ides of March . . . a beautiful spring day.

A new record was set for the three-mile run for a Long Island school that afternoon—and I'm including high schools here. People said afterward that they had never seen anything like it—that kind of speed from a seventh grader.

So I made the varsity team, and had the Big M to keep running, especially since it stayed beautiful for the rest of March as the days grew longer—so long that it was still light when my father and sister came home from Hoodhood and Associates at suppertime. I practiced every afternoon after school with the other varsity runners—me, the only seventh grader—while the sun was yellow and warm, and the sky blue and white. I ran leaning forward, my arms and legs like pistons, head straight and still, hands loose, breathing controlled.

I ran like Jesse Owens with the Big M.

❀

Meanwhile, the story of the rats grew larger. People went to visit the spot where they had met the bus. Doug Swieteck's brother had two teeth that he claimed were from Caliban, and he would show them to you for a quarter.

Mrs. Sidman was the most heroic figure of the story, and even first graders were drawing pictures of her carrying Caliban and Sycorax through the halls of Camillo Junior High. In all of those pictures, she looked like the warrior that Ariel had wanted to be— stern and serious and powerful. A third grader drew a coat of arms for her with two dead rats beneath her feet. Charles, the Fifth Grader of the Lovely Handwriting, inscribed the motto beneath: "To the Death!" The *D* had a whole lot of swirling loops inside it.

The only one who came out badly in the stories was Mai Thi, and honestly, I couldn't figure it out. No one but Mai Thi had stood her ground beside Mrs. Sidman while all the rest of us scrammed across the room. But instead of her getting a coat of arms and being made into a warrior, people started to talk about her, and not just behind her back, but so that she could hear them. About how people in Vietnam ate rats. How she was just hoping for a good meal. How she thought they were ratburgers on the run. Stuff like that.

Until one day, when outside the yellow forsythia branches were weaving themselves together, and the daffodils were playing their trumpets, and the lilacs were starting to bud and getting all giddy, we were going through the lunch line and Mrs. Bigio handed Mai Thi her Tuna Casserole Surprise, and one of the penitentiary-bound eighth graders said loudly to Mrs. Bigio, "Don't you have any Rat Surprise for her?" and then he turned to Mai Thi and said, "Why don't you go back home where you can find some?" and then Mai Thi started to cry, just stood there crying, and Danny took his entire tray—which was filled with Tuna Casserole Surprise and two glasses of chocolate milk and red jello with peaches—and dumped it over the penitentiary-bound eighth grader's stupid head, and then, before the eighth grader could open his stupid eyes to see who had done it, Danny punched him as hard as he could and broke his stupid nose.

Which got Danny a four-day suspension.

Which Mr. and Mrs. Hupfer used to take him to Washington, D.C., because they were so proud of him.

At lunch recess on the day he came back, he told us about climbing the Washington Monument, touring the White House, seeing Hubert Humphrey waving from a limousine, sprinting up the Capitol steps three at a time, running at tempo through the maze of fences the police were putting up to control the demonstration that Martin Luther King, Jr., was bringing to Washington next month, and walking up to President Lyndon Baines Johnson and shaking his hand—all of which we believed except for the last part.

But this next part is no lie: When we got back in from recess, Mrs. Bigio and Mrs. Baker were holding two trays filled with fried bananas. Really. Fried bananas rolled in crushed nuts, dipped in coconut, and topped with caramel sauce. *Warm* caramel sauce. Can you imagine what all four of those together smelled like? Sweet, and fruity, and spicy, and warm, and creamy, and chewy, all at the same time—that's about as close as I can get. It's the kind of smell that makes you hungry just thinking about it.

Mrs. Baker held the tray like she was carrying gold and frankincense and myrrh. "It's a recipe from Vietnam," she said. "Mrs. Bigio has made them for our class." We cheered. "The caramel sauce is called nuoc mau. Did I say that correctly, Mai Thi Huong?"

Mai Thi shrugged and smiled, and Mrs. Baker laughed, and

then she and Mrs. Bigio walked up and down the aisles, and we each took a plate with a fried banana smothered in caramel sauce on it.

And when Mrs. Bigio got to Mai Thi, she stopped, and lifted a plate down onto her desk, and said, "I am so sorry, Mai Thi. I am so sorry."

That night, Walter Cronkite reported that in Khesanh, some of the tunnels the Vietcong were digging now reached to within fifty yards of the marine fences. There were more mortar shells lobbed in. There were more pictures of the marines deep in their bunkers with their hands over their ears. Casualties were light, the White House announced.

In Camillo Junior High, we ate fried bananas with warm nuoc mau. We sang a song that Mai Thi taught us about bananas—though it could have been about elephants and we wouldn't have known it, since we only knew two words of Vietnamese. And when we were done, Mrs. Bigio and Mai Thi held each other tightly, and it seemed to all of us that they did not want to let go.

april

The next week, Mrs. Sidman read the names of the seven members of the Camillo Junior High School varsity cross-country team during Morning Announcements. "We are very glad to have these seven students represent our school," said Mrs. Sidman, "most especially Holling Hoodhood, who will represent the seventh grade. Holling came in with the fastest time during tryouts—almost a minute faster than any of the eighth graders on the team. We wish you all luck, boys!"

This was frightening. It was the kind of stuff that makes you hope that you are never alone in the locker room with the other guys on your team.

And there wasn't much help from anyone in Mrs. Baker's class.

"I wonder why Holling had the fastest time," said Danny after the announcements—a whole lot louder than he had to. "Could it be because he was running away from two rats who were trying to eat him?"

"That might have had a little to do with it," I said.

"A little!" said Danny.

"A little!" said Meryl Lee.

"A little!" said Mai Thi.

"A very little," I said, and everyone in the class ripped out a piece of paper from their notebooks, scrunched it up, and threw it at me—which was unfair, since you can't stop twenty-two pieces of scrunched-up paper at the same time.

You pretty much know from what I just told you that Mrs. Baker wasn't in the room. She'd been called down to the office for a phone call before Morning Announcements, and she'd had Mr. Vendleri stay with us while she was gone.

Which was why balls of scrunched-up paper surrounded my desk by the time Mrs. Baker came back, and since generally the person who is surrounded by balls of scrunched-up paper will be the person blamed for all the balls of scrunched-up paper, I figured I would be the one who had to pick them all up. That's how it is in the world.

But not this time.

Because the phone call in the office was from the United States Army. The Vietcong had abandoned Khesanh, and 20,000 American troops were marching to relieve the marines—and to find missing American soldiers. Like Lieutenant Baker. "It will be called," Mrs. Baker told us, "Operation Pegasus. Now, someone tell me the meaning of the classical allusion."

She never did say anything about all the balls of scrunched-up paper around my desk.

You may have noticed, too, that it was Mrs. Sidman who read the Morning Announcements over the P.A. instead of Mr. Guareschi. That was because Mr. Guareschi was gone. Mrs. Baker had told us he had "received an administrative reassignment," but that only meant that he was gone. And Mrs. Sidman was our new principal. Really. I suppose the school board figured that if Mrs. Sidman could pick up two huge rats by the scruff of their necks and carry them through the halls, she could certainly handle middle schoolers. Which was probably true.

No one saw Mr. Guareschi leave, still looking for a small country to be dictator of.

But everyone saw Mrs. Sidman on the first day she was principal. She stood in the main lobby and watched us come in. She already knew almost all of our names, and she must have said "Good morning" three hundred times. She stood straight, with her arms folded across her chest—which, as any teacher coach will tell you, isn't good for teachers but probably isn't bad for principals.

I heard that she even stared down Doug Swieteck's brother.

While Mrs. Sidman was starting up her new job at Camillo Junior High, President Lyndon B. Johnson was giving up his old one at the White House. Walter Cronkite carried the announcement the last day of March: President Johnson said that he did not want to be distracted by partisan politics "with America's sons in the fields far away, with America's future under challenge right here at home." He had decided that he would not run for the presidency again. His whole face seemed to sag down as he said this.

"He doesn't want to be humiliated," said my sister at the first commercial that night. "He knows he can't win against Bobby Kennedy."

"He knows he can't win against Richard Nixon," said my father. "Not with the whole war on his back."

"Either way, he's getting out because he doesn't want to lose, not because he cares about America's future."

My father sighed a loud sigh. "So is that how all flower children make their judgments—so quick and easy?"

"When they're quick and easy to make," said my sister.

Only the end of the commercial stopped what could have gotten a whole lot louder.

I seemed to see President Johnson's sagging face through the rest of the news. Banquo's face probably looked a whole lot like that just before Macbeth had him killed, when he suddenly realized that everything that he had hoped for was crashing down.

And then, on top of that, we found out after the *CBS Evening News* that President Johnson wasn't the only one giving up his job.

"Kowalski's finished, too," said my father.

We all looked at him.

"What do you mean?" said my mother.

"Finished," said my father. "Done. Over. Washed up. Kaput. I told you he couldn't play for keeps. They'll announce it in a couple of weeks or so. No more Kowalski and Associates. We'll be the only architectural firm in town that matters." He looked at me. "I told you we'd be going places if we got the junior high job, didn't I?"

I nodded. He had told me.

"What about the Kowalskis?" I asked.

My father shrugged. "Architecture is a blood sport," he said.

So at lunch recess the next day, Meryl Lee and I spent a lot of time not saying anything—until Meryl Lee said it for us.

"I might be moving," she said.

I looked at her.

"I'll probably be moving."

"Where?" I said.

"To my grandmother's house. In Kingston."

I nodded.

Another minute or so of not saying anything went by.

I knew I should say something. I guess after reading all that Shakespeare I should know what to say. But I didn't have a single word.

So Meryl Lee said it for us again.

"Toads, beetles, bats," she said. And that was exactly right.

Meryl Lee didn't know how long she had left. Maybe just two or three weeks. So we decided to pretend that it was forever, and we didn't talk about it, and we tried not to think about it. But there were those moments when one of us would look at the other, and we knew what we were thinking, even though we wouldn't say it. Probably sort of how it was between Romeo and Juliet.

It helped to run hard, so hard that you can't think about much of anything else because your arteries are all opened out as far as they can be, looking for some oxygen, any oxygen, because you can't pull enough air into your lungs and there's this coach who has invented an entirely new vocabulary to wrap around the word "faster," a vocabulary that even Caliban would have blushed at. We ran for more miles a day than most commuters drive. We ran through neighborhoods that I don't think are even in Nassau County. We ran past other junior high schools and got jeered at by baseball players who warmed up with a couple of sprints and then shagged balls the rest of the afternoon. We ran past the red tulips in front of Saint Adelbert's and the white lilacs in front of Temple Beth-El. We ran past Goldman's Best Bakery and smelled the latest batch of cream puffs sending their scent through the open windows. One day we ran all the way to Jones Beach, and if Mrs. Sidman hadn't sent a bus after us, I think we would have collapsed on the boardwalk and died.

But I was getting faster. Really. Even though I stayed at the back of the pack of eighth graders.

Let me tell you, when you're in the seventh grade, it isn't healthy to run at the front of a pack of eighth graders. I did it once, and they pulled my shorts down to my ankles in midstride.

You don't let something like that happen twice.

You stay at the back of the pack. And you learn the telltale signs of someone ahead of you who is about to spit off to the side.

Danny understood this, too, since he ran behind the eighth graders on the junior varsity team, and they were angry eighth graders. Angry eighth graders with plenty of spit.

Mrs. Baker did not understand why I was running behind anyone. She decided to give me a month off Shakespeare to coach me, since developing the body as well as the mind, she said, was a humane and educational activity. Every Wednesday, she timed a three-mile run, and I was dropping a couple of minutes with each one. (This didn't include the time I made when Sycorax and Caliban were chasing me, when I think I might have beaten Jesse Owens.) My lean was better, Mrs. Baker said, and my arms a lot looser. But she still wanted to work on my breathing, and so after the three miles we did wind sprints until I almost threw up—which makes you want to get your breathing better in a hurry.

Mrs. Baker didn't care that I had regular practice on Wednesday afternoons, after school, with Coach Quatrini. "If you want to get better, you run," she said. "You can't possibly run too much"—which I do not think is true but probably is some sort of teacher strategy.

Meryl Lee didn't understand why I was running at all, since it meant I wasn't working on the "California Gold Rush and You" project, and she'd already written all the notes for our report and started on the contour map.

"Don't think a rose and a Coke are going to get you out of this," she said.

Which I already knew. Remember, I'm not a jerk like Romeo.

And that was why one afternoon I was in Meryl Lee's kitchen, working on making the California Gold Rush relevant to You, when Mr. Kowalski came home and told us what he had heard on the car radio: that Martin Luther King, Jr., who was in Memphis helping striking sanitation workers, had been shot and killed. He died, Mr. Kowalski said, just after he had asked a friend to play "Precious Lord, Take My Hand."

Meryl Lee took my hand and we went into the living room, where Walter Cronkite was just finishing the news. He told us that it was all horribly true. I thought he was shaking.

"Nothing will ever be the same," said Mr. Kowalski.

Meryl Lee squeezed my hand. Hard.

That night, my sister would not come down to supper. And my father did not call her down. He sat with a face as grim as President Johnson's. Every so often he would look up the stairs to my sister's room, then back down at his lima beans. "How could this happen?" he said.

The next day, there were riots in Chicago, in Savannah, in Washington, in Toledo, in Detroit, in Pittsburgh, and in New York. "We are coming apart," my father said.

And on Tuesday, while everyone at Camillo Junior High watched on a television in the gym, my father stayed home from Hoodhood and Associates to watch on our television two Georgia mules draw the old green farm wagon that carried the body of Martin Luther King, Jr., through the streets of Atlanta. He didn't say a thing at supper. Neither did my sister.

Just before I went to bed that night, I reminded my father that the next day was Opening Day at Yankee Stadium—you probably remember how we got the tickets—and he had promised to drive me there to meet Danny and his father, and Doug and his father, and to write a note to get me out of Coach Quatrini's cross-country practice for that day and to let me leave before school ended.

"Isn't there enough happening in the world that you shouldn't have to go into the city for a baseball game?" he said.

"It's Opening Day," I said.

He shook his head. He never did write the note. So I wrote it myself and got him to sign it in the morning. I told him that he needed to pick me up at 12:00 noon sharp since the game began at 2:00. "Sure, sure," he said—which were the same words that Coach Quatrini used when I showed him the note.

"You expect me to believe that your father wrote this?" he said.

"I wrote the note. He signed it," I said.

"Did he read it before he signed it?"

No, you pied ninny, you blind mole, I wanted to say. He didn't read it. He just signs whatever I ask him to sign. Like blank checks with lots of numbers to the left of the decimal point.

"Yes," I said.

Coach Quatrini scrunched the paper in a ball and threw it at me. "I won't go easy on you at the next practice," he said.

As if this was something I hadn't already counted on.

Mrs. Baker figured that since I was leaving early, I should do the whole day's work in the morning. When I pointed out that neither Danny nor Doug was even in class and that they were probably taking the whole day off and maybe they were sitting in Yankee Stadium already, watching batting practice with Horace Clarke and Joe Pepitone hitting them out a mile, Mrs. Baker pointed out that run-on sentences were improper and I would do well to get started on the nonrestrictive-clauses worksheet. Which I did, since the prospect of Opening Day at Yankee Stadium made even nonrestrictive clauses bearable. (And it probably helped that

Danny and Doug would have to do all the work the next day anyway.)

By the time noon came, my hands were blue with the fresh ditto ink, but I had finished every nonrestrictive-clause exercise, and done the reading comprehension, and even done more to make the California Gold Rush relevant to You by pointing out the perils of the love of money in a brilliantly worded argument for Mr. Petrelli, which I handed Mrs. Baker while everyone went out to lunch recess.

"Why don't you take this down to his room?" she said. "By that time, your father will be here." So I did, and Mr. Pertrelli made me stand there by his desk as he read it over, as he pointed out the powerful use of nonrestrictive clauses, as he advised against the use of clichés, and as he identified more than one historical inaccuracy, and as I squirmed, imagining my father standing in his three-piece suit by Mrs. Baker's desk, large and important, the Chamber of Commerce Businessman of 1967—and probably 1968, too.

When Mr. Petrelli finished, I hurried back to Mrs. Baker's room, since I wasn't sure that I wanted my father to be standing there being large and important.

But I didn't need to hurry, since when I got to the room, my father wasn't standing by Mrs. Baker's desk.

We both looked up at the clock.

12:11.

Eleven lousy minutes after 12:00, and he wasn't here yet.

I ran down to the Main Administrative Office and called Hoodhood and Associates. "I'm sorry," said his secretary. "Mr. Hoodhood has been out at the site of the new junior high school all day, and he isn't expected back until two thirty."

"He has a baseball game at two o'clock," I said.

"No, he has an important meeting with the Chamber of Commerce scheduled for four thirty. He wouldn't miss a Chamber of Commerce meeting for a baseball game."

She was right. He wouldn't.

I hung up the phone and went back to the classroom.

Mrs. Baker was reading in her Shakespeare book when I came back. "Oh," she said when she saw me. She looked up at the clock. "Oh," she said again.

Meryl Lee came back into the room. She stood at the door when she saw me. "Aren't you—" and then she stopped. Because apparently I wasn't.

One by one, everyone came back from lunch recess. One by one, they looked at me and knew what had happened. And what was there to say?

I sat down at my desk, as humiliated as President Johnson would have been if he had lost to Bobby Kennedy. My heart beat against my chest. I was surprised that no one else could hear it.

I suppose there may have been a more miserable hour sometime in my life, but I couldn't think of what it might have been.

Until 1:55, when everyone had left for Temple Beth-El or Saint Adelbert's, and Mrs. Baker said, "Mr. Hoodhood, I think I could get you there for some of the game."

The sweetest words e'er spoken. I almost cried.

I took the two tickets out of my shirt pocket and held them up. "Have you ever been to a Yankee game, Mrs. Baker?"

"Never intentionally," she said. "Call your mother and see if it's all right."

Which I did, except she wasn't home. So I called my sister at high school. "You're calling me at school for that? Why should I care what time you'll be back?" she said, which I figured was good enough.

And that was how Mrs. Baker and I found ourselves on the Long Island Expressway driving toward New York City, me looking at my watch every three minutes or so, and Mrs. Baker moving along at a steady forty-five miles per hour in a sixty-mile-per-hour zone.

"You can go up to sixty-five without getting a ticket," I pointed out.

"I tend not to want to see how far I can break the law before I'm caught."

"You drove a lot faster than this to the hospital."

"Much faster. But I was going to the hospital. Today I am driving to a baseball game."

"On Opening Day, it's just as important," I said. "And I just saw you roll your eyes."

"I never roll my eyes," said Mrs. Baker. "But if I did roll my eyes, that would have been an appropriate time to do so."

The whole way, she never passed forty-five. She fussed at the Whitestone Bridge toll to get the right change. And she fussed at the parking lot, because she wanted to find a space with no cars on either side, which there weren't any of within three miles, and that was about how far away we parked. And we didn't run to Yankee Stadium in seven-minute miles, let me tell you.

So it was the bottom of the third inning by the time that Mrs. Baker and I reached our box seats, which were on the first-base line, right next to the Yankee dugout. You could make out every pinstripe on every uniform, we were that close. Mr. Hupfer got up and let me sit in front with Danny and Doug, and he sat behind us with Mrs. Baker and Mr. Swieteck, and Danny never asked about Mrs. Baker being there, even though I knew he wanted to. But I didn't care anymore because it was April, and it was Opening Day at Yankee Stadium, and the California Angels were out in the field, and the Yankees were up at bat.

The game was everything it was supposed to be. Horace Clarke turned a double play off his heel and Joe Pepitone caught a pop fly over his shoulder. Frank Fernandez had hit the only home run in the second inning, so we'd missed it—which was a big deal since it won the game. And Mel Stottlemyre threw a four-hit shutout. Mickey Mantle had two singles, so Danny and I couldn't boo him like we wanted to. And when Horace Clarke came out of the dugout for the seventh-inning stretch, he tossed three balls to us, and we almost had another one off a Mickey Mantle foul ball except it hit the bar along the box seats and skipped over us. And Mr. Hupfer and Mr. Swieteck bought us all—even Mrs. Baker— hot dogs with sauerkraut and more hot dogs with sauerkraut and Cokes in bottles with the ice still frozen to them and pretzels as big as both your hands together and then another hot dog with sauer- kraut for each of us. And we shouted and hollered when the bum ump made a lousy call on Joe Pepitone that made him strike out and everybody, even Mrs. Baker, stood and cheered when Mel Stottlemyre retired ten batters in a row.

It was just swell.

But what happened afterward—that was just swell, too.

Joe Pepitone and Horace Clarke yelled up to our box at the end of the game! "Hey Danny, Holling, Doug," they called. Just like that. "Hey Danny, Holling, Doug." There wasn't a kid within earshot that didn't wish that they were us.

"Hey!" we called back.

"You want to come down on the field?" asked Horace Clarke, which we didn't need to answer, because we were already climbing over the railing.

That was when Joe Pepitone saw Mrs. Baker.

"You're that dame that got us to come out to that school last December," he said.

Let me tell you, I wasn't sure Mrs. Baker had ever been called "that dame" before, and I was sure she wasn't all that happy about it now.

Mrs. Baker crossed her arms over her chest—even though I had coached her against that. "Yes," she said. "Though it was my brother-in-law who contacted you." She said it in this frozen voice that would have quieted any seventh-grade class in half a second.

But Joe Pepitone didn't notice. He took a step closer. "Aren't you that dame that ran in Melbourne? The women's four-by-one hundred. You anchored, right?"

I was really sure that Mrs. Baker had never been called "that dame" twice in two sentences that came one after the other.

"Yes," she said.

"I saw that race. You were in fifth place when you got the baton, and you almost made it all up in the last hundred. You came in something like three-tenths of a second behind."

"Two-tenths," said Mrs. Baker.

"Hey, Horace," said Joe Pepitone, "do you know who this is? Get Houk over here and see if he remembers that dame we saw anchor the four-by-one hundred relay in Melbourne. And get Cox over here, too."

And that was why when the photographers came to take pictures after the game, they found most of the Yankees around that dame with the legs that almost made up five places in the Melbourne Olympic Games in just one hundred meters. And after she ran the race with them again five times over, she asked the Yankees to show us around the Stadium and they did! Really. Joe and

Horace took us up in the bleachers and to the sky-high seats and then down beneath to the locker rooms (which Mrs. Baker did not go in) and around to the offices and then through the dugout and back onto the field. The people who were still up in the stands saw me and Danny pitch to Joe Pepitone, with Jake Gibbs catching. And I don't think Mrs. Baker rolled her eyes once.

And afterward, I ran around all the bases, from home to first to second to third and back to home. And then I ran to the outfield and sprinted from right to left and then back again. And all the while the green grass and the yellow diamond dust were in my nose, and the sun lowering over Yankee Stadium shone down on me, Holling Hoodhood, playing center field for the New York Yankees and waiting for the crack of the bat.

When you have the chance to run the outfield of Yankee Stadium and you're not exactly sure if you'll ever have another chance, you have to take things as they come.

I ran back to pitch my last pitches. The sun was getting low by the time Joe Pepitone had smacked them out, and Mrs. Baker stood at home plate, surveying the place like she was considering buying it. "What is all that scaffolding up there for?" she asked.

Maybe she *was* considering buying it.

"Repairs," said Joe. "Lots of places in the Stadium need repairs. They're waiting on the boss finding an architect."

"An architect?" said Mrs. Baker.

"Someone classical, the boss says. Real classical."

"I'd like to meet him," said Mrs. Baker.

"If you can hit my fastball," said Mel Stottlemyre, "I'll take you up to meet him."

Mrs. Baker looked at me and rolled her eyes. "Get me a bat, Mr. Hoodhood," she said.

It turned out that Mr. Hupfer drove me and Danny home that night. Mrs. Baker stayed to meet the boss.

Mrs. Baker's picture was in the *Home Town Chronicle* two days later, standing next to Danny and Doug and me, and all of us surrounded by smiling Yankee players. I wore Joe Pepitone's jacket to school, and Danny wore his hat, and Doug wore Horace Clarke's hat. Three sixth graders asked for my autograph on a baseball, which I gave them.

Coach Quatrini, however, did not ask for an autograph. He kept his promise, and the next cross-country practice was about as hard as two practices put together. And since he believed in democracy, he said, he figured that everyone should have the same cross-country practice, and so all seven of the varsity runners ran like Brutus and Cassius were after them with long and pointy knives.

The eighth graders loved me after that. They threw all of my clothes in the showers, and I walked home leaving puddles at every step.

So when spring break finally came, it dropped as the gentle rain from heaven upon the place beneath. Spring break! Were there any two words ever put together that make a more beautiful sound?

Spring break. Let me tell you, the days were warm and green. Danny, Mai Thi, Meryl Lee, and I met at Woolworth's in the afternoons. We ordered Cokes and hamburgers for as long as our allowances held out.

Spring break. The high school was out, too, and so my sister was always in a happy, happy mood. She had a new friend named Chit—that really was his name—and he drove a yellow VW bug with bright pink and orange flower decals. He was mostly legs and arms and hair, and he came over every afternoon and would go down into the basement with my sister and they would listen to her transistor radio and then come upstairs singing about yellow submarines very loudly and laughing like it was the funniest thing in the world. Afterward, Chit would fold himself into his yellow bug and my sister would go driving around with him.

Spring break. Warm and green days. You know they aren't going to last, but when you start in on them, they're like a week of summer plunked down as a gift in the middle of junior high school. They mean the smell of dust and grass on a baseball diamond, the first fresh sea breezes that come all the way inland from Long Island Sound, all the maples decked out in green-gold leaves. They mean checking the tennis rackets to see if winter has warped them while they hung in the garage, and watching the first rabbit running across the lawn, and neighbors putting the first "Free Kittens" signs up on their stoops.

That's spring break. You come back to school thinking that it's no longer just the end of winter; it's almost the beginning of summer, and you figure that you can hang on until the end of June, because the warm breezes are coming in the window like quiet happiness.

Coach Quatrini had made us swear on the lives of our firstborn children that we would run hard during spring break. He promised he would find out if we missed one day—just one day!—and that we would pay dearly.

So when we got back to school, he began the first practice with this announcement: Every runner on the varsity team was going to have to better my tryout time with the rats by thirty-five seconds. No exceptions.

And no rats to help.

Let me tell you, the eighth graders were not happy. Once we got started on our run, there was a whole lot of spitting to the side, timed with the wind, which I had to keep watch for. And I kept well to the back of the pack, since we ran through neighborhoods where there were kids from school who knew me and I didn't want to find myself in front of their houses with my shorts pulled down to my ankles.

I was glad that Doug Swieteck's brother wasn't a varsity runner. Who knew what would have happened then?

It was when we were all back from the run that first day and standing around the gym doors trying not to die that Coach Quatrini gave his second announcement: There was going to be a Long Island Junior High School Cross-Country Meet this spring, just to work up excitement for the fall season.

"It's this Saturday, so you're all going to have to get up early and miss your cartoons," he said. "I feel really badly about that. So badly, I could cry. Boo-hoo. Be here by seven. Bus leaves at seven oh-one. We run at Salisbury Park. Three miles at race pace. Winner gets a hundred-dollar savings bond. Not that I expect any of you ladies to win."

Toads, beetles, bats.

That night at supper, I mentioned the race.

"That will be nice," said my mother.

"Just swell," I said.

"Who's the coach?" said my father.

"Coach Quatrini," I said.

My father considered this a moment. "What's his first name?"

I shook my head. "Everyone just calls him Coach Quatrini."

My father shrugged and went back to eating.

"How far do you have to run?" said my sister.

I told her.

"You'll die," she said.

"I won't die."

"You'll get run over and crushed."

"It's almost happened before," I said. "With a bus."

She smirked at me. "Holling Hoodhood, the local town hero. Do you want a parade?"

"How long is it until you go to college?" I said.

She smirked again. "Not soon enough."

"She's not going to college," said my father.

Silence, since that is one of those lines that gets everyone's attention.

"What?" said my sister.

"You're not going to college," said my father again. "You've got a good job, and you're not going anywhere."

A long pause.

"Did you know that Roy White is batting .429?" I said.

"I am going to Columbia University," said my sister.

My father pressed his fork onto his plate and crushed a lima bean. "Columbia?" he said. "Columbia. Let me think a moment. Isn't that the school that's on strike to protest the war, so there aren't any classes?"

"It's the school where students are striking against the war and against racism."

"The whole world is going crazy," my father said, "and no place is crazier than college. You'll stay at your job and be safe."

"Safe from what? Thinking?"

"You're staying home," said my father.

My sister focused on her meatloaf.

By the way, Roy White really was hitting .429, which was .205

points over his last season's average, which seems to me to be important enough to talk about at supper.

They were all asleep when I left for the cross-country meet on Saturday morning. Actually, I was almost asleep, too, when I left for the cross-country meet on Saturday morning. I think I got to Camillo Junior High only by instinct. It was cold and a little foggy—the kind of foggy that goes all through you, so that everything feels wet, and the cold starts to seep under your skin, and all you can think about is the warm bed that you left to do this to yourself, and you're wishing you had on your thermal underwear, and you're wondering why anyone would want to do this to themselves, and you see Coach Quatrini standing by the bus and shouting at everyone he can see and you wonder even more why anyone would want to do this to themselves.

Neither the fog nor the cold lifted when we got to Salisbury Park. The grass was long and wet, and the fog dripped down from the still fresh green leaves on all the trees. You could see your breath. You could especially see Coach Quatrini's breath, because he was using it a lot, telling us where to leave our stuff, where to wait, where to stop waiting, where to loosen up, where to line up. I guess that was how he stayed warm.

There were something like twenty Long Island junior high schools here, and some of them even had uniforms. Most of us just had the numbers the coaches gave us, pinned to our shirts. My number was 113, which is not a particularly lucky number. Danny Hupfer's was 25—which, as you know, is Joe Pepitone's number. I asked him to change with me.

"Would you change with me if I had 113 and you had 25?" he said.

"In a second," I said.

"Liar," he said.

But when the JV boys' race started, I cheered him on anyway, standing on the sidelines between Mr. and Mrs. Hupfer and a whole bunch of little Hupfers, and Mr. Kowalski and Meryl Lee, who had come out to watch us run on an early Saturday morning.

That's Meryl Lee for you.

It wasn't easy to pick Danny out when they started, since there were about three hundred runners on the line and most of them had on white T-shirts. But after they left and headed into the deep woods of Salisbury Park and the thudding of six hundred feet faded, we all ran to where the trail comes out for a bend and waited for him to pass. He ran through in a clump of runners mostly bigger than him. Eighth graders.

"Keep your arms loose!" I hollered.

"Okay, coach," he called, heading back into the woods.

"And don't talk," I yelled after him. He probably didn't hear me.

We ran to the next bend. When he came past, he was out in front of the clump and running well. He shook his loose arms at me.

"Go, Danny!" yelled Meryl Lee.

"Faster, you dang slug!" I yelled.

And he obeyed. He was sprinting when we saw his back disappear.

Then we rushed back to the starting line, and we all screamed like crazy when he ran past in the top ten and set off for the woods again, the second lap.

There were three more after that.

We ran all over the field to catch him whenever he came in sight—me, all the Hupfers, and Mr. Kowalski and Meryl Lee.

On the fourth lap, he came across the starting line first.

We went berserk. Even Coach Quatrini went berserk—jumping up and down on the sidelines just like one of the little Hupfers.

When Danny disappeared into the woods, followed by the clump of eighth-grade runners pretty far behind him, we ran back to the first bend—for the fifth time—and waited for the sight of Danny.

But it was the clump of eighth-grade runners that came out first.

And then a whole line of other runners, all red and sweating in the cold, foggy air.

"Did we miss him?" asked Meryl Lee.

But we hadn't. Way more than half of the runners had gone by before we saw Danny limping past the first bend. Both of his knees were bloody. He did not look at us.

Mr. and Mrs. Hupfer had their hands over their mouths. And all the little Hupfers asked, "What happened to Danny's knees?"

"I guess he must have tripped," said Mrs. Hupfer.

She didn't know what might happen if a clump of eighth graders caught a seventh grader in the lead.

We ran to the next two bends, and waited. Danny was falling farther and farther behind.

When he finally crossed the finish line, he wasn't last. But almost.

His parents were waiting right there. His father took one arm, and his mother the other. Meryl Lee and I stood back, and we could see that Danny was almost crying. And probably not just because his knees were hurting. He didn't look at us when Mr. and Mrs. Hupfer took him back to the car, followed by the pack of little Hupfers. Some of them *were* crying. "Are Danny's knees going to get better?"

I guess cross-country is also a blood sport.

The varsity race was next, and I lined up behind the eighth graders. *Way* behind the eighth graders. "Get up to the line," hollered Coach Quatrini. I moved up about half an inch.

And probably that was why, among the one hundred and forty runners waiting at the starting line, Mr. Hupfer was able to find me so easily. "I have a message for you," he said, "from Danny. I'm not sure you'll understand it."

"I'll try," I said.

"He said, 'Beat the pied ninnies.' Do you know what he means?"

I nodded.

"Then here's a message from me," he said. He leaned closer. "Run them into the ground."

But it's hard to run one hundred and thirty-nine runners into the ground, especially when the gun goes off and the thunder of all those feet takes over from the thunder in your heart. For a minute, I thought that my sister was right: I was going to get run over and crushed. So I drifted off to the side and sprinted to move ahead before the trail narrowed. By the time I reached the first bend out of the trees, I was just behind the clump of eighth graders from Camillo Junior High. By the time I hit the second bend, we'd passed most of the other runners. By the time we reached the starting line again, the seven of us were out front—actually the six of them were out front, and I was running behind them.

And at the starting line, this is what I saw:

Mr. and Mrs. Hupfer and all the little Hupfers were behind Danny, who had not gone home but was standing there on his bloody knees and hollering as loudly as he could and waving his white shirt high up in the air.

Coach Quatrini was going berserk again, and seemed to be trying to levitate himself off the ground.

Meryl Lee was standing quietly, Mr. Kowalski behind her, and she held up a dried rose with a ribbon as I went by.

And Mrs. Baker was standing next to her, wearing her white sneakers.

So we ran again into the deep woods of Salisbury Park, the damp smell of pine thick in the air.

It was as if we were running alone, the seven varsity runners of Camillo Junior High. When I looked back over my shoulder, I could see only a few runners behind us, and by the time we were on the third lap, we were starting to pass runners still on their second. The fog had lifted, the day had warmed, and at times I could almost close my eyes and let my feet move along the still-dampened grass.

And then I would find that I had come up right behind the pack of eighth graders, and they were looking back at me, and I slowed down.

When we reached the starting line to begin the last lap, Coach Quatrini looked like he was having some sort of fit. I'm not sure that he knew what he was hollering, or if it was even English. Let me tell you, whatever it was, it wasn't Shakespeare. All the little Hupfers were jumping up and down, too, and Danny was still waving his shirt, and Meryl Lee was waving her rose—which was losing its petals—and Mrs. Baker was screaming. Really.

We headed into the deep woods for the last time. In the cool shade of the trees, I came up close behind the eighth-grade pack.

And on the first bend coming out, Mrs. Baker was waiting. Alone.

"Holling," she called.

I looked at her.

"Pass those boys," she said.

And that was all it took.

I glided as we went into the woods again, and stayed close while the trail narrowed and skittered through some thick underbrush. When it widened through a stand of old pines, the eighth graders looked behind and saw me, and they strung out to cover the whole path.

So I went around them, off the trail and through the pines, the needles thick and soft beneath my feet, the dead branches sharp and brittle against my face—and when I hit the trail again I was ahead of them, and we were all sprinting, but they were sprinting on a cross-country trail in Salisbury Park and I was sprinting through the cool grass of the outfield in Yankee Stadium, running down a ball that Joe Pepitone had just hit to right. And I was covering the ground so fast that my feet were hardly touching, and Ralph Houk was shaking his head. "The kid's good," he was saying.

And then everyone in Yankee Stadium was on their feet, and they were screaming and screaming, because now the California Angels were trying to get to a ball I had just hit to deep left, and I was rounding first, and then second, and then third, and Danny Hupfer was waving me home with his shirt, and when I got there, the cheering erupted so loudly that I could hardly hear Mrs. Baker when she picked me up and told me to keep walking, and I could hardly hold the thorny stem that Meryl Lee handed me.

But I sure could feel it when she leaned close to my face and . . .

Well, I don't have to tell you everything.

may

At the beginning of May, Mrs. Sidman told us during Morning Announcements that this would be "Atomic Bomb Awareness Month."

You might think that this would have caught our attention. But it didn't. Every May brings Atomic Bomb Awareness Month to Camillo Junior High, right after the greening grass and the yellowing forsythia. It's so predictable that it's hard to work up enthusiasm.

But Mrs. Sidman had clearly determined that this year—maybe because it was her first year as principal—she would give us the Big M.

"Since we are living so very close to New York City," she said, "Camillo Junior High School is certainly a likely target for an atomic bomb if the Soviet Union should ever choose to attack. It behooves us to be prepared. We will begin a series of atomic bomb drills this afternoon. When the sirens blow, I expect everyone to follow our government's drill procedures precisely."

"Behooves?" said Danny.

"Becomes necessary, Mr. Hupfer," said Mrs. Baker, "as in 'It behooves us to raise our hands before we ask a question.' Now, can anyone tell me what the adjectival form would be?"

Teachers. They can't help it.

I don't think that any of us really believed that Leonid Brezhnev was sitting in the deep, dark rooms of the Kremlin, plotting to drop an atomic bomb on Camillo Junior High. But even so, there was an eerie feeling when the sirens began to wail just before the end of the day, and Mrs. Baker stood up from her desk and clapped her hands at us. (I'm pretty sure she was trying not to roll her eyes.) She told us to scrunch under our desks. *No talking!* She told us to put our hands over our heads. *Absolute silence!* And she told us to *breathe quietly and evenly.* Really. As if we had forgotten how. When we were finally settled—and all this took a while since Meryl Lee wouldn't sit on the floor until she'd spread some clean poster board first—Mrs. Baker opened the classroom door, pulled the shades down on all the windows, turned the lights off, and then patrolled up and down the aisles.

I bet she was rolling her eyes then.

It doesn't take very long when you are scrunched under your desk with your hands over your head breathing quietly and evenly to feel three things:

1. That your spine is not meant to bend like this.
2. That if you don't stretch your legs out soon, they are going to spasm and you'll lose all feeling and probably not be able to walk for a very long time.
3. That you are going to throw up any minute, because you can see the wads of Bazooka bubblegum that Danny Hupfer has been sticking under his desk all year, which now look like little wasp nests hanging down.

But we followed our government's drill procedures precisely and stayed under our desks for eighteen minutes, until the wind would have whisked away the first waves of airborne radioactive particles, and the blast of burning air would have passed overhead, and the mushroom cloud would no longer be expanding, and every living thing would have been incinerated except for us because we were scrunched under our gummy desks with our hands over our heads, breathing quietly and evenly.

We got up when Mrs. Sidman peered into our classroom and told us that we had done quite well and that we were beginning to be prepared.

I guess that was sort of comforting—and I bet it made Leonid Brezhnev tremble in his boots—especially if he really did have it in for Camillo Junior High.

Actually, there seemed to be a lot of people who needed comfort these days—especially the eighth-grade varsity runners, who were taking the Salisbury Park race way too personally. I mean, our whole team came in before anyone else on any of the other Long Island teams. Mr. Quatrini had given us two practices off to celebrate. We got our team picture in the *Home Town Chronicle,* holding the trophy. What more do you want?

Apparently, a whole lot.

Let me tell you, you don't want to open your gym locker and find that someone has squirted shaving cream into it. And you don't want to find that the shoelaces on your sneakers are missing, or tied up in knots that take about a day and a half to get out, or that your shorts are hanging from the rafters in the gym ceiling, or that they're sopping wet—and not from water in the sink.

I think something must happen to you when you get into eighth grade. Like the Doug Swieteck's Brother Gene switches on and you become a jerk.

Which may have been Hamlet, Prince of Denmark's problem,

who, besides having a name that makes him sound like a breakfast special at Sunnyside Morning Restaurant—something between a ham slice and a three-egg omelet—didn't have the smarts to figure out that when someone takes the trouble to come back from beyond the grave to tell you that he's been murdered, it's probably behooveful to pay attention—which is the adjectival form.

Anyway, I stayed way behind the eighth-grade pack in practice these days. They didn't spit anymore, but I figured that if I tried to pass them, they would probably leave my bloody body on the side of the road.

But the eighth-grade varsity runners weren't anything compared with my father, who really needed some comfort because of what the *Home Town Chronicle* reported on May 3.

Here is the headline:

Local Architect Firm to Renovate Yankee Stadium

I guess I don't have to tell you that the Local Architect Firm was not Hoodhood and Associates. It was Kowalski and Associates. The story had words like these: "multi-million-dollar job," "three-year commitment," "highest visibility of any local firm," and "Kowalski a sure bet for Chamber of Commerce Businessman of 1968"—all of which made the job for the new junior high school seem pretty tame by comparison.

Suppers were very quiet for a few days. My father mostly concentrated on his lima beans, until my sister pointed out that a steady diet of lima beans had already killed lab rats, and was probably killing us.

"See?" said my father, looking up. "You can learn all sorts of useful and valuable information without going to Columbia University. And that's good, because no one is going to Columbia University these days, are they? And no one will, since they're going to shut down classes because their students think that life is all about standing on the streets and chanting slogans, instead of working hard and finally getting what they deserve."

"I am going to Columbia University as soon as I finish high school."

"You will be going to Columbia University when lima beans fly."

Which was the moment that my sister demonstrated that lima beans *can* fly, across the table, past my face (mostly), and onto the scale model of the new junior high school.

Toads, beetles, bats.

That was the last night my sister came down for supper. Every night afterward, she'd take her plate and eat in her room, alone with the Beatles and their yellow submarine.

Probably she didn't eat a single lima bean.

Still, my father did find some of the comfort that he wanted: The day after the Supper of the Flying Lima Beans, he came home with a brand-new Ford Mustang convertible. It was white, with a genuine red leather interior. It had an AM/FM radio. Really! It had a 390 big-block V8 engine and a stick-shift four-speed transmission that could take you up to 160 miles per hour if you wanted. The chrome glittering across the front grille gleamed so brightly that you had to take your eyes away from it when the sun struck just right. It made a sound like . . . Power.

It was, all in all, the most beautiful, perfect car that God has ever allowed to be made on earth.

My father and mother went for a drive in it every evening, right after Walter Cronkite was finished. They backed out of the driveway slowly, my mother waving at us and laughing as if she was in high school and going on a date. My father would be concentrating on the road, since he didn't want his Ford Mustang to be near any other car that might come too close and spatter a pebble up at the chrome.

During the day, he left it parked in the driveway—probably because he thought it would look just right in front of the Perfect House, and probably so that Chit wouldn't park his yellow VW bug there. My father wanted to be sure that people didn't think he was driving a bug with pink and orange flower decals, which no one in the running for Chamber of Commerce Businessman of 1968 would drive. At night, after it was too dark to see how wonderful the Ford Mustang looked in front of the Perfect House, he pulled the station wagon out from the garage, drove the Mustang in away from the nighttime dew, and parked the station wagon in the driveway. He did love the Mustang. He watched over it like his Reputation.

I dreamed of driving that car: The AM/FM radio on. The top down and the wind big and loud. Left hand curved around the wheel. Right hand playing on the shift. Seeing if it really could reach 160 miles an hour on a long straight stretch.

But I wonder if even the brand-new Ford Mustang convertible comforted my father any the night my sister left for California to find herself.

We didn't discover anything until the next morning. My father was already at work when my mother went to wake my sister up and found only a note on her bed.

By the time you read this, I will be somewhere on the highway heading toward the Rocky Mountains with Chit. I'll call when I can. Don't worry. And don't try to follow me.

That was all she wrote.

For supper, my mother set only three places. She did not cook lima beans. She did not say anything while my father swore up and down that my sister had made her own decision, that she would have to live with it, that he wouldn't send her a dime—not a dime—if she got into trouble, that she better not call him first because he was likely to tell her exactly what he thought of her. Didn't she realize that this didn't help his business reputation or his chances for the Chamber of Commerce Businessman of 1968, which that creep Kowalski was trying to steal from him? And why weren't there any lima beans for supper tonight?

That evening, my mother did not go for a drive in the Mustang with my father. He drove off alone, without even listening to Walter Cronkite.

And I did the dishes alone.

I wondered what it was like for my sister, cramped into a yellow Volkswagen Beetle with the folded and hairy Chit, heading toward the sunset, going off to find herself. I wondered what exactly she would find. And I wondered if it wouldn't be a whole lot better going off to find yourself in a brand-new Ford Mustang convertible with a 390 big-block engine.

Our house grew quiet and still. My father stopped watering the azalea bushes along the front walk, and they drooped and began to die. There was no music from upstairs. There were no more lima beans—which, let me tell you, didn't cause me much sorrow. But there was hardly any talk. And what words there were felt careful, since there was a whole lot that no one wanted to talk about.

Sort of like things between Claudius, Gertrude, and Hamlet.

You can't say a lot if the whole time you're wondering if everyone else is really thinking about the thing you're not supposed to be thinking about, because you're afraid the thing you're not supposed to be thinking about is going to harrow you with fear and wonder. Or something like that.

As you can tell, Mrs. Baker had me reading *The Tragedy of Hamlet, Prince of Denmark* for May—which I think was punishment for taking off April. This was slow stuff, and even Romeo had it all over Hamlet. The ghost was okay, and the gravediggers, but when you write about characters who talk too much, the only way that you can show that they talk too much is to make them talk too much, and that just gets annoying. So anytime I saw a speech by Hamlet or Polonius or—well, just about anybody—I skipped over it pretty quickly, and I don't think I missed a thing.

I shared this insight into reading Shakespeare with Meryl Lee— who, by the way, was not going to move, who now knew who Mickey Mantle was, and who had memorized the entire Yankee roster.

"I don't think that's a good way to read something," said Meryl Lee.

"Why not?"

"You can't just skip the boring parts."

"Of course I can skip the boring parts."

"How do you know they're boring if you don't read them?"

"I can tell."

"Then you can't say you've read the whole play."

"I think I can still live a happy life, Meryl Lee, even if I don't read the boring parts of *The Tragedy of Hamlet, Prince of Denmark.*"

"Who knows?" she said. "Maybe you can't."

I tried my insight into reading Shakespeare on Mrs. Baker.

"I see," said Mrs. Baker. "But doesn't this play in particular pose a problem for your new method, Mr. Hoodhood?"

"What problem?"

"That there are no boring parts in this, Shakespeare's greatest play of all." She looked at me, and she almost folded her arms across her chest but stopped at the last second.

"I guess that would be a problem," I said.

"Read it all," said Mrs. Baker. "Even Polonius."

"And if it gets boring?"

"It won't get boring."

"It already is boring."

"Then I suggest you start again. This is the story of a son who is asked to take vengeance for what has happened to his father, who has been dreadfully murdered. But he's not sure that he can trust anyone in his family. What might you do in such a situation?"

"I'd run over the murderer with a Ford Mustang."

"Short of that colorful extremity."

"Well," I said, "I guess I'd start by looking around for someone to trust."

Mrs. Baker nodded. "Now," she said, "begin the play."

The next day, right after lunch recess, the atomic bomb sirens wailed again in Camillo Junior High. I guess Leonid Brezhnev was still at it.

We scrunched under our desks again and put our hands over our heads. *No talking! Absolute silence! Breathe quietly and evenly!*

"This rots," said Danny Hupfer.

"No talking, please," said Mrs. Baker.

"I have a question," said Danny.

"After the drill," said Mrs. Baker.

"This is important," said Danny.

Mrs. Baker sighed. "What is it, Mr. Hupfer?"

"Isn't it dangerous for you not to be under your desk?"

"Thank you for your concern. I will take the risk."

"But suppose an atomic bomb was really coming down, right on top of Camillo Junior High?"

"Then," said Mrs. Baker, "we wouldn't have to diagram any sentences for the rest of the afternoon."

"It might be worth it," whispered Danny.

If Danny sounded a little snippy, you have to realize that his bar mitzvah was coming up, and he was more terrified of his bar mitzvah than an atomic bomb. He was really touchy about it, even when you tried to encourage him.

"You've been taking Hebrew lessons for this for a year," I'd remind him.

"Years."

"So how hard can it be?"

"How hard can it be? How hard can it be? How hard do you think it can be if your rabbi is standing right next to you, and your parents and grandparents are watching you, along with every aunt and uncle and cousin and second cousin—even some you've never met—and two great aunts who immigrated from Poland in 1913 and a great uncle who escaped the tsar, and every one of them is looking at you and crying and waiting for you to make a mistake, and if you do, they'll holler out the right word and stare at you like you've shamed the whole family and they'll never ever be able to walk into the synagogue again. How hard do you think it could be?"

"Maybe it would help," I said, "if you scrunched under your desk and breathed quietly and evenly."

"Maybe it would help," he said, "if I stuck this gum up your nose."

Meryl Lee and Mai Thi and I decided that we should find better ways to help Danny than putting gum up our noses. So every lunch recess for most of May, we sat inside and listened to him recite what he was going to read at the service—even though we had no idea if the words he was saying were coming out right or not.

At the end of every recess, he was always ready to run away to California.

"I can't do this," he'd say.

"You *can* do this," we'd say.

"I don't want to do this," he'd say.

"You *want* to do this," we'd say.

"I don't even care about this," he'd say.

"You *care* about this," we'd say.

It was sort of like a play—which, as you know, I have some experience at.

That's how it went every day.

You can see how that didn't put us into the mood for atomic bomb drills, which was too bad, since in May there wasn't a single day that went by that we didn't practice for an atomic bomb. Meryl Lee and Mai Thi spent most of the time under their desks softly singing the music from *Camelot*—which Mrs. Baker didn't seem to mind, even though there was supposed to be *absolute quiet*. Danny practiced his Hebrew, which is hard to do when you have your hands clasped over your head. I threw spitballs at him, which is even harder to do when you have your hands clasped over your head. And Doug Swieteck went to sleep, and when he went to sleep, he really went to sleep. Let me tell you, you don't want to be in the seventh grade and have people hear you snore. What you hear when you wake up is humiliating. Not as humiliating as yellow tights with white feathers on the butt, but humiliating enough.

One of the atomic bomb drills came on a Wednesday afternoon, about halfway through the month, right about the time the Yankees were batting .187 as a team and were stuck in ninth place again—just like last year. It was one of those hot, still days that come before summer and that remind you what July is going to be like. When I scrunched under the desk, I could feel immediately that the air there was kind of heavy and steamy, and that I was going to start sweating pretty quickly—which I did. This was really unfair, since everyone else had already left for Temple Beth-El or Saint Adelbert's.

I think that Mrs. Baker probably agreed.

"This, Mr. Hoodhood, is ridiculous" she said—and she wasn't even scrunched under her desk.

I leaned out from under my desk. My hands were still clasped over my head.

"Mrs. Baker?" I said, even though I was supposed to be breathing quietly.

"Yes," she said.

"Would you mind not calling me 'Mr. Hoodhood'? It sounds like you're talking to my father."

Mrs. Baker sat down at Danny's desk. "You're still angry about Opening Day," she said.

"I just don't want to be him already."

"But you have similarities. Meryl Lee showed me your drawing. It was wonderful. Anyone can see that you have the soul of an architect."

"Maybe," I said.

"But you want to decide for yourself," said Mrs. Baker.

I nodded. I wanted to decide for myself.

"And you're afraid," said Mrs. Baker, "that you won't get the chance."

"That I won't get the chance to see what I can do with the slings and arrows of outrageous fortune," I said.

"Not many people do," said Mrs. Baker. "Even Hamlet waited too long."

The sirens wailed, as if to remind us that there was supposed to be *absolute silence*.

"This is ridiculous," Mrs. Baker said again. "Here we are in the middle of Act III, and we have to leave Shakespeare to curl up underneath a desk for an atomic bomb drill, which is, by my count, the sixteenth time you've practiced curling beneath a desk, as if anyone needed to practice curling beneath a desk."

She rolled her eyes.

Then she seemed to make a sudden decision.

She gave up patrolling the aisles and walked back to the Coat Room. She seemed to be rummaging around. And then suddenly, there was a crash and a splatter, and almost instantly the entire classroom smelled like Long John Silver and his crew were yo-ho-hoing over bottles of rum. Lots of bottles of rum.

Mrs. Baker's voice came out of the Coat Room. "It seems that the crock with Mrs. Kabakoff's pilgrim cider has fallen from the top shelf. Would you please run and bring Mr. Vendleri?"

I did. When he came into the classroom, his eyes widened. "Smells like a brewery in this classroom," he said.

"Indeed," said Mrs. Baker. "You'll have to air it out after you mop up the cider."

"You can't stay in here with a smell like this," he said.

"Do you think so?" said Mrs. Baker. She looked at me. "Then we shall have to go on a field trip."

"A field trip?" I said.

"We are going to survey points of local architectural interest."

I thought for a minute.

"Are there any?"

Mrs. Baker had pulled her white sneakers out from her lower desk drawer. She looked up at me. "Yes," she said.

We walked together to the Main Administrative Office—where all the secretaries were scrunched up under their desks—and Mrs. Baker explained to Mrs. Sidman that our classroom smelled like a brewery, and that she certainly did not think that she could keep a student there, and that she would like to take the opportunity to go on a field trip while Mr. Vendleri cleaned the room.

Mrs. Sidman had one eyebrow raised the entire time she was listening, but Mrs. Baker had her arms crossed, and you know how convincing that can be. So Mrs. Sidman agreed, and Mrs. Baker filled out a form, and one of the secretaries crawled out from beneath her desk and called my mother, and then we got into Mrs. Baker's car and she drove me around and showed me all the points of local architectural interest.

We crossed over the Long Island Expressway to the north side of town, and meandered down side roads until we stopped beside the Quaker meetinghouse. "This was built in 1676. Think of that, Holling. When it was built, people were still living who had been alive when Shakespeare was alive. A hundred and fifty years ago, it was a station on the Underground Railroad. Escaped slaves hid right here."

We meandered down more side roads. "That's the first jail house on Long Island," Mrs. Baker said. "It has two cells, one for men and one for women. The first man to occupy the cell had stolen a horse. The first woman had refused to pay the church tax because she was not a member of the church. She wanted to define freedom for herself. Think of that. You can see the bars in the windows where she would have looked out."

We drove out to the east side of town and circled Hicks Park. "This has changed a great deal over the years, but it was once Hicks Common, where the first settlers of the town grazed their cows and sheep. Those larger oaks—no, the oaks, Holling, over there—were probably saplings then. And the building backing up against the park—that clapboard building there—is Saint Paul's Episcopal School, where British soldiers were housed during the American Revolution. The silver communion ware it owns was made by Paul Revere, and one of the original Hicks family members hid it in a cellar so it wouldn't be stolen during the war."

On the south side of town, we passed Temple Emmanuel. "That is the fourth temple on that same site," said Mrs. Baker. "The first building was burned by lightning, the second by British soldiers who found out the congregation was supporting the Revolution, and the third by arsonists. In all those fires, the ark holding the Torah was never damaged. It's still there today."

And on the west, on the far outskirts of town, we drove past what looked like a garden shed. "The first abolitionist school," Mrs. Baker said, "where Negro children could come to learn to read and write and so escape the ignorance that slavery wanted to impose. Right there, Holling, is the true beginning of the end of slavery."

I never knew a building could hold so much inside.

On a bright blue day when there wasn't an atomic bomb on any horizon, when the high clouds were painted onto blue canvas, when tulips were standing at attention and azaleas were blooming (except for the ones in front of the Perfect House) and dogs were barking at all the new smells, I saw my town as if I had just arrived. It was as if I was waking up. You see houses and buildings every day, and you walk by them on your way to something else, and you hardly see. You hardly notice they're even there, mostly because there's something else going on right in front of your face. But when the town itself becomes the thing that is going on right in front of your face, it all changes, and you're not just looking at a house but at what's happened in that house before you were born. That afternoon, driving with Mrs. Baker, the American Revolution was here. The escaped slaves were here. The abolitionists were here.

And I was here.

It made me feel sort of responsible.

Before we got back to Camillo Junior High, we passed Saint Adelbert's—"built almost a century ago with the pennies of Italian immigrants," said Mrs. Baker.

"Let's go in," I said.

Mrs. Baker paused. "Would your parents approve?" she asked.

"It's a point of local architectural interest," I said.

So we went in.

It was the first Catholic church I'd ever been inside, mostly because Catholic churches are supposed to be filled with idols and smoking incense that would make you so woozy that you'd give in and start praying on your knees, which Presbyterians know is something that should not be done. But it wasn't like that at all. We came in, Mrs. Baker dropped some money into the offering box, and we walked down the main aisle. The afternoon light slanted down through the high windows, so that up close to the ceiling the air was flecked with glowing gold specks. Down below where we were, it was shadowy and warm. I ran my hand over the dark wood of the pews, worn smooth. There was no carpet, so we could hear our own footsteps as we walked toward the altar, where a crucifix hung suspended—a pale white Christ with bright red wounds.

For a hundred years, people have been coming together in this dark, I thought, breathing quietly and evenly. For a hundred years. It made me wonder.

"Mrs. Baker," I said.

"Yes, Holling."

"I have a question."

"Yes."

"It doesn't have anything to do with points of local architectural interest."

"That's all right."

"After the game at Yankee Stadium, when Mel Stottlemyre took you up to meet the boss, did you ask him to have Kowalski and Associates do the renovations so that Meryl Lee could stay?"

A pause.

"Whether or not I spoke about the renovations to Yankee Stadium is not something you need to know, Holling."

"Then I have a second question."

"Does this one have anything to do with points of local architectural interest?"

"Yes."

"What is it?"

"If an atomic bomb drops on Camillo Junior High, everything we've seen today will be gone, won't it?"

Another long pause.

"Yes," she said, finally.

"And it really doesn't matter if we're under our desks with our hands over our heads or not, does it?"

"No," said Mrs. Baker. "It really doesn't matter."

"So why are we practicing?"

She thought for a minute. "Because it gives comfort," she said. "People like to think that if they're prepared, then nothing bad can really happen. And perhaps we practice because we feel as if there's nothing else we can do, because sometimes it feels as if life is governed by the slings and arrows of outrageous fortune."

"*Is* there anything else we can do?"

She smiled. Not a teacher smile.

"Two things," she said. "First, learn to diagram sentences—and it is rude to roll your eyes, Holling. Learn everything you can—everything. And then use all that you have learned to grow up to be a wise and good man. That's the first thing. As for the second . . ."

I lit a candle in a Catholic church for the first time that afternoon. Me, a Presbyterian. I lit a candle in the warm, dark, waxy-smelling air of Saint Adelbert's. I put it beside the one that Mrs. Baker lit. I don't know what she prayed for, but I prayed that no atomic bomb would ever drop on Camillo Junior High or the Quaker meetinghouse or the old jail or Temple Emmanuel or Hicks Park or Saint Paul's Episcopal School or Saint Adelbert's.

I prayed for Lieutenant Baker, missing in action somewhere in the jungles of Vietnam near Khesanh.

I prayed for Danny Hupfer, sweating it out in Hebrew school right then.

I prayed for my sister, driving in a yellow bug toward California—or maybe she was there already, trying to find herself.

And I hoped that it was okay to pray for a bunch of things with one candle.

That afternoon when I came back home, the station wagon was gone, and the Mustang was gone, and the whole house was empty.

Even the mailbox was empty, except for a flyer for my sister from the Robert Kennedy campaign, announcing that he would be stopping on Long Island before the New York primary. My sister would have flipped.

And I realized that the biggest part of the empty in the house was my sister being gone. Maybe the first time that you know you really care about something is when you think about it not being there, and you know—you really know—that the emptiness is as much inside you as outside you. For it so falls out, that what we have we prize not to the worth whiles we enjoy it; but being lacked and lost, why, then we rack the value, then we find the virtue that possession would not show us while it was ours.

That's when I knew for the first time that I really did love my sister. But I didn't know if I wanted more for her to come back or for her to find whatever it was that she was trying to find.

See, this is the kind of stuff you start to think about when you're reading *Hamlet, Prince of Denmark*. You just can't help being kind of melancholy—even though if you had to play him on stage at the Festival Theater, at least you'd be a prince and wearing a black cape instead of being a fairy and wearing yellow tights.

And that's why, when my sister called that night—long after my mother and father had gone to bed, when she knew that I would be the only one awake to pick up the phone—I started to cry right away.

And she did, too.

Both of us not saying anything, just crying into the telephone.

What jerks.

Somewhere in between all the crying, I heard that she was in Minneapolis—which I guess is on the way to California—that she was alone, that she had exactly $4 left in her pocket, that she didn't know what she was going to do since a bus ticket to New York City cost $44.55, that I couldn't ever, ever, ever, ever, ever tell Dad or Mom that she called because she couldn't bear to hear what they would say to her and she wasn't sure if they even would say anything to her, and what was she going to do now?

I guess she hadn't found herself.

"Where are you?" I said.

"In the bus station. How else do you think I'd know that a ticket to New York City costs $44.55?"

"Is there a Western Union window there?"

"Of course there's a Western Union window here. All bus stations have a Western Union window." She paused a moment. I guess she was looking around. "Holling?"

"Yes."

"I don't see a Western Union window here."

The operator told us that we were almost out of time and we should deposit thirty-five cents for another three minutes.

"I don't have any more coins!" yelled my sister.

"Get to the nearest Western Union station tomorrow morning," I said quickly. "I'll—" Then the phone went dead. All because of a stupid thirty-five cents in coins. Like Bell Telephone was going to go bankrupt because of one phone call from Minneapolis to Long Island in the middle of the night.

I didn't know if my sister had heard what I'd said at the end. But the next morning, I was waiting outside the Commerce Bank on—I'm not kidding here—Commerce Street when it opened at 10:00. This may not sound like a big deal, but if you knew that

Commerce Street was only a block over from Lee Avenue, and that I'd been hiding from eyes that would have wondered why I wasn't in Camillo Junior High for the last hour, you'd be impressed.

I handed my $100 Salisbury Park savings bond to the teller.

"Aren't you supposed to be in school?" she said.

"I'm a little worried that an atomic bomb might drop on it," I said.

"Probably the school will make it through the day," she said. "What do you want to do with this bond?"

"I need to turn it in for cash."

She looked at the date. "If you turn it in for cash now, you'll only get fifty-two dollars. If you hold on to it, in just a few years it will be worth a hundred dollars."

"I don't have a few years," I said.

"Because of the atomic bomb?"

"No."

She turned the savings bond over and looked at it again. "Do your parents know that you're cashing this in?"

"Yes," I said.

I know, I know. You don't have to tell me.

The teller fingered the savings bond. "All right," she said finally. "Fifty-two dollars. I hope you're going to do something worthwhile with the money."

I nodded, and she counted the bills out onto the counter.

Further down on Commerce Street was the Western Union. I put the money up on the counter.

"I need to send all this cash to Minneapolis," I said.

"It's going for a visit, is it?" said the Western Union man. This was worse than a teacher joke. This was even worse than a nurse joke.

"I need to send it to my sister."

The Western Union man counted it out. "That's a lot of money," he said. "Where are you sending it exactly?"

"To the Western Union closest to the Minneapolis bus station."

"Huh," he said. He pulled out a directory and thumbed through it. It took about half an hour before he found Minneapolis.

"Well," he said slowly, taking his glasses off, "looks like they've got two bus stations. There's the one on Heather Avenue. And there's the one on LaSalle."

"Heather Avenue," I said. "Send it to the one on Heather Avenue."

The Western Union man put his glasses back on. "It'll cost you $1.75," he said.

"Fine."

"And what's the name of the recipient?"

I told him, and he took the money and sent $50.25 to Minneapolis, Minnesota, to a Western Union station on Heather Avenue, even though I didn't know if my sister was at that station or if she even knew that money was coming. I thought of her sitting alone in a place where everyone else was going somewhere, or wandering the streets of Minneapolis, looking for a way to come home to a place that was emptier without her.

Sort of like Hamlet, who, more than anything, needed to find a home—because he sure couldn't find himself.

I spent the afternoon hiding around town—which is not easy, since this isn't that big a town, and it would take a whole lot less than an atomic bomb to make it disappear, and since anyone who saw me might tell the Chamber of Commerce Businessman of 1967 or Mrs. Baker. And if either of them heard . . . well, put me under that bomb.

I waited for a call from my sister that night. But it didn't come until late Friday night. From Chicago.

On the way.

On Saturday morning, I told my parents at breakfast that my sister would be at the Port Authority in New York at 10:50 that morning.

They looked at me like I had just chanted Hebrew.

"She'll be in the Port Authority at ten fifty?" repeated my mother. Her hand was up to her mouth, and her eyes suddenly filled.

"Yes," I said.

"How is she going to get home from there?" asked my father.

"I guess she was hoping you would go and pick her up."

"Of course," said my father. "Of course I'll drop everything and pick her up. Of course I have nothing else to do." He stood up. "If she went out in a yellow bug, she can come home in a yellow bug."

"She's alone," I said.

"You're not going to see me driving all the way into the city on a Saturday. She can take the train."

"She may be out of money."

"Well, whose problem is that?" he said.

"It doesn't matter whose problem it is. She can't get back home unless you go get her," I said.

He looked at me. "Who do you think you're talking to?" he said.

"She needs help."

"Then you go get her, Holling. The car keys are up on my dresser." He laughed.

"Okay," I said.

"Okay," he said, and went outside to start up the lawn mower.

I went upstairs and got the car keys. The Ford Mustang car keys—not the station wagon.

"Holling," said my mother when I came back down. "I think he was being sarcastic."

I went to the front closet and found my jacket.

"Holling, what are you doing?"

I held up the car keys. "I'm driving into New York City to pick up my sister from the Port Authority Bus Terminal at ten fifty."

"You don't know how to drive."

"I've seen movies."

I went to the front door.

"Holling," said my mother.

I turned around.

"You can't drive in by yourself."

"Then come with me."

She looked out to the backyard. "We can't do that, either," she said, and her voice was as sad and lost as Loneliness.

I went out to the garage and sat in the Mustang. The red leather still smelled new. The steering wheel felt right in my hands.

It wasn't like I'd never driven before. My mother had let me drive the station wagon around parking lots—the big ones down at Jones Beach, where you can go for two or three miles before you hit anything more dangerous than a seagull. I'd gotten out of first gear plenty of times, and even up into third gear twice. And the Mustang was smaller and handier than the station wagon. I probably just had to think about turning and the car would feel it.

But driving around Jones Beach parking lots is a whole lot different from driving on the Long Island Expressway into New York City. And even if I could get on to the expressway, I wouldn't know what exit to get off.

Toads, beetles, bats.

I came back inside. I threw the keys on the kitchen counter. My mother was putting out a cigarette and starting to make pound cake for lunch.

Outside, the mower fussed at the edges of the lawn.

I went into the living room and sat down on the couch.

And Meryl Lee called.

Because her father was going in to Yankee Stadium.

Would I like to come?

"Can I get to the Port Authority from Yankee Stadium?" I said.

Meryl Lee asked her father.

"It's too far, but he says that if you can leave right now, we'll have just enough time to drop you off." She was quiet a moment. "I think he feels like he owes you something," she said.

I went into the kitchen. "I need money for two train tickets," I said.

"Train tickets?" my mother said.

"And money for two lunches."

She stared at me.

"Big lunches," I said.

She went upstairs for her pocketbook.

I was there when the bus from Chicago pulled in at 10:50.

The Port Authority was all noise and rushing. The accumulated combustion from the buses had thickened the air. The whoosh and squeak and hollering of the brakes and the distorted announcements over the P.A. system and the newsboys hawking and the pell-mell of more bodies than belong in any one building gave the place a general roar. As for the floor, you couldn't have found a greater confusion if the ceiling had been lifted off and the sky had rained down ticket stubs and newspapers and Baby Ruth wrappers.

But as soon as the 10:50 bus from Chicago parked itself, everything stopped. The rush, the roar, the squeak, the whoosh—they all stopped. Really. Like Leonid Brezhnev had sent over an atomic bomb and wiped it all out.

They did not start up again until my sister got off the bus, and she ran out of the diesel combustion and right to me, and we held each other, and we were not empty at all.

"Holling," she said, "I was so afraid I wouldn't find you."

"I was standing right here, Heather," I said. "I'll always be standing right here."

For lunch, we had grilled cheese sandwiches and Cokes and chocolate doughnuts at a counter in the Port Authority. Outside, we bought pretzels from a stand, and then we walked to Central Park, hand in hand. We lay down in the Sheep Meadow, and my sister told me about driving west, with the sun on your face. We got up and walked around the Pond, and stopped at an outcropping of boulders that fell out of the woods. Around us was every shade of green you could ever hope to imagine, broken up here and there with a flowering tree blushing to a light pink. All the colors were garbled and reflected in the tiny ripples of the water. Then through the wandering paths of the Ramble, looking as if we were up in the mountains of California, and then across Bethesda Terrace, where we sat on the stone walls and traced the carvings with our fingers until someone hollered at us to get off there! Then back along the Mall underneath tall elms, until we passed the statue of—no kidding—William Shakespeare, who stared down at us sternly, probably because he is wearing tights and is embarrassed doing that in front of everybody.

We walked slowly. We talked a little. I told her about our atomic bomb drills and about our town and about *The Tragedy of Hamlet, Prince of Denmark*. She told me about Minneapolis and how she got out of the yellow bug and wouldn't get back in and how Chit drove away, and about going to the Western Union and finding the money for the ticket, and falling asleep for the first time in two days on the bus to Chicago. But mostly we didn't talk. It was spring in Central Park, and being there with my sister was enough.

We took the train out of the city and walked from the station. When we got back home, it didn't matter that my mother had made us burned grilled cheese sandwiches for supper. It was just so good that the house wasn't empty anymore.

My father said only one thing during supper:

"Did you find yourself?"

"What?" said my sister.

"Did you find yourself?"

"She found me," I said.

By the end of *The Tragedy of Hamlet, Prince of Denmark*, Laertes is stabbed, the queen is poisoned, and the king is poisoned *and* stabbed—which is pretty much the same thing that happens to Hamlet. By the time it's all over, there are these dead bodies all over the stage, and even though Horatio is hoping that flights of angels are coming to sing Hamlet to his rest, it's hard to believe that there's any rest for him. Maybe he knew that. Maybe that's why he dressed in black all the time. Maybe it's why he was never happy. Maybe he looked in the wrong places trying to find himself.

Or maybe he never had someone to tell him that he didn't need to find himself. He just needed to let himself be found.

That's what I think Shakespeare was trying to say about what it means to be a human being in *The Tragedy of Hamlet, Prince of Denmark*.

And speaking of being found, that's what happened to Lieutenant Baker, too!

Really.

After almost three months in the jungles of Vietnam, he got found.

I was there on the last Wednesday afternoon of May, a cool and blue day, when Mrs. Sidman came in with an envelope and handed it to Mrs. Baker. She took it with hands that were trembling. She tore the top slowly open, and then stood there, holding the telegram, unable to pull it out to read it.

"Can I help?" said Mrs. Sidman.

Mrs. Baker nodded.

"And then I'll take Holling to my office so that you can be alone."

Mrs. Baker looked at me, and I knew she wasn't going to send me to Mrs. Sidman's office so that she could be alone. You don't send someone away who has lit a candle with you.

"I suppose not," said Mrs. Baker.

Mrs. Sidman took the envelope, then held out the opened telegram to Mrs. Baker.

But Mrs. Baker closed her eyes. "Read it," she whispered.

Mrs. Sidman looked at me, then down at the telegram. Then she read the first line: "Sweet eyes . . . stop."

Think of the sound you make when you let go after holding your breath for a very, very long time. Think of the gladdest sounds you know: the sound of dawn on the first day of spring break, the sound of a bottle of Coke opening, the sound of a crowd cheering in your ears because you're coming down to the last part of a race—

and you're ahead. Think of the sound of water over stones in a cold stream, and the sound of wind through green trees on a late May afternoon in Central Park. Think of the sound of a bus coming into the station carrying someone you love.

Then put all those together.

And they would be nothing compared to the sound that Mrs. Baker made that day from somewhere deep inside that had almost given up, when she heard the first line of that telegram.

Then she started to hiccup, and to cry, and to laugh, and Mrs. Sidman put the telegram down, held Mrs. Baker in her arms, nodded to me, and took her out of the classroom for a drink of water.

And I know I shouldn't have, but I picked up the telegram and read the rest. Here is what it said:

SWEET EYES STOP OUT OF JUNGLE STOP OK STOP
HOME IN TIME FOR STRAWBERRIES STOP LOVE TY STOP

Shakespeare couldn't write any better than that.

June

Mrs. Baker hated camping.

You could tell this because her eyes rolled whenever the subject came up—which was plenty lately, since that's what her class was going to do to celebrate the end of the school year. Two nights of camping up in the Catskill Mountains. Beside a waterfall. In deep woods.

"On soggy ground," said Mrs. Baker.

"It'll be great," said Danny.

"With mosquitoes," said Mrs. Baker.

"Mosquitoes?" said Meryl Lee.

"Sleeping on rocks," said Mrs. Baker.

"Terrific," I said.

"Dew all over us," said Mrs. Baker.

"Great," said Doug Swieteck.

"Let's get back to sentence diagramming," said Mrs. Baker.

You might wonder why Mrs. Baker was going to take us camping when she thought that camping meant soggy ground, mosquitoes, sleeping on rocks, and dew. But every year since she had first begun to teach at Camillo Junior High, Mrs. Baker had taken her class camping in June. Lieutenant Baker had come along—probably because he loved camping, and Mrs. Baker was willing to put up with soggy ground, mosquitoes, sleeping on rocks, and dew for his sake. Maybe she wanted to go this year because *he* would have wanted to go. Maybe she thought that if she kept every routine the same, then he really would be home in time for strawberries.

So Mrs. Baker was taking us camping, even though she hated camping.

But let me tell you, Mrs. Baker would have had to hate camping a whole lot more to keep herself from smiling through all of her classes—even when she was rolling her eyes or crossing her arms or fussing that Mr. Vendleri had still not gotten all the spilled cider mopped up, so that it was sticky on the feet when you walked into the Coat Room.

She was still smiling anyway, because Lieutenant Baker was coming home.

It was in all the papers. Even Walter Cronkite talked about it on the 6:30 news. How Lieutenant Baker's helicopter was shot down. How he jumped out before the helicopter hit the ground and shattered. How his leg was caught by one of the broken blades. How he hid in the jungle near Khesanh trying to keep his wound clean and eating chocolate bars from his pack. How he followed a river until he couldn't go any further. How he was found by a woman who already had two sons killed and didn't want anyone else to die, so she took him back to her house. How he hid there for three months until an American helicopter came over and he signaled. And how the crew pulled him out.

It was, said Walter Cronkite, a miraculous rescue.

I guess it's like Prospero pulling back the curtain for the king and there's Prince Ferdinand, who the king thought was dead, playing chess with Miranda like he was on vacation. Or maybe, a little like a phone call late at night from your sister, who isn't all that interested in finding herself anymore. She just wants to find you.

So Mrs. Baker was smiling because no one can help smiling at miracles.

The camping trip was going to be on Thursday and Friday of the second week of June. Everything before that, said Mrs. Baker, would be work. Work like we had never known work. Work that would make us drop. Work that would make us beg for mercy.

It was hard to worry too much about this since she was smiling the whole time she said it. But she really did work us like we had never been worked before. Sentence diagramming, short stories by John Steinbeck, the spelling and construction of adverbs and adjectives with Latinate endings, declining strong verbs, more short stories by John Steinbeck—who wrote a whole lot of short stories—and an essay report on any three poems written before 1900—because Mrs. Baker thought that no one had written any poems worth writing about since then.

All this in two weeks. And that doesn't count Mr. Petrelli's "Westward Expansion and You" report. Or Mr. Samowitz's pre-algebra final examination.

And it didn't count *Much Ado About Nothing,* which should have counted for the whole shebang, since it advertised itself as a comedy—but let me tell you, it wasn't.

"Of course it's not always funny," said Mrs. Baker. "Why would you ever imagine that a comedy has to be funny?"

"Mrs. Baker, if it's a comedy, it's supposed to be funny. That's what comedies are."

"No, Holling," said Mrs. Baker. "Comedies are much more than funny." And she smiled again.

Whatever it was supposed to be much more than, *Much Ado*

About Nothing wasn't funny. Maybe a line or two here and there, but other than that, pretty much not funny. I mean, talk about jerks. Claudio and Hero—Shakespeare wasn't all that good about his names—Claudio and Hero would have a whole lot to do just to get up to where Romeo and Juliet were. First they're in love, then they're not in love, and Hero has to pretend to die (Does this sound familiar? Don't you think Shakespeare needed some new material?), and Claudio has to pine away at her tomb, and then Hero has to come back to life, and then they fall in love again just like that. Really.

Can you believe this stuff?

Because you don't have to be Shakespeare to know that's not the way it happens in the real world. In the real world, people fall out of love little by little, not all at once. They stop looking at each other. They stop talking. They stop serving lima beans. After Walter Cronkite is finished, one of them goes for a ride in a Ford Mustang, and the other goes upstairs to the bedroom. And there is a lot of quiet in the house. And late at night, the sounds of sadness creep underneath the bedroom doors and along the dark halls.

That's the way it is in the real world.

It's not always smiles. Sometimes the real world is like Hamlet. A little scared. Unsure. A little angry. Wishing that you could fix something that you can't fix. Hoping that maybe the something would fix itself, but thinking that hoping that way is stupid.

And sometimes the real world is more like Bobby Kennedy, who was a sure bet for the Democratic nomination and probably would have been president of the United States and stopped the war, but who got shot at point-blank range.

After she heard the news, my sister locked herself in her bedroom. She put on the Beatles singing "Eleanor Rigby" and played it over and over and over again, low, so that I could just barely hear it through her door.

I knocked after something like the fiftieth repetition. "Heather?"

No answer. The song started over.

I knocked again, but she turned up the volume, and the Beatles sang about all the lonely people and wondered where they all came from. As if we didn't know.

But I kept knocking, until finally the music stopped, and the door jerked open, and it looked for a moment like my sister was going to take my head off. But she didn't. Behind her, the Beatles sang of Father McKenzie, walking away with the dirt of a grave on his hands.

I took Heather's hand, and we left the house together.

We walked to Saint Adelbert's. We waited on a long line to light two candles, and though we both were crying—everyone was crying—we kept holding each other's hands, and we said the same prayer.

But it's not always miracles—as if we didn't know that, too.

Bobby Kennedy died the next morning.

We heard it together on the transistor radio, Heather and me. She cried, and I held her, gut-crying, not knowing what at all to do except to be together. And if I hadn't heard that Lieutenant Baker was going to come home and that some miracles stand a chance of being real, I think I might have given up on the whole Presbyterian thing right then, sort of like Julius Caesar giving up on Brutus and going ahead and dying.

Early the next Thursday morning, a bus pulled up to take Mrs. Baker's class to the Catskill Mountains. We taunted the other seventh graders going on into their classrooms. Then there was running onto the bus to pick out our seats, and a lot of running back out to help load the hot dogs and buns and chili and water bottles and juice-powder mix and marshmallows and more marshmallows and loaves of bread and wool blankets for everyone and extra wool blankets for just in case, and then running onto the bus again to make sure that no one had stolen our seats, and then running out again to go to the bathroom one more time, since the only bathrooms where we were going had branches on them. It took Mrs. Baker and Mr. Vendleri and even Mrs. Sidman—who was coming along with us to lend Mrs. Baker moral support, she said—to get us finally herded onto the bus. Then it bumped into gear, and we were out onto Lee Avenue.

We sang as we drove to the Long Island Expressway. We got to Old Miss O'Leary taking a lantern to her shed, and the flea on the fly on the hair on the wart on the frog on the bump on the log in the hole in the bottom of the sea, and the bullfrog stubbing his toe and falling in the water. When we reached the Throgs Neck Bridge, Doug Swieteck started "One Thousand Bottles of Beer on the Wall," until Mrs. Baker came down the bus aisle and didn't need to say anything. She had her arms crossed.

A very ominous beginning.

After an hour, the bus went from the highway to the Thruway, then—an hour later—off a sharp exit to a two-lane road, then to a gravel road, and then to a dirt road. Finally, we ended up on a two-track path that the bus could never have gotten out of if the path didn't double back on itself. When we reached the end of that—and let me tell you, this took a while—we climbed out and Mrs. Sidman tried to keep us corralled together as Mrs. Baker issued a pack to each of us.

The pack Mrs. Baker gave Danny was full of cans of chili—which weighed enough to make Danny stop smiling pretty quickly.

The pack she gave me held four cans of chili—big cans of chili—and all the utensils. "If something happens to this pack," she said when she hefted it onto my shoulders, "we're all going to eat with our fingers."

"What could happen?" I said.

"That is probably what Hero's father was thinking after the wedding date was set," she said.

Which, if you haven't read *Much Ado About Nothing* lately, was Mrs. Baker's way of saying that a whole lot could happen.

In small groups we followed Mrs. Baker onto a path that went mostly uphill while jutting up as many tree roots as it could to trip us. It wasn't too long before we were all stretched out, a long and straggling line that got longer and stragglier the farther we went.

Still, it was a June day to be blithe and bonny in. The leaves up in the hills still had that fresh color they have when they're just a couple of weeks old, and they give off that green smell that mixes so well with sunshine in June. A few big billows of clouds floated ahead of us. We could see them piled up when the maples thinned out to birches, carried on winds that were way too high to reach us below the trees. Top branches rubbed together now and then, their creaking and cracking the only sound we heard except for the group up ahead that was singing about Napoleon's army of fifty thousand men climbing up a hillside. They probably weren't carrying hefty cans of chili.

I was the very last person on the path. And let me tell you, after a while that bugged me. It wasn't that I was alone. Mrs. Sidman walked in front of me, picking up sweatshirts and canteens that hadn't been tied to the packs very well, and handing them to Danny and Meryl Lee when her arms got too full. But you put all the utensils for an entire class in one pack, and four big cans of chili, and you're carrying quite a bit, and that's going to slow you down. And it was an old pack, and it smelled old. I had to keep hefting it back up around my shoulders because the straps wouldn't hold tight, and every time I did that, another fork or knife found a way to poke into my spine. And when you have to do that while you're climbing mostly uphill, and the straps of your backpack are cutting grooves into your shoulders, and Doug Swieteck is carrying a pack filled with bags of marshmallows, you don't get in the best of moods—even if it is a June day off from school.

The path heaved in short, quick spurts up through some stands of old birches, and then out into more sunlit spaces. We crossed some open rock, and since it had become much warmer, I was glad when the clouds hid the sun and dropped the temperature. Then we climbed into some scrub pines, where the wind came on and cooled our backs. Even my pack began to feel a whole lot lighter, and the forks and knives had stopped jabbing into me whenever I hefted it up again.

It was past noon by the time our group got into camp, and I have to say, Mrs. Baker had picked a great spot—though probably Lieutenant Baker had picked it out years before. An egg-shaped clearing beneath high pines rounded out a bend in a running stream. A waterfall on one side threw its water over mossy stones and into a small, deep pool; on the other side we set our camp. The ground was not soggy, and there were no mosquitoes and not too many rocks, which I pointed out to Mrs. Baker.

"Just wait," she said.

Mrs. Baker organized the whole site. She gave Doug Swieteck a camp shovel and had him dig out a fire pit. I lined it with stones from the streambed. Mai Thi and Danny built a teepee fire, and Mrs. Baker put two large pots for chili beside it. Mrs. Sidman took everyone else to search for wood, and she organized what was brought back into a pile that slouched from the biggest logs to the smallest twigs. Then Mrs. Baker marked out the sleeping places with long branches—the girls on one side of the fire, the boys on the other—and she and Mrs. Sidman set up a big tent in between while everyone picked spots to lay out their sleeping bags.

After the tent was up, Mrs. Baker waved at Danny and me. "The chili," she called, and we brought our packs and dropped them beside her. Meryl Lee filled a fry pan with hot dogs and slid it on a grill over the fire. They began to sizzle right away.

You had to hand it to Mrs. Baker. For someone who hated camping, she knew exactly what to do. She even had latrines built in the woods, and she posted signs shaped like little hands with GENTLEMEN and GENTLEWOMEN written on them pointing to two thin paths that led away from each other. While the hot dogs cooked, I followed the path from the GENTLEMEN sign down a sharp ridge, over a dry streambed, up another ridge, and behind a boulder the size of Camillo Junior High. It was peaceful and comfortable. Doug Swieteck had used his camp shovel to dig a hole in the middle of some bright green vines, and he had set three rolls of toilet paper on three dead branches of a tree beside the hole. The vines that ran up the trees almost covered them. He left a shovel in the pile of dirt—to use as needed.

It was the kind of place where you could sit for a while within the vines and watch the green world be green.

Then Mrs. Sidman hollered, "Holling Hoodhood!"

You already know what had happened, don't you?

Let me tell you, it wasn't my fault that Mrs. Baker had given me an old pack. And it wasn't my fault that its seams were starting to split. And when you're hiking up a path that's pretty steep and hefting an old pack onto your shoulders, you don't feel stuff falling out.

"You didn't notice it was getting lighter?" said Mrs. Sidman.

"Well," I said, "I did notice it wasn't getting any heavier."

She held up a spoon. "This is our entire set of utensils," she said.

"We can stir the chili," I said.

"The can opener was in your pack, too," said Mrs. Sidman.

Mrs. Baker picked up four cans and handed two to me. "Come with me, Holling." We went down to the streambed. "Look for some large stones that are sharp at one end," she said.

And that's how we got the cans of chili opened. We smashed into them with rocks, which is what I think people did during the Westward Expansion. At first, the cans just bent over and started to collapse into themselves, but after a few blows they split open, and chili spattered out. By the time Mrs. Baker and I were done, we looked liked someone had thrown a whole can over us both.

But from the way Mrs. Baker was laughing, you couldn't tell that anything was wrong.

Or that she hated camping.

Mrs. Sidman was grumbling more than a little by the time we got back, and it didn't help much that she cut up the ends of three of her fingers trying to get all the chili out of the battered cans, which were pretty jagged. Every time she cut one, she would glare at me, and I don't think she was thinking thoughts about nurturing one of her students in wisdom and learning.

Any lunch after a long hike tastes good. Especially if it's on a day off from school. And if you take two hot dogs and hold them together, one in each hand, you can scoop up the chili between them, and shovel it all up to your mouth. If you lean way over while you do this, most of it won't even drip onto you—which is something that Mrs. Sidman didn't seem to understand.

And again, it wasn't my fault that she was wearing her favorite sweater, and that streaks of chili don't exactly go with mango, which is a color that you shouldn't wear on a camping trip anyway.

I think this is why I was the one who ended up carrying all the pots and pans down to the stream to wash them.

Meryl Lee helped. She didn't have to, but she did. So it wasn't bad at all, scrubbing at the pots together and her splashing me a little and me splashing her a little until we finally gave up and splashed each other all over so that it looked like we had jumped in—which washed all of the chili off me. Which is more than I can say for Mrs. Sidman's mango sweater.

But by the time we were done, there was a breeze skimming over the top of the stream, and it wasn't warm. We stacked the pots near the rest of the food, and then stood by the fire—Mrs. Sidman did not seem to mind me adding a few sticks to make it blaze up. Still, we were pretty wet, and the problem with getting warm by a fire is that one side of you is always cold, and the other side is always roasting. So you have to keep turning around and around.

We were supposed to go swimming in the afternoon, but the breeze that sent me and Meryl to the fire got stronger when a few of the clouds stacked themselves up between us and the sun, and so we played Capture the Flag instead, which our side won because Danny cheated and hid our flag about three stories up in a pine tree. And after that we climbed down past the waterfall and followed a deer track that led out from it and then climbed back above the waterfall and explored an abandoned stone house in a field beyond it. There were supposed to be rattlesnakes in the basement, but none showed.

It was a whole lot colder when we got back, and so Mrs. Sidman sent us to bring in more wood, and while we did, Mrs. Baker heated up pots of hot chocolate—which tastes better in the woods by an open fire than it does anywhere else—and Mrs. Sidman started unpacking the hamburger patties and glaring at me again, since she wasn't sure whether she could cook them with only one spoon to turn them over.

Anyone would know that she couldn't, and I think that even Mrs. Baker knew it wasn't right to blame me entirely when four of Mrs. Sidman's remaining seven healthy fingers got burns on the ends.

Let me tell you, she made a big deal of it.

After supper, Meryl Lee and I did the pots again.

It was hard to tell when night came on. We got the fire going pretty high—almost as high as where Danny hid the flag—and the crackling and snapping and small explosions of pine resin sent out sparks that looked like rising stars. The clouds had gotten so thick now that there was no sunset to see, and the breeze had picked up to a kind of steady rhythm, steady enough that not even a single mosquito was brave enough to fly out into it.

"Just wait," said Mrs. Baker.

But all through the singing that we did that night, no mosquito showed its face. Which just goes to show that even Mrs. Baker isn't right all the time.

Mrs. Sidman tried some ghost stories after the singing, but there's something about principals that makes it impossible for them to tell ghost stories. I mean, you can't spend your days in the Main Administrative Office and then hope to scare someone with a story about a headless ghost. You don't have a chance. She tried to make her voice all low and quavery, but she just got to sound like old Pastor McClellan at Saint Andrew's grumbling out a hymn. When she finally got to the end and shouted out the climax—which was supposed to make us all scream in fascinated terror—not much happened. So she sat back down and looked at us like she was going to make us all repeat seventh grade next year. There's a special kind of principal look for that, and even though she had only been a principal for two months, she had it down.

So when Mrs. Sidman got up to give her what-you-should-be-careful-about-in-the-woods speech, we didn't pay much attention, either. After all, that's what happens when you have teachers and principals along on a camping trip: You hear about all sorts of disasters, like mosquito bites, bee stings, what to do if you trip over a stone and get blood on your knee. You're told not to wander so far from camp at night that you can't see the firelight—as if that's going to be a real issue. And you're reminded where the latrines are, and how you shouldn't use too much toilet paper since there wasn't a whole lot, and what the shovel is for—stuff like that.

But when she came to the snake part, she got our attention.

"There are poisonous snakes all around here," she said. "If they bite you, your leg will swell up until you have ankles like cantaloupes and shins like watermelons. If you get bitten, you have to swallow this very quickly"—she held up a small glass vial—"so that you can make it to the hospital. You have to swallow it within thirty seconds for it to work. And even if you get it swallowed in thirty seconds, there is no guarantee. So in addition to this vial, I'll have to cut between the fang marks"—she held up a knife that Long John Silver would have been proud of—"and hope that some of the venom will ooze out along with your pus and blood."

I felt my throat start to close up. Meryl Lee took my hand.

Doug Swieteck moaned.

"This is what she should have used for her ghost story," said Danny.

"So be careful to check your sleeping bags before you get into them," said Mrs. Sidman. "It might be a good idea to turn them inside out once, just in case. And be sure not to sleep directly under a low branch. Snakes can climb trees, and sometimes they crawl out onto branches and fall, and you don't want a snake to fall across your face while you're sleeping."

By the time she was done, no one was talking. No one was moving. And Doug Swieteck was close to passing out.

"I'm going to stay up all night," said Danny.

"We can keep the fire going," said Mai Thi.

"I'll help," I said.

Meryl Lee squeezed my hand. Hard.

And that's why long after midnight, after everyone else had turned their sleeping bags inside out, shaken them, then turned them back and crawled in and zipped them up over their heads, Danny and Mai Thi and Meryl Lee and Doug and I and Mrs. Baker—I guess the part about the snakes got to her, too—were sitting around the fire as the flames faded and the blue and gold embers glowed like jewels. We sat in close, with blankets over our backs.

None of us said anything. We sat beside each other by the fire, silent, watching the jewels change and glow first into white diamonds, then into sapphires, then into rubies. Sometimes Mrs. Baker got up and threw another piece of wood on the fire, and the sparks shattered up into the night darkness and we watched them ascend until they disappeared like the stuff of dreams. The breeze clicked the branches above us together, and the water farther away tumbled and dropped into the pool below.

It was about as far away from the Perfect House that you can get and still be in the same universe.

We probably would have stayed there all night—if it hadn't started to rain.

Actually, "started" isn't really the right word. It didn't come on like rain usually does, a little at a time until first you realize that you're feeling a drop or two, and then you realize it's more than a drop or two, and then you know you need to get someplace because it's going to really come down in a minute. Here, one second it was all ascending sparks, and the next it was all rain. It must have been something like the moment the doors closed on Noah's Ark.

We threw our wool blankets over our heads, but it was already too late. We held the blankets tight around us as a cold wind dropped down with the rain, and while every single seventh grader from Mrs. Baker's class was hollering and trying to keep already soggy sleeping bags from getting a whole lot soggier and asking if snakes came out in the rain, Danny and I loaded more wood onto the fire to keep it from going out.

And that's pretty much what we all did for the rest of the night—hollered and wrung out sleeping bags and kept throwing wood onto the fire. Except for Mrs. Baker, who went inside the tent with Mrs. Sidman.

When dawn finally came—which we were all ready for, let me tell you—every bit of ground around the campsite was wet. Every bit. Puddles everywhere. It squelched while we walked, though sometimes it was hard to tell. Sometimes it might have been our sneakers squelching.

Mrs. Baker came out of the tent and looked at us with half-closed eyes. "Awfully soggy, isn't it," she said.

Why is it that when teachers go on campouts, they have tents?

Mrs. Sidman came out with a dark green poncho that covered her head and reached down to her ankles. She looked around the miserable campsite. We all had mud up to our knees, and most of us had draped our sleeping bags on pine branches above us; water dripped from their corners.

"You look like refugees," she said.

"Perhaps we should move toward breakfast," said Mrs. Baker.

Mrs. Sidman nodded. "You used a lot of wood last night," she told us.

"I'll find the eggs," said Mrs. Baker.

That morning, we had scrambled eggs spiced with pine bark, which came from the sticks we used to stir them. The orange Kool-Aid we drank was muddy, because the rain had stirred up the river before we filled our jugs. The bread was soggy, so we dripped honey onto the slices and rolled them and they didn't taste too bad.

Mrs. Sidman warmed the rest of the chili over the fire again, in case anyone wanted it. Only Doug Swieteck did—which was a mistake, as it turned out.

I think if it had kept on raining, we would all have gotten in under Mrs. Sidman's poncho and walked back home. But after Meryl Lee and I had carried all the pots to the stream—we waded right on in with them, since we were wet through already—the clouds started to shred, and sunbeams slit through. Each beam stabbed at the cold winds, until one by one they whimpered and died. The whole sky grew yellow, and we threw off the wet blankets—nothing smells worse than a wet woolen blanket—and then squelched around the campsite gathering more wood for the day, until suddenly it was so warm that someone said, "Let's go swimming," and we all ran a little way down the paths to the latrines and put on shorts and came back to the water and stepped carefully in—it was still cold—until Danny finally let himself slide down with the high current and over the waterfall ledge and into the pool. When he surfaced, he was laughing and snorting with water up his nose.

"It's great!" he said. And so we all went over the waterfall and got water up our noses.

Even Meryl Lee.

Even Mai Thi—holding Meryl Lee's hand.

That's what we did most of the morning, while Mrs. Baker and Mrs. Sidman stood above us and watched.

I could tell that Mrs. Baker was wanting to try it. It was probably getting hot on the open rocks above the falls, with the sun coming straight down now. Everything in the woods around us was steaming and glistening. The ferns, the pines, the leaves, the moss—everything. Even the teachers.

It's got to be hard to be a teacher all the time and not jump into a pool of clear water and come up laughing and snorting with water up your nose.

We ate lunch—chicken salad sandwiches and cucumber spears, which didn't need utensils—and then we headed back to the water, where Danny was throwing dives that the rest of us tried to match but couldn't. He could flip one and a half times and land headfirst right where the falls hit the pool, disappearing in white spray. Once he got around two full turns, which no human being should be able to do, and came up laughing and snorting so hard he could barely breathe.

That's all we did most of the afternoon. Not a diagrammed sentence in sight. Swimming and diving in a waterfall through the heated hours. Until finally we came back up to the campsite and Mrs. Baker started to assign our chores.

Now, you have to understand that we'd been here for a day and a half, and in all that time Doug Swieteck hadn't followed the GEN-TLEMEN sign and used what was over the two ridges. It was pretty clear he wanted to. Actually, it was very clear he wanted to. But he wasn't going to use a hole in the middle of the woods, he said, even if he had dug it himself.

Still, when you've eaten chili the night before, and chili for breakfast, you can't hold it off forever. Even Doug Swieteck knew that, and that's why he finally gave in. He didn't have any choice.

He was gone for a long time. No one said anything, but everyone watched down the path.

And no one was surprised when he came back smiling—which you can understand.

He probably had no idea what had found him, and what was now following him.

Even we couldn't tell.

"It looks like smoke," said Mai Thi.

"But it's *following* him," said Danny.

Mrs. Baker sighed. "It's not smoke," she said.

"It's mosquitoes," I said.

Mrs. Baker rolled her eyes.

We all ran. Doug Swieteck couldn't quite figure out why, until the first ones landed on him. He looked down and saw his arms covered. That was until they flew into his eyes. Then he ran, too, and probably hit a whole lot more trees than he would have if the world was a fairer place.

The mosquitoes followed us like little airplanes. You could hear them buzzing.

We ran down to the water and splashed at them.

They hovered above us and laughed.

We ran toward the woods and swatted at them with pine branches.

They laughed some more.

Then we ran toward the fire, since Mrs. Baker said they hated smoke.

They don't. Hiding in the smoke helps about as much as scrunching under a desk during an atomic bomb attack.

"Keep moving and stay in groups," said Mrs. Baker, which is the same strategy to use if you're floating in the ocean and surrounded by sharks. It means that anyone on the outside of the group gets picked off. So we took turns getting in close to the center—except I gave Meryl Lee my turn since she had helped me with the pots. She said that I saved her about a pint of blood—which was worth it the way she smiled at me when she said this.

And that's how Mrs. Bigio found us when she hiked in at dusk—all huddled into small groups, swatting hopelessly at hordes of mosquitoes, nothing cooking on the fire. (Mrs. Sidman was in the tent, with the entrance zipped up.)

Mrs. Bigio unslung her backpack, whipped out a can of insect repellant, and went to work on us. Then she loaded wood onto the fire and sent half of us out for more. "The rest of you, bring me three large flat stones from the river. And scrub them clean! And bring back two pots of water, too. Who's been cleaning these?"

When we came back with the stones and pots of water, she unloaded garlic and carrots and potatoes and turnips and chuck beef and tomatoes.

Mai Thi stared at it all. "Thit bo kho?" she asked.

"It will be by the time we're done," said Mrs. Bigio. "The curry and gingerroot are in the front pocket there. I couldn't find any lemongrass, so we'll have to make do."

She and Mai Thi made do. In a little while, the water was boiling, and they had chopped up the potatoes and turnips into one pot, and the chuck beef into another. And then they combined them and added everything else that Mrs. Bigio had brought. And even if there wasn't any lemongrass, it all smelled as wonderful as any food cooked over an open fire can smell—which is pretty wonderful, let me tell you.

Just as we saw the first star, Mrs. Bigio and Mai Thi ladled the stew out into bowls—that Mrs. Bigio had packed—and gave us spoons—that Mrs. Bigio had picked up all along the trail. "You can never be too careful about your supplies," she said to Mrs. Sidman, who, because she was eating hot thit bo kho, was happy enough not to blame anything on me. Even though I still was the one who carried the pots down to the stream to clean them out.

With Meryl Lee.

And neither of us minded at all.

We were still there when Mrs. Bigio and Mai Thi came down to wash Mrs. Bigio's cutting knives—which she wouldn't let anyone but Mai Thi touch—and when Mrs. Bigio said to Mai Thi that she had meant to be up to the campsite earlier but that she had taken the morning to speak with the Catholic Relief Agency that had sponsored Mai Thi when she came from Vietnam. She wanted Mai Thi to know that the house where she was living with the relief sisters was very nice, but if she wanted, that is, if Mai Thi would like to, Mrs. Bigio had a small house and she was living all alone now and she thought that maybe, if Mai Thi would ever, could ever imagine that—until Mai Thi put her arms around Mrs. Bigio, and Mrs. Bigio put her arms around Mai Thi, and the ripples of the water replaced all words.

Good Lord, for alliance!

That night, I lay awake. It seemed that the soggy ground had sunk down and left a whole lot of rocks to poke up into me. I watched the bazillion stars amaze the sky above. I watched until they fell asleep themselves. Half my mind on sea, half on shore. Thinking about Mai Thi and Mrs. Bigio. And Lieutenant Baker coming home to Mrs. Baker. And Danny Hupfer getting ready for his bar mitzvah. And Bobby Kennedy. And Martin Luther King, Jr. And how in five years I'd have to register for the Vietnam draft.

And how the dew was starting to soak my sleeping bag.

So I was still awake when the dawn started to think about showing herself. The air was coloring everything gray, and the fog was coming up from the ground in white shreds and billows, as if the whole campsite had lifted itself up into the clouds overnight. I slipped out of my dewy sleeping bag and walked through the white and the gray to the water. When I reached it, the stream rippled happily, as if it had been waiting just for me all this time. I knelt down and lowered my palm into it. Cold. Frigidly cold. But I rolled up my pants and waded in. Beneath me, the rocks of the streambed felt smooth and slick, even soft, as the water rushed past, carrying itself away.

Then I looked upstream.

The disk of the sun had just come up, and the billows of fog had bowed to it and backed away. The river was a sudden ribbon of silvery light, flickering and sparkling and flashing, carrying the new light on its back all the way down from the high mountains. It was so bright that you couldn't see below the surface until the water was right up to you, and then it was suddenly clear, and buoying me up in its rush. And it never stopped, this rush of bright water from the mountains, these flashes and chunks of light from the sun. There was so much of it to come.

❧

I didn't tell anyone about the river that morning. Not even Meryl Lee. I think that if I had told Pastor McClellan, he would have said it was a vision. I think if I had told Mrs. Baker, she would have said that it was a miracle, that all dawns were miracles—miracles being much on her mind lately, as you can understand. I think that if I had told Shakespeare about the river, he would have said, "All this amazement can I qualify"—but he would have been wrong, since what I saw was something more beautiful than has ever been written.

But I didn't tell anyone.

Not even Danny, who was hoping for a miracle, right up to the day of his bar mitzvah.

You could see him waiting for the worst to happen when he stood up in the synagogue a week later—a synagogue that was full, mostly with Hupfers. Mrs. Baker and Mrs. Bigio and Mrs. Sidman sat near the front. Mai Thi and Meryl Lee and Heather and I sat behind a group of ancient Hupfers—I was trying to keep my borrowed yarmulka on the back of my head, because it felt like it was slipping down all the time. And our parents were there, too—even my father, who, I guess, figured that Mr. Hupfer might someday need an architect, and so he had better show up. It was sort of like an investment. He sat as far away from Mr. Kowalski as he could.

We all watched as Danny pulled the prayer shawl his great-uncle had given him around his shoulders. The tassels reached below his waist. Then he wound the tefillin around his arm and across his forehead. You could see him still waiting for the worst, hoping for a miracle. Then the prayers. Still waiting. Then he walked with the rabbi and cantor back to the altar and took out the Torah. We all stood—I reached up to press down my yarmulka—and he carried the Torah back to the reading desk. The rabbi drew it from its mantle, untied the scroll, and rolled it open.

A huge breath from Danny. Still waiting.

And then—can you believe it?—the miracle came after all.

He lifted one of the tassels, touched it to the scroll, kissed it. He took the handles of the Torah in his own hands. And he began to sing.

Baruch et Adonai ha'mevorach.

And everyone around us sang back.

Baruch Adonai ha'mevorach l'olam va'ed.

And Danny sang again, deep and steady, until he got to *"Baruch ata Adonai, noteyn ha'torah,"* when everyone sang back, just as deep and just as steady, "Amen."

Then Danny took a deep breath and began to read from the Torah.

Okay, so maybe sometimes the real world *is* smiles and miracles. Right there in front of us, Danny Hupfer was no longer Danny who stuck wads of gum under his desk. Or Danny who screamed out of his skull at soccer games. Or Danny who ran cross-country on bloody knees and waved sweaty T-shirts.

He was more than all of those things. He sang the words, and he was everyone who had sung them before him, like he was taking up his place in this huge choir and it wasn't Miss Violet of the Very Spiky Heels but God Himself leading the music. You saw Danny covered with weight.

Then the cantor and Danny's father stood over him and blessed him. More weight.

And Danny chanted again, this time from the Prophets. More weight.

And then he reached into his back pocket and took out his speech, his Dvar Torah. "Today," he said, "I am become a man."

And he had.

You could see it afterward, when he recited the blessings over the challah, and over the wine, and everyone shouted *"L'chayim!"* "To life!"

Danny had become a man. You could see him take up his place. And he was smiling. And crying, too.

After the service, my parents and Heather decided not to stay for the party already starting in the reception hall. When they asked if I wanted a ride, I told them I would walk home instead. But I went to the parking lot with them anyway.

As he unlocked the car, my father said, "I bet you're glad you don't have to go through something like that."

"I guess I am," I said.

"What do you mean, 'I guess I am'?" he said. "Would you want to stand up there with all that stuff all over you and chant at everyone?"

"It was a whole lot more than chanting at everyone," I said.

"Let's get in the car," said my mother.

"No," said my father. He put his arms up on top of the station wagon's roof. "I'd like to know what Holling thought was a whole lot more."

My stomach got tight. "He became a man," I said.

"You think that's how you become a man, by chanting a few prayers?"

"You think you become a man by getting a job as an architect?"

My father straightened. "That's *exactly* how you become a man," he said. "You get a good job and you provide for your family. You hang on, and you play for keeps. That's how it works."

"I really do think we should get in the car," said my mother.

"I don't think so," I said to my father. "It's not just about a job. It's more. It has to do with choosing for yourself."

"And you didn't even have to go to California to figure all that out," said my father. "So who are you, Holling?"

I felt Heather looking at me. And somehow—I don't know how—I thought of Bobby Kennedy, who could have made all the difference.

"I don't know yet," I said finally. "I'll let you know."

"What a barrel of mumbo-jumbo," said my father. He got into the station wagon and slammed the door. My mother blew me a kiss—really—and then she got in, too.

And my sister got in last of all.

She was smiling.

I could hardly breathe.

When they drove away, I went back inside Temple Beth-El, where the sounds of the miracle were still loud. Danny was still smiling— and it wasn't just because Mr. Goldman had brought huge trays of brown, light, perfect cream puffs. He couldn't stop smiling. And after a while, I couldn't, either—especially once the dancing started and Meryl Lee took my hand. And even more especially after Meryl Lee said, "You look different," and I said, "Maybe it's the yarmulka," and she said, "No, something else."

Meryl Lee. Can the world buy such a jewel?

It was when I had gone to find her a Coke that I saw Mrs. Baker, standing alone beside a pile of sugared strawberries. She was holding one in her hand, smiling, too.

Now, I know that you're not supposed to talk to a teacher outside of school activities. It's a rule that probably no one has ever broken. But I decided to break it anyway.

"Do you think Lieutenant Baker will really be home in time for strawberries?" I said.

Mrs. Baker, smiling Mrs. Baker, did not look away from the strawberry. "I'm sure of it," she said.

Now I smiled. "Do teachers always know the future?"

"Always," she said. "Shall I tell you yours?"

Standing there in the music of the bar mitzvah party, feeling the weight of what had happened in the synagogue, I saw again the glittering stream, with its light rushing toward me. "Don't tell me," I said. "But how do you know?"

She looked away from the strawberry and at me. "Do you remember Don Pedro, standing alone at the end of the play?"

I nodded. "Claudio has Hero, and they'll be fine. Benedict has Beatrice, and they'll be fine. Everyone else has everyone else, and they'll all be fine. The only one who's left alone is Don Pedro. And they all go off to dance and leave him behind. And they don't even remember that he's the one who has to deal with a traitor tomorrow, or that he hasn't got anyone."

"That's right," said Mrs. Baker. "And maybe his whole country will split into pieces. He doesn't have any idea what's going to happen to him."

"Great comedy," I said.

"A comedy isn't about being funny," said Mrs. Baker.

"We've talked about this before."

"A comedy is about characters who dare to know that they may choose a happy ending after all. That's how I know."

"Suppose you can't see it?"

"That's the daring part," said Mrs. Baker.

"So you think Don Pedro ended up all right," I said.

"I think he became a man who brought peace and wisdom to his world, because he knew about war and folly. I think that he loved greatly, because he had seen what lost love is. And I think he came to know, too, that he was loved greatly." She looked at the strawberry in her hands. "But I thought you didn't want me to tell you your future."

The music started again. A quick ring dance. Danny Hupfer was going to dance with Mrs. Bigio, and Mai Thi was doubled over, laughing. Mrs. Sidman had stepped into the ring beside Doug Swieteck—who didn't look all that happy. The Kowalskis and the Hupfers had come in together, Mrs. Hupfer and Mrs. Kowalski giggling and in their stocking feet, since you can't dance in high heels. And Meryl Lee . . .

Everyone was laughing and jostling to their places. I needed to go find mine.

"*L'chayim!*" I said to Mrs. Baker.

And she smiled—not a teacher smile. "Chrysanthemum," she said.

Eleven days later, on Wednesday, Lieutenant Tybalt Baker came home.

It was the day that President Lyndon B. Johnson announced that the marines were abandoning Khesanh.

I was at the airport. Me and Danny and Mai Thi and Meryl Lee and Doug and the whole class. Standing on the tarmac when the military plane landed.

We all held boxes of sweet strawberries.

I guess you want to know what Mrs. Baker did when Lieutenant Baker came out of the plane. And I guess you want to know what Lieutenant Baker did when he saw Mrs. Baker on the tarmac.

But toads, beetles, bats. If you can't figure that out for yourself, then a southwest blow on ye and blister you all o'er.

Because let me tell you, it was a happy ending.